"Were you wearing this last night?" Damian asked softly

Alexa looked at the sleep shirt in Damian's hand, then into his eyes. "No, I was wearing a long cotton nightgown." Frantically, she turned over the bed covers, dislodging the pillows. *No nightgown.* "It's not here," she said in a fractured whisper.

"Don't panic, Alexa," he returned gently. "Maybe you were sleepwalking on the balcony. Maybe you took it off yourself when it got wet in the rain."

"Then where is it?" An icy lump formed in Alexa's stomach. Had her nightmare been a reality—one from which even Damian's gentleness and strength couldn't save her?

Had she really killed a man while she'd been sleeping?

ABOUT THE AUTHOR

Tina Vasilos has successfully written romantic suspense for many years. She has traveled widely around the world, and she uses her trips to research her novels. Tina and her husband live with their son in Clearbrook, British Columbia.

Books by Tina Vasilos

HARLEQUIN INTRIGUE

68–UNWITTING ACCOMPLICE
101–WOLF'S PREY
132–PAST TENSE
235–CRY OF THE PEACOCK

Lost Innocence

Tina Vasilos

Harlequin Books

TORONTO • NEW YORK • LONDON
AMSTERDAM • PARIS • SYDNEY • HAMBURG
STOCKHOLM • ATHENS • TOKYO • MILAN
MADRID • WARSAW • BUDAPEST • AUCKLAND

ISBN 0-373-22274-2

LOST INNOCENCE

This edition published by arrangement with Harlequin Enterprises B. V.

Printed in U.S.A.

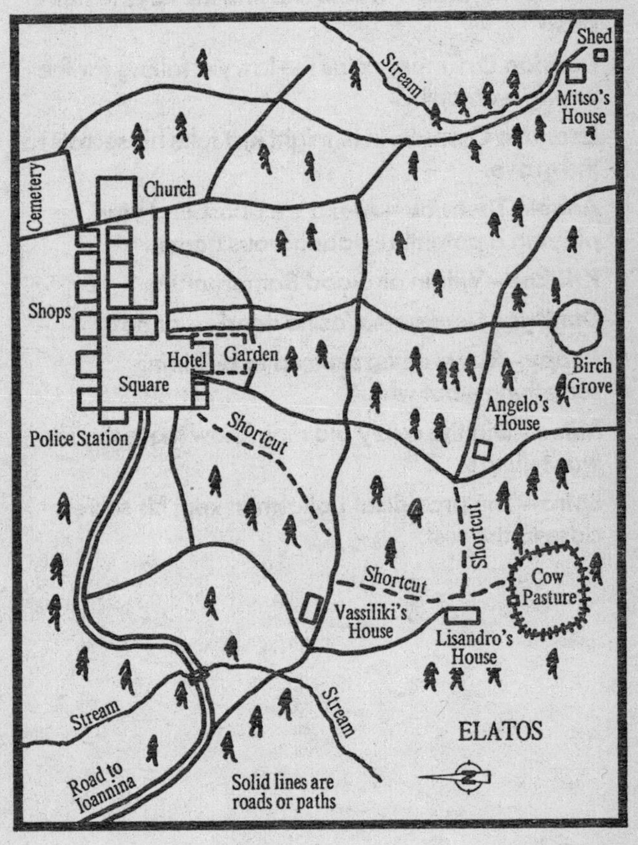
Shed
Stream
Mitso's House
Cemetery
Church
Shops
Hotel
Garden
Square
Birch Grove
Angelo's House
Police Station
Shortcut
Shortcut
Shortcut
Cow Pasture
Vassiliki's House
Lisandro's House
Stream
Stream
ELATOS
Road to Ioannina
Solid lines are roads or paths

CAST OF CHARACTERS

Alexa Thetalou—Would she find the keys to her past?

Damian Orfanos—Was the lawyer falling for the wrong woman?

Lisandro Cosmos—He might just take his secrets to the grave.

Angelo Thetalou—Alexa's ex-husband was playing a potentially dangerous game.

Kritikos—Villain or Good Samaritan?

Dimitrios Doukas—Was he dead . . . or not?

Poppy—The woman seemed to be hiding something—but what?

Mitso—Did the crazy old man know more than he was telling?

Spiro—The provincial policeman kept *his* secrets close to the vest.

Chapter One

"Your father is alive."

The words beat a painful tempo in Alexa's brain, blocking out the roar of traffic on the busy Volos street behind her. She stared at the man who had uttered them.

He looked back at her, face expressionless, dark eyes hooded. She didn't like his eyes; they were cold and hard, like wet pebbles on a beach, the kind of eyes she imagined a reptile having.

Her father alive? A chill ran over her skin despite the heat of the October sun. She shook her head. She must have misunderstood—that, or her lingering jet lag was worse than she'd thought. The statement was too fantastic, and there was no reason for her to believe this stranger.

She stood up, the sturdy café chair teetering. "It's not true." Her thigh bumped the small table and water sloshed in the glasses.

Before she could get away, a large hand gripped her wrist. "Please, you must listen."

"Let go of me," she said tightly.

"If you'll stay for just a moment." He withdrew his hand. Against her better judgment, she sank down on her chair.

The heavyset man leaned forward, gazing at her earnestly. "My dear Mrs. Thetalou, your father, Dimitrios Doukas, is alive."

Tears pricked her eyes but she blinked to control them. With effort, she kept her voice steady. "That's impossible. He died over twenty-five years ago. His brother came back and told us." His brother, her uncle, who was also dead.

The man shrugged. "Greece was in a state of turmoil at the time. Mistakes were made. You've seen the Albanians who've come into Greece in the past year since the border was opened?"

She nodded. How could one help it? Poor, ragged, sleeping in the woods or in abandoned buildings, mostly men but some women and children as well—there were thousands of them, wandering the countryside and gathering in the cities. Refugees, looking for a better life.

The man sipped from the cup of coffee he'd ordered. Hiding her impatience, Alexa watched as he fastidiously blotted his upper lip with a white handkerchief. A thin mustache sat below a prominent nose, the ends joining a neat salt-and-pepper goatee that gave definition to his moon-shaped face.

"I hired a group of Albanians to work on my property," he said finally. "One of the men seemed to be better educated than the others, and I put him in charge of the crew. He reported to me every evening. I asked him how he'd learned Greek. There are, of course, many Albanians who speak the language, but it's a kind of dialect. This man's Greek was pure. He told me that years ago he'd had a friend who had taught him Greek, a man named Dimitrios Doukas. After eight or nine years in Albania, this Doukas left. He said goodbye to the family he lived with and walked down the road. They didn't hear from him again."

He paused. His dark eyes searched Alexa's face as if trying to gauge her reaction. Hoping her features remained expressionless, she clenched her hands tightly in her lap to hide their trembling.

"Until a year ago." The words dropped into the silence like a bomb. "The family received a letter, postmarked

Ioannina, telling them he was well and settled back in Greece. A sum of money was enclosed, an amount that to them seemed large, although in fact it was only the equivalent of one thousand American dollars. But there was no return address, no way they could trace him."

Alexa shook herself. She wasn't convinced, not without some kind of proof. She had been six when her father was reported dead, killed in an accident after fleeing political enemies. He had left a letter, to be opened after his death, advising her mother, Olympia, to leave Greece, to go to Canada where Dimitrios and Olympia had lived in the early years of their marriage. There was money in a bank account. Realizing that she and Alexa were also in danger, Alexa's mother had packed their few belongings and had taken her daughter to Vancouver.

This was the story she'd told Alexa. Alexa didn't remember any of it, not Elatos, the village where they'd lived for less than a year, nor the long journey to the West Coast of Canada. She only remembered her mother crying sometimes at night, when she was tired from a long day of work in a restaurant kitchen.

Surely if her father had been alive, they would have heard from him. Alexa had only dim memories of him, a gentle man who had told her stories in a deep voice that rumbled in his chest when she sat on his knee and laid her cheek against him. She had loved her Papa, and hadn't understood why he had to leave. But her mother had explained to her that bad men wanted to hurt him and that he needed to go far away to hide from them.

"How did you find me?" she asked the man sitting across from her. "And what did you say your name was?"

He smiled briefly. She saw that his right incisor was crooked, almost overlapping the tooth next to it. The imperfection made his lip curl, almost turning the smile into a sneer. She thought she detected a sly gleam in his eyes and vowed to be even more on her guard.

"Kritikos," he said. "Pavlo Kritikos. I know your aunt Eleni. She told me you'd gone shopping, that you liked to watch the ships come in, so I was likely to find you here on the waterfront. At this time of year, after the tourist season, one doesn't see many blondes. You were easy to find."

And an easy mark? Alexa wondered. She didn't trust the man; he was too glib, too friendly.

And his story, of course, was crazy.

"Why didn't my aunt tell me this?"

"She didn't know. I only heard it myself a short time ago. We knew you were coming to Greece, so I decided to wait until you were here. As you probably know, your aunt Eleni doesn't think kindly of your father deserting his family."

Alexa straightened in her chair, grimacing as she tasted her cold coffee. Bitter, like the taste of this tantalizing string of lies. Still, she couldn't think of a possible motive; perhaps she should give him the benefit of the doubt.

For now.

"Where is this Albanian?" she asked. "I'd like to talk with him myself."

The broad face took on a look of regret. "I'm so sorry, Mrs. Thetalou. That's impossible. Regrettably, his papers weren't in order and he was deported back to Albania."

"That does it." Alexa stood up, her emotions churning until anger was uppermost. She dropped a handful of coins onto the table for her coffee. "Find someone else to tell your lies to. I'm not buying it."

The man remained seated, unperturbed. "If you want to check it out, go to Elatos."

DESPITE HER MISGIVINGS, four days later Alexa found herself in a tiny rented Renault, lurching along a road that resembled a dry riverbed. The mountains of Epirus towered around her, jagged ramparts thrusting into a hard blue October sky. Near the road, the slopes were clothed in a blanket of trees that did little to soften the forbidding gray crags glowering in the distance.

She'd driven for an hour since leaving the main highway northwest of Ioannina, and not encountered another soul. The only evidence of human activity was the neatly trimmed logs stacked at intervals along the road, awaiting collection by a logging truck. She prayed the pickup wasn't scheduled for today; she wasn't sure there was room for her to pass a truck on the narrow track.

Protruding rocks and tree roots scraped against the bottom of the car. A four-wheel drive vehicle would have been more practical, but the rental agency in Volos had not run to anything sturdier than the Renault.

She hadn't expected the difficult conditions. Her map had shown the road to be at least partially paved; it had been, for two kilometers, but from there had deteriorated steadily.

How did people live here? she asked herself for the tenth time. She laughed, more to hear a human sound than out of humor. Maybe they didn't. Maybe she was on a crazy wild-goose chase, all as a result of an absurd story from a stranger.

One thing in Kritikos's favor, though. Her aunt Eleni, her mother's sister, did know the man. Which wasn't to say she liked him. "He was in politics years ago," she'd said, her mouth turning down in contempt.

Not much of a recommendation, Alexa thought. But he'd once had connections in Elatos, friends or relatives, Eleni had assured her, so the story might be true. And furthermore, wasn't Alexa curious about her father's native village? Even if nothing came of her quest, she would see the country, gain insight into her own heritage.

Originally Alexa had planned to stay in Greece only a couple of weeks, visiting her aunt in Volos and seeing the sights in Athens. She didn't remember Elatos, and her mother had hardly mentioned the village over the years. It was Alexa's father's people who had come from there, and none of them was alive anymore. Alexa knew her mother didn't have happy memories of the place, only nightmares that had lingered for years, about war and destruction and senselessly spilled blood. Olympia only wanted to forget and, unknowingly, Alexa had absorbed this attitude.

Yet, here she was, delving into virtually unmapped mountains, searching for a man who had been dead for more than twenty-five years.

Alexa glanced at the sky. Cobalt blue, cloudless. The sun was hot now, but early this morning in Ioannina, her breath had formed clouds in the cold air when she'd walked from the hotel to the car.

The road began to climb again, smoother but narrowing as rocks gave way to a pale, sandy gravel. The snaggled teeth of the mountains loomed closer. Deciduous trees crowded in on the edges of the road. Alexa shivered as the lush, dark green foliage blotted out the sun. All the travel posters portrayed Greece as a land externally bathed in a drenching Mediterranean sun. She wasn't prepared for the lush green gloom that enveloped her, as oppressive as a month of rain.

In the deep shadows ahead she saw movement. A deer, perhaps, if they had deer in Greece. She couldn't remember. There were foxes here. They were supposedly nocturnal but she'd seen one earlier, crossing the road at a leisurely pace, its bushy tail brushing the ground.

Again. A tall shrub stirred violently. She slowed the car. Two men, one of them carrying a pack, darted across the road and disappeared into the forest, too far ahead for her to make out details of their appearance.

Sweat broke out on her palms. Brought up with a sense of her own independence while her mother worked, she'd never thought of herself as vulnerable. She did now, and apprehension was drying her throat. All they had to do was block the road and she would be helpless.

Before she'd left Volos her aunt had filled her head with the dangers of traveling alone, stories of drivers picking up hitchhiking refugees and being robbed—or worse. Alexa had ignored most of it, dismissing the tales as exaggeration; it occurred to her now that she should have listened more carefully.

The road leveled off and then began to wind down into another valley. Needing all her attention to negotiate hairpin turns, Alexa stifled her momentary fear.

She steered around a curve and abruptly slammed her foot onto the brake. The little car jerked to a stop. In the middle of the road, a tan-and-white cow regarded her with mild brown eyes, its jaw swinging as it placidly chewed its cud.

Rolling down the window, Alexa waved her arm at the cow. Only its tail moved as it whisked a fly. "Shoo, cow," Alexa muttered, debating whether to get out of the car. A short debate in which caution won; she didn't like the looks of those sharp horns.

A shrill whistle sounded from the dense shrubbery beside the road. The cow turned its head, fuzzy brown ears rising to attention.

A man burst out of the bushes, his headlong rush carrying him straight into the side of the car. His sturdy boots scrabbled on the sandy road surface as he fought to regain his balance.

Bracing a hand on the roof, he bent down to the window, his nose an inch from Alexa's. "That's a dumb place to park a car."

"No dumber than where you parked your cow," she retorted. "If you'll kindly move it, I'll be happy to get out of your way." She broke off. "You spoke English," she exclaimed. "How—?"

He grinned briefly, a flash of white teeth that transformed his narrow, dark face from anger to a somewhat wary friendliness. "Your hair. Not many Greeks are so blond, not even around here."

The grin faded, his gaze sharpening as he took in the dusty car, the single suitcase on the back seat, the map beside her. "Are you lost? You're awfully far off what one might call the beaten track."

His accent was faint but noticeable. The muscular forearm that rested on the window ledge was bare and tanned, sprinkled with soft black hairs and trapped beads of sweat. He smelled warm, spicy.

Her stomach tensed and she leaned back, although it was impossible to put any real distance between them unless he moved away. She looked up and found his eyes locked on her face. Remarkable eyes, they were a very dark, deep blue, still and watchful, filled with shadows, as if he'd seen things others ran from. She met his gaze and felt a strange stirring in her soul. Instantly she knew that however long she lived, she would remember the haunted beauty of his eyes.

He blinked, breaking the contact with her. The long, curling black lashes were the only soft feature in his narrow face, a face that was a little too angular to be called truly handsome. A hard face, strong bones and more than a hint of cynicism around the thin mouth.

He had a surprisingly full bottom lip, she mused irrelevantly. A mouth made for kissing. Something dark and primitive moved inside her, a sexual reaction she hadn't allowed herself since her bitter divorce.

Get real, she told herself sternly. He's probably got a wife and six children. So he's the sexiest man you've seen lately. He's not for you.

Besides, she'd only be here for a day or two. She had business to do, business that did not include daydreaming about one of the local residents.

"No, I'm not lost," she said crisply, banishing her errant thoughts. "This is the road to Elatos, isn't it?"

He stepped back and gestured with his arm. "Just ahead. Cross the bridge and you'll see the first houses. Are you looking for someone in particular?"

She hesitated. Her aunt's words echoed in her head. There had been a lot of political turmoil in Epirus during the Greek civil war and again in the sixties and seventies. Eleni was not from the area and hadn't been involved in the dispute; she had no way of knowing whether sympathy might lie with Alexa's father or with his enemies.

With this in mind, Alexa had decided to keep her own counsel until she learned more about present sentiments. "My parents lived here years ago," she said carefully. "I thought I'd have a look at the countryside."

"Oh?" His brow lifted and she could see curiosity in his eyes. "Maybe I've heard of them."

"Not likely," she said. "When they left, you would have been a child. I trust there's some sort of inn or hotel in the village?"

"Just drive straight through. You'll see it on the square." He walked around the front of the car, tapping the cow's flank with the palm of his hand.

Alexa allowed herself a moment of distraction as he strode gracefully after the cow. He was only a little taller than her own height, she judged, lean and fit, narrow hips clothed in faded jeans, and surprisingly muscular shoulders filling out a white T-shirt.

As if he sensed her eyes on him, he turned and waved before disappearing into an unseen path off the road. Chagrined at her behavior, Alexa engaged the gear more forcefully than necessary, spinning the wheels as she clattered across the metal Bailey bridge that looked too flimsy to support the car.

HIDDEN IN THE SHRUBBERY, Damian watched the little car trundle around the corner.

Pretty tourist? Or trouble?

Visitors rarely came to Elatos in summer, except for a stray hiker or two. By October, even some of the villagers began to make plans to spend the winter in the city.

Who was she? He didn't believe she'd just stumbled on the last unspoiled mountain village in Greece.

Well, tongues would be wagging by nightfall. A beautiful woman with blond hair could hardly go unnoticed or untalked about. What was her real purpose here, he wondered. A search for her roots? Maybe. Maybe not. He'd sensed a reserve, a secretive evasion in her hesitation, when he'd asked who she was looking for.

He shrugged. None of his affair, as long as she wasn't a land developer looking to build a tourist hotel that would spoil the peaceful ambience, which wasn't likely; the cost of building a proper road was enough to deter the most ambitious resort scout.

A cold nose nudged him. He absently pushed the cow's head aside before she could wrap her tongue around his arm to taste the salty sweat. Setting his feet into motion, he herded the animal toward the village.

He would find out soon enough who the woman was.

And learn the color of her eyes, which had been hidden by dark sunglasses.

THE VILLAGE CONSISTED of widely scattered houses, sturdily built of the local gray stone. Even the roofs were tiled with slate slabs. The entire effect would have been bleak except for the surrounding trees and the pots of bright geraniums and marigolds that decorated patios and balconies.

Quaint and picturesque, Alexa thought, pleasantly surprised. Even if the report about her father came to nothing, exploring the village would make up for the difficulty of the drive.

The square was laid with flagstones, and birch trees at the corners had started to turn a pale autumn gold. She saw the hotel, rooms on the second floor above a small restaurant and the village office. Scarlet geraniums in window boxes splashed color against the gray stone walls.

A bell tolled the hour, eleven. Oddly, the church was not on the square, but was situated a block away, its bell tower visible down a narrow street lined with small shops. The street and the square bustled with people doing their morning shopping. Alexa was enchanted to note that some of the women wore the heavy skirts and ornate vests of years ago. And several old men sitting on a bench wore the white leggings and pleated kilt often thought to be the national Greek costume.

She parked the car and climbed the wide steps leading into the hotel, blinking in the gloom of the lobby.

"*Kalimera.* Good morning." An attractive young woman with masses of dark hair greeted her from behind the restaurant bar.

"*Kalimera,*" Alexa said politely. "Do you have a room?"

"You speak Greek," the young woman exclaimed. "Where are you from?"

"I spoke little else until I was six," Alexa said. "I'm from Canada."

"How nice. A number of people from here went to Canada, but that was many years ago." She laughed, retrieving a book from under the counter. "Before I was born, you know. Yes, we have a room. How long are you planning to stay?"

"I'm not sure. Is that a problem?"

"Not in October. We stay open all year because we get business people occasionally, wool buyers mostly, but it's quiet in winter." The girl pushed the book across the counter. "If you would sign here, please. And show me your passport."

Alexa signed her name and handed over the passport. The girl flipped it open, pen ready to jot down the information. Her hand stilled in midair, the smile sliding off her face.

"Thetalou?" the girl said in a voice barely above a whisper. Avoiding Alexa's questioning look, she scribbled the number into the book and briskly handed back the document. "Have you come to visit relatives here?" she asked, an odd, almost hostile note in her voice. "Thetalou is a local name."

Alexa bit her lip against a torrent of questions. She said quietly, "I have no relatives here, and Thetalou was the name of my husband."

The girl's expression lightened marginally. "Come, I will show you your room."

They climbed a creaking wooden staircase. The upstairs corridor was lit by a window at one end, through which the sun laid a golden swath across the floor.

The room was unlocked; a key extended from the old-fashioned keyhole. The girl pushed open the door, revealing a high-ceilinged, square chamber simply furnished with a bed, a wardrobe and a small desk. "Okay?" she asked in English.

Alexa smiled. "Okay."

The girl handed her the key. "Keep it with you. The outside door is always open. You can get your meals downstairs. I'm afraid it's the only restaurant open in Elatos at this time of year, but I promise you won't be disappointed with the food. Our cook is very good." She smiled. "My name is Poppy. Call me if you need anything."

UNPACKED AND SETTLED IN, Alexa left the hotel a short time later. A luridly decorated truck drove by, its speaker blaring an atonal melody played on violins and wailing clarinets. The driver leaned out of the cab, whistling. "Hey, pretty lady. Where did you get that hair?"

She ignored him, smiling inwardly. All her life, among her mother's circle of Greek friends, she had been teased about her blond hair. It was impossible to tell the shade of Alexa's father's hair in the single, much-handled black-and-white photograph Olympia had of him. "Almost blond it was," she'd told Alexa. "Not as light as yours. His mother, your grandmother, who died when you were two, was blond until her ninetieth year."

It was odd, Alexa reflected now as she started down a path leading from the hotel. Both her parents and her father's had had their children late in life. Dimitrios had been fifty, Olympia thirty-eight, when Alexa, their only child, was born. "And you were a real surprise," her mother often told her. "We'd been married so long, we'd almost given up hoping for a child."

It was still early for lunch, although tantalizing smells drifted from the houses she passed on the narrow, rocky path. The sun, its heat magnified in the clear mountain air, beat down on her from a sapphire sky.

She decided to walk around the village, to get her bearings and perhaps stir long-buried childhood memories. The path was steep, the smoothly worn cobblestones hazardous underfoot; it became more narrow, winding through a wooded area where there were no houses.

Again, she had a feeling of unease as the dense trees shaded her from the sun. She was being irrational, she told herself. She had no reason to feel unsafe. Even now, she could hear people talking lower down the path, see the golden-green birch tree at the corner of the square.

Talking about her, perhaps? She'd been conscious of speculative glances as she crossed the square earlier, and of the silence that followed her. Some mystery about the name Thetalou, to go by Poppy's reaction, a curiosity only a trace short of hostility. Was it directed at her, or at anyone who bore that name?

She shivered, a sense of watching eyes pricking her consciousness. Trees arched over the path; the patch of sky visible between the green boughs seemed lower, pressing down on her like a heavy blue lid.

She whirled around, the hair standing up on her skin. There was no one in sight, but she couldn't shake her funny feeling as she hurried down the path.

"Alexa!"

She froze in her tracks. The voice was male, familiar, instantly recognizable although she hadn't heard it in over a year.

"Alexa, wait."

Her heart cramping in her chest, she turned. And stared into the hard, coffee-brown eyes of Angelo Thetalou, the last man on earth she expected or wanted to see.

Chapter Two

Alexa stared at the man who had once been her husband. "What are you doing here?" she finally blurted out.

"I might ask you the same, dear *ex*-wife," he said in a malevolent drawl. His English was good; during his years in Canada he'd worked hard to master the grammar and the idioms. He smiled, his handsome features lighting with every appearance of friendliness. "I live here," he added, flippantly casual. "Welcome to Elatos."

Outrage boiled in Alexa's stomach. Wasn't it enough that he had harassed her for five years after their divorce? Did he have to show up in her life again, just when she was beginning to think she was finally free of him? "Get out of my way, Angelo. We have nothing to say to each other."

He scowled, the smooth charm evaporating like noxious smoke. "Don't we?" he said in an ugly tone. He grabbed her wrist with hard, hurting fingers. "And if I say we do?"

"Let her go." A voice spoke harshly behind her.

Angelo froze. "Keep out of this, Damian."

Alexa twisted free, pain shooting up her arm. She rubbed her wrist. There would be a bruise there tomorrow; it wouldn't be the first bruise Angelo had inflicted.

Angelo, with the face and charm of an angel. Poor, misguided fool she'd been, she hadn't seen below the surface when she'd met him at eighteen. Spellbound, she'd married him at nineteen—and regretted it forever after.

She turned. The man she'd encountered on the road stood behind her, scowling. "Are you all right?" he asked, not taking his eyes off Angelo.

"Yes. Thank you."

"Get lost, Damian," Angelo said. "This is a private discussion."

"Looked like more than a discussion to me," Damian said. "You have a bad habit of grabbing people, don't you, Angelo? Better watch it next time."

Angelo glared at Damian, then turned his gaze on Alexa. "I'll see you again. We have a lot to talk about."

She backed away. "There's nothing to say," she said evenly, knowing an angry reaction would only further provoke him.

Angelo opened his mouth as if to respond, then snapped it closed. He turned and stamped down the path.

"Thank you," she said to Damian when Angelo disappeared around a bend. "I could have handled it, but thank you, anyway."

She gave him a dazzling smile which he didn't return. His eyes remained on her, dark and speculative. She took a step back, remembering too late that they stood on an isolated path and that she might have traded one problem for another.

But her misgivings were short-lived. Damian's face softened and he gestured with his arm. "The square is that way. I'll see you safely to the hotel."

DAMN ANGELO. Damn him, damn him, Alexa repeated in her mind like a mantra. And damn her own insecurities, which her ex-husband still had the power to reawaken after all this time.

She'd been sure Angelo had finally resigned himself to the end of their relationship. She hadn't heard from him in a year, and therefore had assumed he'd given up his campaign of mental torture—late-night phone calls and nasty letters in the mail.

She glanced at Damian, keeping pace with her. He hadn't said a word during the walk. Alexa was grateful for his silence, but his dark, brooding eyes warned her he might change his mind at any time, when curiosity won over courtesy.

The contrast between him and Angelo was striking, even at short acquaintance. Damian might lack Angelo's charm, but he also lacked his deceit. She felt a sense of quiet stability coming from Damian, giving her the conviction that he could be depended upon.

Perhaps it was her experience with Angelo that had made her able to read people more accurately.

Angelo. If she'd known she would meet him again, here in Elatos, she would never have come. And if she had half a brain, she would get into her car and drive out of here. At once.

Your father is alive. Kritikos's words echoed in her head. No, she couldn't leave. Not yet. Not until she had some answers. She would just have to stay out of Angelo's way.

She squared her shoulders. She was no longer emotionally bound up with him, no longer intimidated, first by the overwhelming attraction that had trapped her, and later by his cruel manipulation.

She was strong now; she could handle Angelo.

"Here we are." Damian's low, deep voice washed over her.

Startled out of her gloomy thoughts, she noted they'd reached the hotel steps. A flush heated her cheeks. What must he be thinking of her, not saying a word all the way here?

"Thank you," she said brightly, banishing the bad taste Angelo left in her mouth. "I'm sorry—"

"Don't be," he said.

She shifted nervously from one foot to the other. "Did you get your cow home all right?"

"Yes." He let out an exasperated breath. "She'll probably get out again, though. The fence posts are rotted and she just pushes them aside. Did you find a room?"

"Yes, thanks."

"Are you planning to stay long?"

She looked straight at him, her eyes almost on a level with his. She'd been right; he was only a couple of inches taller than her own five feet nine inches. "Why?" she asked with a light laugh. "Are you the mayor, keeping track of visitors?"

"Hardly." He grinned at her, the quick grin that came and went like a burst of sunlight through clouds. "I don't even live here."

"Then what were you doing chasing a cow through the woods?"

"Making sure you didn't run over it," he said wryly. "If you're staying for more than a couple of days, I'm afraid you'll find there's not much to do here."

He was fishing. She knew it, but subterfuge was as foreign to her as flying without an airplane; her face gave away her every thought. "Are you warning me off?" she asked bluntly.

He threw up his hands. "Not me. Just being honest."

She nodded, unsure what to make of him. He saved her from having to make a reply by putting out his hand to shake hers. His palm was warm and hard, his fingers gripping hers with gentle strength. "I'm Damian Orfanos. I hope you enjoy your stay in Elatos, that you don't find it too boring."

"If you don't live here, where do you live?" she asked, deciding that he'd been nosy enough that she had a right to reciprocate.

He looked startled for a second. Then reluctant amusement sparked in his eyes. "In Ioannina. I'm a lawyer. What about you?"

"I live in Vancouver, Canada. I'm an investment broker. Are you here on holiday, too?"

A shadow darkened the storm-colored eyes to black. "Not exactly a holiday," he said without elaborating.

"Damian," Poppy called from the doorway. "The soup is ready. You can pick it up in the kitchen."

He turned his head briefly. "Thanks." He took a step toward the door, then paused. "You didn't tell me your name."

Poppy's appearance had reminded Alexa of the young woman's reaction to her passport, the uneasiness she'd conveyed. Angelo's presence explained it. At least, so she guessed. Angelo, whose baser qualities were probably well known in a place this size.

Dragging her sunglasses up onto her head, she kept her gaze fixed on Damian's face. "I'm Alexa Thetalou."

He didn't so much as blink an eyelid. "A relative of Angelo's?" he asked, his casual tone belying the tension that clenched his hands into fists.

She walked past him, didn't turn until she'd crossed the lobby and reached the foot of the stairs. "You might say that," she said evenly. "A long time ago I was married to him. In another lifetime."

HER EYES WERE BROWN, Damian thought inanely as she disappeared up the stairs. A rich chocolate brown, unusual in a blonde, but perhaps not surprising considering her Greek heritage.

Angelo's ex-wife. The former Alexa Doukas, descendant of one of the founders of Elatos. A lot of things suddenly fell into place.

Particularly Angelo Thetalou's interest in the site of the small house that Damian's foster father had had built in

Elatos last spring. The house that sat on the former Doukas property.

From the day Lisandro moved into the house, Angelo had shown an interest in him, waylaying Damian several times with requests that he might speak with him. Damian had put him off. Lisandro was ill; he saw no one. He had come to Elatos for peace and quiet.

Curious, Damian had asked around about Angelo. Information was sparse, due to the fact that few of the townspeople had lived in Elatos for more than ten or fifteen years, after reviving what had been a virtual ghost town. He'd discovered that Angelo's father had once been a prominent citizen of Elatos who had died tragically more than twenty-five years ago. Angelo himself had left Elatos after his mother's death, six or seven years later. He'd been a troublemaker throughout his youth, gossip said, the despair of his widowed mother whom he'd always been able to charm into covering for him.

He'd returned to Elatos a year ago, fixed up part of the family house—hovel, if truth were told—and moved in. Damian hadn't grown up in Elatos, but he'd seen enough to put credence to the gossip he'd heard—Angelo's casual cruelty to Poppy, for instance.

And now to Alexa.

He scowled. That beautiful, self-possessed woman who'd just gone up the stairs couldn't be Angelo's ex-wife.

"Damian."

Poppy's call brought him out of his introspection. He went into the kitchen and picked up the container of soup. Damian usually cooked for himself and his foster father. Or their part-time housekeeper, Vassiliki, made a meal, but once in a while he ordered from the excellent menu at the restaurant. "Thanks, Poppy."

"Did she tell you her name?" Poppy asked.

"Yes. She's Angelo's ex-wife."

Poppy's dark brows lifted. "She told me she didn't have any relatives here. I wonder what she's up to."

Damian shrugged. "Just visiting the family village, maybe? Isn't that what we all do on occasion?"

"Probably," Poppy agreed. "Say hello to Lisandro."

"I will, thanks."

Lost in thought, he walked through the village, absently acknowledging acquaintances' greetings. He was accepted, but he was aware he didn't quite fit into the tightly knit village society. Neither he nor Lisandro had been born in Elatos, and they weren't related to any of the village families. Lisandro never went down to the square because of his poor health, never attempted to socialize. Other than the doctor, the priest and Vassiliki, Lisandro saw no one. Thus, he and Damian were destined to remain outsiders.

The small, comfortable cottage sat on a knoll at the edge of the village. Surrounding trees protected it from the cold mountain storms and gave it the appearance of coziness. Lisandro had bought the land years ago, when Damian was away at university. Last winter, when he had learned of his illness, he'd had the cottage built. He'd only come to the village briefly to check out the site, placing the task of building in the hands of a contractor. Damian had come up several times to check progress. In July, Lisandro had moved in, and miraculously his health had improved in the fresh mountain air.

For a time. Already Damian could see signs of deterioration in him again. Pleasant as it was, the cottage was the place where Lisandro had come to die.

Damian grinned in delight at seeing the old man sitting next to the open front door. Lisandro's thick white hair gleamed above a weathered face tanned a deep bronze. Only the faint blue tint of his lips gave evidence of his illness. "I brought your soup, Papa. Would you like to eat out here?"

"Thank you, Damian. I felt better today. The sun called me outside." His voice was strong, only a little unsteady.

Once he had been a tall, robust man. It pained Damian to see him weak, often bedridden, but he supposed that was to be expected in a man who'd lived more than eight decades.

It didn't make it any easier to accept that the one person he loved in the whole world would soon be taken from him.

"I met a woman today," he said when they were eating the soup along with crusty chunks of bread.

"About time," Lisandro said, his deep brown eyes twinkling. "Who is she?"

"Angelo Thetalou's ex-wife."

Lisandro choked on his soup. Damian took the spoon from his lax hand and patted him on the back. "Papa, are you all right?" He held a glass for the old man to sip a little water.

Lisandro waved Damian back to his chair. "Alexa Doukas...." he said in an odd voice. "That's why he was asking about this land."

"She and Angelo are no longer married." Damian frowned thoughtfully. "I wonder if she knew Angelo was here."

Lisandro leaned forward, his soup forgotten. "Tell me, Damian, what's she like?"

Hiding his surprise that Lisandro would be interested in the woman, Damian said, "Blond. Well dressed. Sophisticated."

Lisandro still looked pale, and lines of strain were etched around his mouth. "Papa, are you all right? Would you like me to help you inside?" asked Damian.

"It's okay." To Damian's relief, the color began to seep back into Lisandro's face. He picked up his spoon. "Let me finish this. Then I'll lie down. I am a little tired."

Some time later Damian sat on the chair by the stoop. The book he was reading lay idly on one knee, the ginger cat that seemed to have adopted their house was stretched out on the other. He purred, winking at Damian with wide amber eyes, his claws occasionally flexing to dig into Damian's leg through his jeans.

Damian barely noticed the sharp pricks as he considered the events of the morning.

He had to see her again. This decided, the next step was easy. He would give Lisandro his supper early, then go down to the restaurant. She was bound to be dining there. He would casually come in, speak to her, and she would ask him to join her.

He tilted back the chair, closing his eyes. Yes, a simple plan, but simplicity usually worked best.

"*KALISPERA*. Good evening."

Alexa glanced up from the menu she was studying to find Damian Orfanos standing beside the table. For a moment she stared at him, tongue-tied. The T-shirt and jeans were gone, replaced by gray trousers, a tweed sport coat and a white shirt set off by a tasteful striped tie. The lawyer. She could picture him in the courtroom, those intense dark eyes convincing a jury that what he told them was the truth.

"Good evening," she said coolly, valiantly hiding her thoughts.

Not very successfully. As usual.

"Didn't expect me to clean up so well, did you?" he asked with a slow smile. "Do you mind if I join you?"

She gestured at the chair opposite. "Go ahead."

He sat down, smiling at Poppy when she brought another menu. "Did Lisandro like the soup?" she asked.

"Yes, thank you," Damian said.

"Lisandro?" Alexa asked when Poppy left them.

"My foster father. He's ill. I'm taking care of him."

"So Lisandro adopted you?"

Damian gave an ironic laugh. "Something like that. He caught me breaking into his house when I was sixteen." Now why had he told her that, a story even his closest friends didn't know? Mentally he shrugged. In a couple of days she'd be gone. What did it matter? "Instead of calling the police, he took me into his house, said I could live there as long as I went to school and kept out of trouble."

Her dark brown eyes were avid with curiosity. "And you accepted."

"Not that easily. He made it clear the alternative was jail. Since I'd already spent a night or two in the hole they called a jail at that time, I figured I'd at least go through the motions. But I found a warm bed at night was better than sleeping in a drafty doorway. And he had a whole library of books I could read. So I stayed."

"And now you're taking care of him." Her voice was warm, understanding, and a lump formed in his throat.

"Yes," he said shortly, uncomfortable talking about emotions that lived deep inside him. When he'd heard Lisandro's illness was going to be fatal, he'd wanted to scream. To curse God. Lisandro had taken the doctor's verdict calmly, accepting his imminent death as part of life, God's plan, and Damian had finally found his own peace, if not resignation.

To his relief, Poppy came up to take their order.

"What about you?" he asked after she'd gone. "Your parents came from Elatos?"

"My father did, although he married my mother in Canada. They lived in Vancouver for a while, then he brought her back to Greece and they lived in Athens. I was born there. When Athens became dangerous for my father, he moved us here, but less than a year later he died and my mother took me to Canada."

"Then you don't know anyone here except Angelo?"

Anger flashed in her eyes. "I don't want anything to do with Angelo. If I'd known he was here, I wouldn't have come."

Why *had* she come? The question gnawed at him.

"I hate Angelo," she added vehemently.

"Then why did you marry him?" He wished he could retract the words as soon as they left his mouth. He braced himself, waiting for her to tell him off, walk out, something.

Instead, she laughed bitterly. "I was young. He was charming. He seemed like a connection to Greece, not that I remembered much. My mother, whom I adored, approved of him. She'd been friends once with his mother, when I was a child. What can I say? I married him and lived to regret it."

Damian saw her pain and wished he'd never mentioned Angelo. He toyed with his water glass, making a pattern of wet circles on the tablecloth. "What does your mother say now?"

"Nothing. She died six months ago."

"Oh. I'm sorry." He would have taken her hand, but she pulled it back just as he reached across the table.

Her mouth trembled, and he could see tears glossing her eyes. "I'm sorry, too," she said jaggedly. "I loved her so. For years it was just the two of us. She worked hard after she came to Canada. In a restaurant. She always said cooking was what she knew, so that was what she did. But she also had an excellent head for business and eventually she owned five restaurants. She made sure I never went without anything I needed. The only thing that went wrong was Angelo. She regretted that until her dying day, said she should have seen him for what he was from the beginning."

"From what I understand," Damian said deliberately, "Angelo can play any role the occasion warrants. I had a few words with him when we were building Lisandro's house last spring. Seems he felt he had a claim to the land, although I showed him the title, proving Lisandro the legal owner. They say he became the village bad boy after his father died."

"Well, his reputation didn't follow him to Canada," Alexa said bleakly. "What about you?" she added with forced brightness. "Are you married?"

His brows rose. "No. Are you always this blunt?"

A pink flush raced across her cheekbones, but she answered steadfastly. "I try to be. Saves time, don't you think?"

"Mmm," he said noncommittally, thinking how different she was from the women he knew. She was refreshingly open and honest, straightforward. Which made the feeling he had that she was hiding something all the more disturbing.

He pushed the thought away. Today they would just get to know each other. Tomorrow he would find out her secrets.

He smiled at her with practiced ease. "Here's Poppy with our food."

THEY WERE DRINKING tiny cups of after-dinner coffee when Angelo came in, sauntering over to their table with that arrogant walk of his, the walk that had seduced Alexa once but now merely bored her.

"Good evening, Alexa, Damian," he said with a friendly smile, as if the encounter at noon hadn't happened.

"Evening, Angelo," Damian said coolly.

Without waiting for an invitation, Angelo pulled out a chair and sat down. His eyes rested on Alexa for a long moment, the predatory stare of a wolf about to pounce on a rabbit. She willed herself not to squirm and met his gaze with a hard look of her own. "What do you want, Angelo?"

"You, perhaps," he drawled with a sly grin and a wink. "I'm still thinking about it. But at the moment, it's Damian I need to talk to."

"I doubt if we have anything to say to each other." Damian's tone was mild, but Alexa heard an undercurrent of animosity.

Angelo's affable expression disappeared like a torn-off mask. His eyes glittered with hatred. "Actually, it is Lisandro I need to speak with. You say he's not well enough to receive visitors, but I heard he was sitting outside early this afternoon. I need to see him. If you try to stop me again, I'll wait until you're not around."

"Is that a threat?"

"Not yet," Angelo said. "But I can make it one. I can't wait much longer."

Alexa shivered as she saw the stillness that froze Damian's face. Dangerous. She wondered what hardships Damian had endured to develop that edge of controlled violence.

"Lisandro doesn't want to see you," he said in an even voice. "And I won't let you upset him, even from a distance. The man is dying. Can't you let him live his last days in peace?"

Angelo got to his feet, resting his palms on the table as he leaned toward Damian. "Let me talk to him and he'll have peace. That's my final word."

He stalked toward the door, then veered away to the kitchen instead, intercepting Poppy in the middle of the room. He took hold of her wrist, stopping her as she tried to walk around him.

"I'll see you later, won't I, Poppy?" he said without bothering to lower his voice. The click of cutlery and the hum of voices ceased as the fifteen or so townspeople in the restaurant focused on the drama, like an audience at a play.

Her eyes skittering left and right, Poppy said nothing, but Alexa could see her lips compressed in pain. Damian half rose in his chair, intending to intervene, but Angelo let go of the woman's wrist. She ran back into the kitchen. Angelo turned, smirking in Damian's direction before striding out. The door slammed behind him.

Scene over, the other diners turned their attention to Damian and Alexa's table. Alexa could feel their eyes on her, but she couldn't guess whether they were sympathetic or censorious. After a moment, their conversations resumed, but a strange uneasiness still lay over the room.

"One day he's going to regret it," Damian muttered.

"I gather that's not the first time something like this has happened?" Alexa said, forcing a calm she didn't feel. Under her skin, her nerves were jumping. Poor Poppy. Another of Angelo's victims.

"No. I think they were friends when he first came. But something happened. He's still pushing himself on her but she usually tells him off, or manages to avoid him. He doesn't seem to understand when he's not wanted."

"What's all this between him and your foster father?"

Damian drew in a long breath. "Ever since Lisandro came here in the summer, Angelo has been after me to let him talk to him. Lisandro is adamant. He won't see Angelo. It can't be about the land again, not after all this time."

"Why would Angelo think he has a claim on the land?"

"Through you, Alexa. Your maiden name is Doukas, isn't it?"

Alexa jumped as if she'd been stung. "How did you know that?"

Damian shrugged. "Ever since he came back a year ago, Angelo's been bragging that he married Dimitrios Doukas's daughter. Local gossip has it that the families were enemies at one time."

"Enemies? My mother liked Angelo's mother."

"That may be. It's an old story. Who knows what the truth is? However, your old house stood on that land."

"Mine?" she said in a bewildered tone.

"Yes. I thought you might have come back to look at the place you once lived in."

Alexa shook her head. "I came to see the town," she hedged. "I don't remember the house. I was only six. How did Lisandro come to buy the property?"

"He bought it from your uncle Elias, your father's brother. After you and your mother left, Elias lived in the house for several months. There was some sort of skirmish between communist party members and the Greek military and the house was badly damaged. Your uncle moved to Ioannina."

"Now I remember," Alexa said thoughtfully. "Angelo even asked about the property at the time of our divorce. My mother told us that she no longer owned it. She'd signed it over to my uncle when we went to Canada, long before I met Angelo. Did you know my uncle Elias?"

Damian shook his head. "Lisandro has owned the property for a long time. I didn't know anything about it until he decided to build a house there earlier this year."

"In any case," Alexa said, "it's impossible for Angelo to have any claim on the land."

Damian shook his head. "All I know is that he seems very anxious to see Lisandro, and he's becoming more persistent."

"What about now? Is Lisandro alone? Should you be getting back in case Angelo tries to get to him?"

"Lisandro is okay. Our neighbor, Vassiliki, is with him." He smiled faintly. "Angelo is not likely to tangle with her. She's bigger than he is and has a tongue like a razor." He pushed back his chair. "But I'm sure she'd like to get home, so I'd better be going."

He picked up the bill and walked Alexa to the foot of the stairs. "Good night, Alexa."

She walked slowly up the stairs, thinking about what he had told her, about the property on which her father's house had stood, about Angelo and his lack of consideration for a dying man. Everyone seemed to know who she was, which meant there was no point in keeping her quest a secret any longer. Tomorrow she would ask some questions.

Her mind drifted to Lisandro. How long did he have left? she wondered. Damian was worried about him, despite the optimistic front he put up. The deep love he had for the man had been obvious.

It must be excruciating to watch someone you loved dying before your eyes, she thought. Painful as her mother's death had been to her, it hadn't been drawn out. Olympia had died within hours of suffering a stroke. Unable to talk, she'd said goodbye to Alexa with only a squeeze of her hand. Later Alexa realized Olympia must have had a premonition of her death; she'd left her affairs in meticulous order, every detail spelled out with no way for Angelo to get his hands on a penny of her considerable estate.

Shaking off her morbid thoughts, she reached the landing and pulled the key from her pocket. The light suddenly went out; probably a burnt-out bulb.

She could barely make out the rectangle that was the hall window. Her door was next to it. Carefully avoiding a small cabinet set against the wall, she edged toward it.

From the shadows, a heavy body hurled itself at her. She crashed to the floor, pain shooting through her head as her temple connected with the cabinet.

Chapter Three

A new pain sliced into Alexa's brain as the light flared on. Dazed, she shook her head before scrambling to her knees.

"Take it easy." Damian set a hand on her shoulder.

"I thought you'd gone," Alexa said inanely. She lifted her head. Black-and-purple spots spun before her eyes.

"Give it a minute. You don't want to faint," Damian said as he kept her head low with a gentle hand on her neck.

His voice was deep and reassuring, and Alexa focused on it until her vision cleared. Poppy, her eyes wide with horror, stood behind Damian. Face pale, she appeared closer to fainting than Alexa felt. "Maybe you shouldn't get up," she said shakily. "I'll call the doctor."

Alexa braced her hand against the cabinet. Her other hand grasping Damian's, she hauled herself to her feet. She paused, assessing the damage. Except for a slight buzzing in her head and an ache in her wrist, which she'd extended to break her fall, she seemed to be all right. "I don't need a doctor." She looked past Poppy, down the brightly lit hall. "Did you see him?"

"See who?" Poppy spun around, then turned back to Alexa.

"Someone ran into me. It was dark."

Poppy shook her head. "I didn't see anyone."

"Is there another way out?"

"Yes, down the hall branching off this one. The fire stairs. The door is never locked from the inside, but you can't get in from outside."

"Just a minute," Damian said. "Can you stand alone?"

Alexa nodded. He let go of her and strode down the hall. A moment later he came back, shaking his head. "The door was still slightly open. That's how he got away, all right."

Alexa chewed her lip. "He must be long gone by now. Didn't you hear anything?"

"I was just paying the bill when I heard a crash," Damian said. "When you fell, I guess. I heard nothing else. The light was out—I turned it back on to come up the stairs."

"The light is supposed to be on at all times," Poppy said worriedly. "I wonder who turned it off."

Damian took Alexa's elbow solicitously in his hand. "Let me help you to your room. You must have a bump on your head. Are you sure you don't want a doctor?"

Alexa pushed her fingers through her hair, gingerly feeling the bruised area. "It's only a little bump. The skin isn't broken."

They all stopped short as they reached the end of the hall. The door to Alexa's room stood ajar.

She might have expected it, Alexa thought fatalistically. Someone skulking in a dark hallway, and hers the only occupied room—who else could have been the target?

Pushing the door wider, Alexa looked inside. The drawers in the bottom of the wardrobe hung open, her clothes were scattered on the floor in front of them. Her suitcase teetered on the edge of the bed, as if that was the last thing the intruder had searched.

Beside her Poppy gasped in dismay, her hand coming up to cover her mouth. "This is terrible. Nothing like this has ever happened before."

"I haven't been here before," Alexa said dryly.

"No, no," Poppy stammered. "I'm sure it's not you. It must be some stranger in town, thinking a tourist has money lying around. None of the villagers would do such a thing. We have a long tradition of hospitality."

What about Angelo? The thought shot into Alexa's head. He had apparently left. He could have gone around the building and sneaked in through the kitchen entrance at the back. The main stairs were only partially visible from the dining room. By waiting for the right moment, he could have gone up unobserved.

But why? She had nothing that could possibly interest him.

She checked her purse, which she'd remembered to pick up from the floor after her fall. Her passport, wallet, the rental agreement for the car—all of it appeared intact. Not that the intruder had had much time to rifle through it. She'd only been stunned for an instant, not knocked out.

"Is anything missing?" Poppy asked.

Alexa gathered up her underwear and T-shirts, throwing them back into the drawers. Her other clothes, hanging on the rod, were undisturbed. She checked her suitcase, setting it upright. The paperback books and magazines that had been in it lay on the floor. "Everything's here."

Damian prowled around the room, looking into the bathroom and rattling the locked French doors leading to the little balcony. "All secure here," he said.

Poppy twisted her hands together. "If you'd like another room," she said diffidently, "I can give you one. Not as nice as this but..."

"This room is fine," Alexa said. From the inside, the door could be secured by a sturdy bolt, insuring privacy when the room was occupied. The outside locks were the same on every room; in fact, Alexa wondered if one key didn't open them all. Obviously petty theft was not a problem in Elatos.

Until now? Her mind went back to the man in Volos, what was his name? Kritikos. She hadn't trusted him. Could he have followed her up here, told her the story about her father to lure her to Elatos? Crazy notion, but no crazier than running into Angelo.

"I'm so sorry," Poppy said, more than a little distressed. "I'm just glad nothing was taken. Are you sure you'll be okay? I'll be right downstairs—I live in a flat behind the office—so please call me if you need anything. Or if you feel ill. Any time."

"Thanks, Poppy. But I'm sure I'll be fine."

Poppy walked to the door, with many backward glances. Alexa threw her a wide, reassuring smile. "Good night, Poppy. And don't worry about a thing."

Poppy's smile was tentative. "Good night, Alexa." She flushed, her cheeks turning vivid pink. "I'm sorry. I—"

"We're friends, aren't we?" Alexa said. "A little late for formality. Oh, and don't worry about Angelo. If he bothers you again, I'll have a word with him."

Instead of looking relieved, Poppy's brows knitted in a worried frown. "It's all right, Alexa. I can handle Angelo."

She went out, leaving Damian behind. He stared intently into Alexa's face, his dark eyes unreadable. "Please be careful, Alexa," he said. "I don't know why this has happened but I don't like it."

"It's not my fault."

"No, of course it isn't," he said gently. He touched her cheek with his forefinger, smiling, although his eyes remained watchful. "You've a smudge there."

At the door, he paused. "Lock up. I'll see you tomorrow."

He left, closing the door. Alexa's gaze remained fixed on the white painted panels. Tomorrow. A promise? Why did that fill her with an almost breathless anticipation? He had meant nothing more than kindness. She was crazy to stand there mooning about a man simply because he had beautiful eyes that made her heart beat faster when she saw the gentleness in them.

She shook herself, dragging her thoughts back to the more serious matter of the intruder. Had her unwelcome guest been Angelo up to some sadistic game? It wouldn't be the first time. She'd been a victim of Angelo's self-serving manipulations often enough.

Until the day she'd rebelled and walked out on him, an act of defiance he'd never forgiven her for.

She bolted the door, put away her clothes neatly, then showered in the small adjoining bathroom. She crawled into bed, expecting her thoughts to dwell on the bungled burglary. Instead, when she closed her eyes, she kept seeing Damian's face, the intense, dark eyes that were by turns cynical and tender. She sensed a darkness in his soul, but also vulnerability.

If she weren't leaving in a few days, would their acquaintance expand into friendship? The thought was tantalizing. And disturbing. More so, because after Angelo she hadn't allowed herself to become involved with any man. Hadn't even been interested. Until Damian, who had neither the time nor the emotional energy for her. Nor could she afford the luxury of an interest in him.

No matter, she told herself firmly. Tomorrow she had to find out about her father.

IT WAS THE CHILL that told her something was wrong. Her feet were frozen. She looked down and realized she was standing on frigid marble, not on the hooked rug that covered the wooden floor of her room.

"Oh, no," she groaned inaudibly. This hadn't happened in months—why now?

In the damp air her nightdress clung to her, clammily sticking to her skin. The pungent scent of chrysanthemums drifted up from the pots below the steps. She looked up at the sky, glittering with stars. Her breath puffed into a cloud. Sometime after midnight, she judged, but nowhere near dawn.

She walked slowly back inside, up the stairs and through the open door of her room. She'd undone both the lock and the bolt. Of course, that was minor compared to the escape she'd accomplished as a child, when she'd managed to wander out of their house, which was locked with a double-cylinder dead bolt. She'd retrieved the key from the drawer where it was kept and opened the door. A cruising policeman had returned her home from three blocks away, waking her mother and giving her a lecture on child safety.

The sleepwalking had become less frequent as she grew up, but in times of stress, even as an adult, she'd experienced occasional lapses. During the stock market crisis of 1987, she'd put obstacles between her bed and the door so that she would wake up before she got outside.

The last episode had been after her mother's funeral. She'd found herself in the garage ready to get into her car, but the sound of the garage door opener had awakened her. She'd been free of the affliction for several months now.

Until tonight.

She locked the door and set a chair in front of it. Back in bed, she pulled the blankets up to her chin and rubbed the circulation back into her cold feet. She guessed the intruder tonight had thrown her nervous system into overload; she just hoped nobody had noticed her late-night excursion.

She had to see Damian—that should relieve some of her stress. Last night at dinner she'd debated whether to tell him why she was there. After Angelo's interruption, there hadn't been an opportunity. But he might be able to help her.

DOWNSTAIRS, POPPY WAS sitting at one of the tables in the empty dining room, poring over a large, old-fashioned ledger.

"Do you run this place all by yourself, Poppy?" Alexa said by way of greeting.

Poppy looked up, smiling, her finger marking her place. "Good morning, Alexa. Yes, at the moment I'm here alone, except for the cook. We're lucky with our cook. The restaurant is popular with the townspeople all year and gives us most of our income in winter. My brother and I are partners, but he's in Athens for a month taking a course in computers." She gestured at the ledger. "So we can streamline our accounting. It's quiet now so I can manage all right. How are you feeling?"

Alexa smiled. "I feel fine. No headache."

"I'm so glad." For a second a worried frown creased Poppy's forehead, but then she smiled again. "Shall I bring you some breakfast?"

"Just toast will be okay. And coffee, please."

After breakfast, Alexa spent nearly an hour wandering around the village. None of the streets looked familiar. She dredged the murky depths of childhood memories but came up blank. It was as if she had never been there before.

She ran into Damian at the greengrocer's where he was buying beets and shaggy heads of lettuce. He grinned at her, gesturing for her to wait until he paid for the vegetables. Again she felt the disconcerting flutter in her chest at the sight of him, a feeling she firmly squelched.

"I don't understand it," she said dejectedly. "I can't remember the layout of the village at all. And I should."

"You were very young," he said. She still looked young, her cheeks flushed from the sun, her hair tangled by the breeze. He had a sudden urge to pull her close and kiss those luscious pink lips, touch the skin that looked as lucent as pearls.

"It's been more than twenty-five years," he added, putting a rein on his thoughts. "The population is twice what it was then. And virtually none of the residents of that time are here now." He gestured at the busy shops around them.

"Most of these buildings are less than ten years old. During the fighting here at the time you and your mother left, the village was virtually destroyed. That's why you don't remember."

"I'd like to see the place where our house stood," Alexa said. "That is, if you and your foster father don't mind."

"Mind? Why, Lisandro wants to see you. I was coming to look for you as soon as I finished the shopping." He shifted the bags to one hand and took hers in the other. "Come along. He was feeling quite well this morning."

Alexa tried to convince herself that the heat of his palm wasn't causing the turmoil in her thoughts as they walked up one narrow path after another. He was only being friendly. His manner was courteous, without disturbing undercurrents, a pleasant change from Angelo's suave charm.

"Are you feeling okay? Any more disturbances last night?" Damian asked as they walked up the path.

"I'm fine. And, no. Nothing more happened in the night." Except for her sleepwalking, she added to herself, the familiar frustration stirring within her.

THE HOUSE WAS SMALL but exquisitely crafted from the native stone, its square lines relieved by the pots of red geraniums flourishing in window boxes and large terra-cotta pots.

They were met at the door by an enormous woman with steel-gray hair and a merry twinkle in her deep-set eyes. "He went in a few minutes ago, said he wanted to rest before he met the young lady."

Damian's brow furrowed. "He's all right, isn't he?"

"Overexcited, I'd say."

"Angelo hasn't been around?"

"No, he hasn't." She folded her arms beneath her massive bosom. "And he'd better not come around while I'm here. I'll be back if you need me, Damian." She strode off down the path.

"Come in, Alexa," Damian said. "I'll put this stuff away and then I'll take you in to see him."

Sunlight flooded in through the window where Lisandro sat in a rocking chair. The room was large, furnished as a bed-sitting room. Shelves of books lined the walls, and the fireplace was laid with wood and kindling for cool evenings. It was obvious that Lisandro spent a lot of time there.

He turned toward them as they came in, his face lighting up with a smile as he saw Alexa. He extended his hands to her, and Alexa, delighted by the warm welcome, took them in both of hers. His grip was surprisingly strong.

"Damian told me about you," the old man said. "I'm so happy you came."

"Thank you," Alexa said.

He turned his head to greet Damian and the light hit his face. Alexa stifled a gasp as she saw the long jagged scar that ran up his cheek from jaw to temple. The puckered skin, livid against his tan, was crisscrossed with white lines, old stitch marks showing where the deep wound had been crudely sewn.

Lisandro must have seen the shock on her face. He lightly touched the scar, lifting his shoulder in a faint shrug. "An old war wound. It's nothing."

"I'm sorry," Alexa said awkwardly. The moment passed as Damian made the introductions.

"Alexa," Lisandro said slowly, as if savoring the name. "I understand your mother died recently." He squeezed her hands. "I'm sorry. I know that sounds inadequate, but what can one say? Damian, please bring Alexa a chair."

She sat down next to the old man, who retained his hold on one of her hands. He was lonely, she thought. He must not receive many visitors.

"And your father died when you were a child. Some say he was a hero."

Alexa smiled. "To my mother, he was. Did you know him?"

An odd expression crossed the old man's face. "I'm not from here," he said. "Do you remember him?"

"Just a few impressions." Alexa smiled. "He told wonderful stories. I loved him." A long-buried memory jumped into her mind. "I was angry when he left and didn't come back. I'd forgotten."

"That's understandable." Lisandro's deep voice was calm, yet she sensed an undercurrent of strong emotion. "I have something to give you, Alexa, which we found in the wreckage of the original house, something your mother left behind when she fled."

At Alexa's startled look, he chuckled. "Yes, Alexa, your mother stole away in the middle of the night, walking with you through the mountains until she caught a bus on the main road in the morning. The next day soldiers came." His eyes became shadowed and the lines of his face deepened. "No one was allowed to leave the village for weeks and then winter came. She was lucky to get away when she did."

"How did you know this?" Alexa asked.

"Your uncle Elias told me. I bought this land from him years ago. Such courage your mother had." He tilted up her chin and looked into her eyes. "I think you have it, too." He gestured toward the fireplace. "Do you see that knife hanging there?"

Alexa nodded. On the massive chimneypiece hung not only an ornate knife but also two long crossed swords. "Damian, show Alexa the knife."

He took it down and handed it to her. It was heavy for its size, the curved blade still sharp. "The hilt is silver, made by smiths in Ioannina," Lisandro said. "I believe this was your father's. I found it with the other items. It rightfully belongs to you. Come to see me before you leave and you may have it."

"But I couldn't," Alexa stammered, overcome. Her eyes burned with unshed tears.

Lisandro clasped her hand. "You must, my dear. Indulge an old man." He took the knife and gave it to Damian, who hung it beneath the swords. Leaning back in the chair, Lisandro closed his eyes. "Now I must rest. Damian will give you the box with the other items in it. Guard it well."

"Damian," she said urgently when they stood outside the bedroom door. "Is all that true about my parents?"

Damian nodded somberly, his face remote. "I would bet on it. Lisandro has studied the history of the area. Whatever he tells you will be as close to the truth as he knows it. You probably don't know how it is here—there is always gossip, but Lisandro isn't one to repeat mere rumors."

Tears burned in her eyes. "It's so sad that they couldn't have left together, been together in Canada."

"Yes, it is." He hugged her shoulders reassuringly, a gesture as natural as if they were old friends. In the other room, the chair creaked as Lisandro shifted his weight. Damian glanced down the hall, his eyes wistful. Alexa's heart ached for him.

"You'll miss him, won't you?"

"He's been more than a father to me," Damian said, his voice rough. "Even though I should be used to the idea that I'll lose him, it still doesn't feel real. And we'll be lucky if he lasts until Christmas. He hasn't been able to get around much for a year. In fact, he only spent part of the summer here. He was in a hospital in Ioannina for a time, and then bedridden at home. We only came up here when I was in a position to take some time off so I could stay with him."

He led her into the kitchen, a sunny room lined with rustic oak cupboards. "When was Lisandro wounded?" Alexa asked.

Damian shrugged. "I don't know. World War II, I imagine. He never talks about it, and I don't even notice the scar anymore. The box is in the pantry. I'll get it."

She didn't know what she expected, but the metal box he brought out looked too small to contain much of value. "Here's the key," Damian said. "I can carry it down to the hotel for you, or you can open it here."

"I'd rather open it." She took the key, which was heavy and cold in her palm. A shiver ran up her spine. Pandora's box? She laughed at the fantasy, but couldn't shake a feeling of apprehension.

The key turned easily but the lid creaked on rusty hinges when she forced it open. Inside lay two small books, the cracked leather covers spotted with mildew. Her heart pounding in her throat, she lifted them out. She opened the cover of one, staring down at the spidery handwriting, the foreign script.

Hands shaking, she passed it to Damian. "The diary of Georgia Doukas, 1821," he read aloud. "Don't you read Greek?"

"Yes, but handwriting gives me difficulty." She took the book and held it in her hands. "Georgia Doukas. She's an ancestor of my father's. My great-great-whatever-grandmother. And 1821 is the year Greece began the war of independence against the Turks. This will be interesting."

"What about the other?"

She slowly opened it. "Why, it's in English. The diary of Olympia Doukas. That's my mother, of course. I wonder when she wrote this. The date is blotted, must have gotten wet at some time. It says 1960 something."

"Probably 1967," Damian said. "Wasn't that the year your mother took you to Canada?"

"Yes." Alexa tapped her finger on the metal box. "How did this escape the destruction of the house?"

Damian leaned back against the counter, crossing his ankles. "The original house was constructed from sun-dried bricks, a material not used much up here since there's plenty of stone. It was badly damaged during the fighting the winter after your mother left. Over the years, with half the roof gone, the structure just collapsed. The kitchen, added onto the back, had stone walls that remained standing under the rubble. The box was found under the marble slab that covered the lower cupboards." He stroked his hand over the counter at his side. "I had the workmen use it as part of this counter when Lisandro had the new house built."

"And the key?"

Damian frowned. "I guess it was in the lock. Lisandro was here when they discovered it. I wasn't. Will you have trouble translating the older diary?"

"Are you offering to help?" she asked lightly.

"I could," he said, his face serious. "If you let me."

"We'll see," said Alexa. "I should be able to figure it out once I get used to the script." She placed the diaries into the box and closed it. "I guess I'd better get started on it."

"I'll walk you back," Damian said.

"Better not leave Lisandro alone. I know the way now."

"Then you'll know the way back, and come and see Lisandro again."

Impulsively, Alexa laid her hand on his arm. "Of course I will."

To her surprise, Damian lifted her hand and kissed the back of it, a light brush of his lips over her skin. A tingle whizzed up her arm. The tingle became a buzz when he turned her hand and planted another kiss in her palm, tickling her with the tip of his tongue. He closed her fingers over it, his eyes dark and sober as they gazed into hers.

"Damian," Alex said breathlessly.

He touched her lips with his fingertip. "Please. Don't say anything. I'll see you later."

She was halfway back to the hotel before she realized she hadn't told him about her search for her father.

SHE TACKLED her mother's diary first. The handwriting wasn't completely clear, but at least the language was English. This didn't surprise her, because her mother had spent most of her school years in Canada, only returning to Greece after her marriage to Alexa's father.

Dampness had blurred some of the lines, but she estimated the diary covered five or six months, from the time Alexa and her parents arrived in Elatos to the day before her mother had fled to Canada. This confirmed the year as 1967, the year of infamy, Olympia had written. Dimitrios, Alexa's father, had spent little time there once he'd installed Alexa and Olympia, making many trips back and forth to Athens. Alexa's eyes filled with tears at the poignant statement of how much her mother had missed him.

Still, as Alexa knew, Olympia's outstanding personality trait had been her optimism. The political situation would change. But the optimism changed to despair when Dimitrios, hounded by political enemies, had gone north.

The tone grew darker, more desperate. Dimitrios's brother, Elias, had followed him but had returned within weeks. Alexa wept as she read of her mother's soul-wrenching grief when she received the news that Dimitrios was dead.

But, realizing greater political storms were brewing, within days Olympia had gathered herself and put into motion the instructions her husband had left her in a letter.

Because of Dimitrios's and Olympia's Canadian connections and his prior preparations, the arrangements were routine. Still, she was torn, caught between the need to stay home in case the death report was false, and her fear for Alexa if they stayed. In the end, she had decided they would leave.

"It's too dangerous for a small child now," Olympia had written, "and what future will she have? I must go, for Alexa."

The diary ended on this note. Only one more sentence had been added. "I will hide the book in the house, for Dimitrios to find, if this all turns out to be a bad dream and he is still alive."

But he wasn't alive, unless Kritikos told the truth, and others had found the book.

Tears blurring her eyes, Alexa leafed through the remaining blank pages, her fingers shaking.

At the back of the book, in the middle of a page, she found a single line, crookedly scrawled, as if the writer had been in a hurry. She couldn't tell if it was her mother's writing because it wasn't in English.

It was written in Greek: *Where is the sword of Dimitrios?*

Chapter Four

The sword of Dimitrios. What was the sword of Dimitrios?

The question rang in Alexa's brain all through lunch, even while she was conversing quietly with Poppy, who finally sat down when Alexa insisted she wanted company.

"There was another stranger in town this morning," Poppy said. "From Volos. Didn't you say your aunt lives there?"

"Yes." Alexa frowned, that feeling of uneasiness resurfacing.

"He was looking for a small house to rent," Poppy went on. "I can't imagine why anyone would want to stay here now. It'll soon be winter and there's nothing to do."

"Maybe he's a skier," Alexa suggested.

Poppy clicked her tongue. "No skiing here."

"So what did you tell him?"

"I told him to ask around the square." She pointed to the two small books beside Alexa's plate. "I see Lisandro gave you the diaries."

Alexa's eyes widened. "How did you know about the diaries?"

"Oh, everyone knows. When the workman cleared the rubble from the old house, he found the box. He gave it to Lisandro since he now owned the property. Of course, the workman couldn't resist opening the box first and looking at what was inside. And it was too good a story to keep to himself. It was all over the village in an hour."

"Everyone knew and I didn't," Alexa said ruefully.

"Angelo should have given Lisandro your address so he could send them to you, but you know Angelo. He never does anything that isn't to his advantage. And he wanted the diaries himself. Something about family history."

That might explain why Angelo wanted to talk to Lisandro, Alexa thought with sudden insight. Only it was Alexa's family history, not Angelo's. Unless— "Have you seen Angelo today?"

Poppy shook her head. "No, which is kind of odd. He's usually sitting in the square drinking coffee in the mornings."

Maybe Angelo wasn't going to be a problem, after all, Alexa thought. She pushed back her chair. "I need to check out the village records. Could you lock the diaries in the safe for now?" Even if the diaries turned out to have nothing more than sentimental value, Alex wasn't going to risk leaving them in her room when she wasn't there. Maybe they weren't even safe when she *was* there, if she continued to wander in her sleep.

"Of course," Poppy said.

Alexa followed her into the office, where Poppy knelt before the small safe and manipulated the combination lock. Alexa laid the books inside. "Thanks."

Poppy locked the safe. "I'll come with you. There's probably no one in the village office right now and I have the keys."

The office, next door to the hotel restaurant, smelled of dusty ledgers and chrysanthemums, yellow, mop-headed blossoms nodding in a crystal vase on the front desk. To Alexa's surprise, Damian sat behind the desk.

He glanced up from the file spread out in front of him. At the sight of her, his questioning look changed to a broad smile that sent a zing along her nerve endings.

"You *are* the mayor," she said facetiously.

"No, I'm not," he said, getting up. "I'm just looking over some land records. The clerk isn't here, but maybe I can help you."

"Births and deaths," she said. "Not that they're likely to be of much help, since the records in Ioannina weren't."

Damian took a large leather book down from a shelf, blowing off the dust. "Here you are. Goes back almost a hundred years."

She found the names easy to recognize. More conveniently, they were listed in alphabetical order by months, births in one section, deaths in another, marriages in between.

After an hour, she had found the entry for her father's birth, more than eighty years ago. It hit her suddenly that the chance of him being alive was remote; by now he was a very old man. She pushed away the thought even as she turned to the deaths. As she had expected, her father's was listed, in the summer of 1967. In the late seventies, she saw the entry for her uncle Elias's death, although it was noted that he wasn't buried in the village cemetery.

She found an entry for the death of Constantine Thetalou, also in 1967. In fact, there had been a lot of deaths in 1967 and 1968. Constantine's age was a surprise. Although Angelo had been eight years older than Alexa, his father had been a good twenty years younger than Alexa's father. She turned to the marriages. Yes, he'd married young, in his early twenties, and Angelo had been born six months later.

She turned back, looking for more Thetalous. The name recurred several times, and the most interesting fact she gleaned was that Constantine had had a brother, five years younger than he was. But his birth was the only entry—no listing of marriage or death. Obviously he had left Elatos before the trouble began.

Eyes weary, she handed the book back to Damian. "Find anything interesting?" he asked as he returned it to the shelf.

"Nothing new."

He touched her shoulder. "Don't be discouraged, Alexa." He smiled, taking her hand. "Come, I'll show you our museum."

He led her through an open door into the next room. Along the wall stood a carved chest with many shallow drawers. The top was a glass-covered display case, containing a collection of weapons from, she estimated, the last two hundred years. She knew little about guns, although she recognized an old flintlock pistol that looked like a weapon for a duel. Two swords lay side by side, one straight-bladed, the other curved. Turkish? she wondered. Next to those lay a row of smaller knives.

"Quite a history here, isn't there?" Alexa said, her eyes on the intricately fashioned knife handles, some of which were set with jewels. Did their beauty make up for their use, maiming and killing, shedding blood and destroying souls? "Too many wars, though."

"Yes," Damian agreed. "But usually it was necessary."

"Not always." She went back to the first case. "Those knives look like the one Lisandro showed me, the knife he said belonged to my father."

"The design indicates it's from before your father's birth. Must be a family heirloom."

"What about the swords Lisandro has hanging over the fireplace?" Alexa asked.

"They're Lisandro's. He had them in his Ioannina house. Actually, if I'm not mistaken, they're older and more valuable than the swords displayed here. They belonged to an ancestor of his from the Middle Ages, or even earlier." He pointed to a rectangle of black velvet that lay in the center of the case. "That's where the prized artifact sat until it disappeared."

"Disappeared?"

"Yes, Alexa," Poppy said. "No one could believe it. It was quite a scandal at the time."

A chill feathered up Alexa's spine, as if someone had walked on her grave. "Scandal?"

"Poppy—" Damian began, a warning in his voice.

"What scandal?" Alexa demanded, cutting him off.

Poppy shrugged. "It was a long time ago. No one would hold you responsible for your father's actions."

"My father was a good man," Alexa said, biting her lip.

"Oh, no one ever said he wasn't. Some people even say he was a saint. After all, he did it in the hope that it would prevent further bloodshed. Actually, I think far too much fuss is made over these old artifacts, and keeping feuds alive for generations is ridiculous."

More vague innuendos, but if her father were involved in a scandal, that explained the odd looks she'd been getting. "What did he do? Tell me."

Poppy tapped her fingers on the glass case. "I only know what I heard. I was a baby at the time. They say he took the sword. It hasn't been seen since, all these years."

"The sword?" Alexa waited with an oddly detached dread, already knowing the answer.

"The sword of Dimitrios."

The phrase in the diary. "My father's name was Dimitrios," Alexa said tonelessly as she sank down onto a chair.

"My father, who was interested in history, told me about the sword," Poppy said. "Your father was not the Dimitrios the sword was named after. The weapon goes back to the Byzantine era, and was probably carried on the Crusades. It belonged to the founder of Elatos and was kept in the village office. During the War of Independence, the family records were lost in a fire. When things settled down, many years later, several families got into a feud over the sword, each of them claiming to be the descendants of the original Dimitrios. After your father left, the sword was discovered missing."

"He didn't steal it," Alexa declared forcefully. "Maybe he hid it for safekeeping."

Poppy nodded. "That's possible. But we'll never know, will we?"

Unless Kritikos's story was true. She needed to think, and she did that best in the fresh air.

Taking her leave of Damian and Poppy, Alexa walked around the village to clear her head. Up one narrow trail, down another; if she got lost, she didn't care. After about an hour, she found herself in a tiny meadow carved from a grove of white-trunked birches. The gold-green leaves rustled above her head as she sat down on a patch of grass baked to a soft tan by the summer sun.

Her father was not a thief. He was an honorable man. Her mother had told her a thousand times how brave he was, fearless even when all his friends turned against him. It was his unimpeachable honor that had made it necessary for him to flee Elatos. If he hadn't gone, he would have been killed, and many others with him.

Slowly peace came to Alexa. She glanced around the little glade, struck by a feeling of familiarity. Perhaps she'd come here as a child, pretended she talked to fairies in the grass.

Then, all of a sudden, she heard a shrill cry and a chill washed over her, shattering the pleasant fantasy. An eagle hung in the clear dome of the sky, its wings motionless as it searched for prey. Suddenly the wings folded and the great bird plummeted toward the earth. A moment later she saw it rising through the trees, a small furry creature clutched in its talons.

Shivering despite the heat of the Indian summer sun, she started back toward the village, taking what she assumed was the shortest path back to the square. She must have gotten turned around, she realized presently. She'd asked Damian earlier where Angelo lived and had deliberately avoided passing his house. Yet here she was, standing outside a rusting chain-link fence. The house was little more than a shack set in a garden that grew only tall dried-out thistles. Several windows were boarded up, and plaster was peeling off the walls, leaving ugly holes that exposed the cement blocks underneath.

Two cars stood at the side of the garden, a little jeeplike affair she assumed must be Angelo's, and another car, a dusty gray Escort with a sticker advertising a Volos car dealership.

Volos. The car must belong to the stranger Poppy had mentioned? But what was he doing here, at Angelo's house, if indeed this was Angelo's house. She might have misunderstood, but the chain-link fence convinced her. Damian had specifically mentioned that it was the only such fence in the village. And one of the few houses not built of stone.

Her mind jumped back to Poppy's words of last evening. No one in town would break into anyone's room. But a stranger might. Maybe this stranger had come last night. Maybe he had followed her from Volos.

Without disturbing the stones on the steep path, she hurried away from the house. Apprehension quickened her steps. She hadn't heard the last of Angelo. Of that she was convinced.

AS SHE ATE DINNER that evening, her eyes kept wandering to the doorway, taking note of each person who entered. She felt an acute disappointment when none of them proved to be Damian.

He was eating with Lisandro, of course. She couldn't expect Damian to leave him alone every evening.

It would be easier if she went to him.

The widely scattered streetlamps cast circular pools of light along the paths, separated by immense tracts of shadow. Alexa wove in and out of them, casting frequent, nervous glances behind her and to the sides of the path. She thought she heard footsteps, a furtive shuffling of shoes against stone, but each time she spun around she saw nothing, only the dark images of trees stirring in the breeze.

She chided herself for an overactive imagination, wiping her sweating palms on her jeans. The village was probably safer than any Vancouver street, including her own.

The front shutters were closed at Lisandro's house, but she could see the light shining through the louvers, laying golden bars on the veranda floor. She knocked on the glass-paneled door, shifting from one foot to the other as she waited.

Damian opened the door. His face immediately lit up with a smile and she was glad she'd come. "Alexa, come in."

"Just for a moment," she said, denying her longing to get to know him better. She couldn't let herself become involved with this man, never mind how much that intriguing combination of cynicism and sweetness pulled her. She had a life in Canada, a life she had to go back to. There was no way they could be together.

"For a moment, then," he said, faintly mocking. "Lisandro's asleep."

"At this hour?" she asked, surprised.

Damian nodded soberly. "I'm afraid so. He tires very easily these days. Meeting you excited him. He didn't rest enough during the day."

Alexa dipped her head, contrite. "I'm sorry."

Damian touched her hair—she felt the brush of his fingers all too briefly, as if he'd thought she might not welcome the closeness from someone she barely knew. "Don't be sorry. He enjoyed it so much."

"Did he know my mother, by any chance?" Alexa asked as he led her into the living room and gestured toward a chair near the windows.

"I don't think so. As far as I know he's never been in Elatos except to plan this house last spring." He frowned. "I suppose he must have been here to look over the property when he bought it, but that was long ago, and certainly after your mother left. I don't really know. Lisandro never talks about the past."

The lace curtain over the window billowed into the room, driven by a quickening breeze. Alexa jumped as the weighted hem flicked over her arm. "Oh!"

"What's wrong?" Damian rose from his chair, walked over and closed the window.

"Just jumpy, I guess. I thought someone was following me when I came up the path."

Damian laughed. "What? In little Elatos? Where nothing's happened since the sixties? Even then they called it only a political difference."

"Someone was in my room last night, remember?"

His eyes narrowed, giving his face a hard, closed look. "The locks are a joke. I know. I stayed there when I was supervising the building of this house for Lisandro." Raking his fingers through his hair, he paced from the window to the kitchen door and back again. "You didn't discover afterward that anything was taken, did you?"

"No, but I wonder who it was and what he was after."

"Could have been one of the refugees who've been hanging around," Damian suggested. "Not that I'd accuse them, just like that. Up to now we've had no trouble with them, and they work hard at whatever jobs they can get."

"Well, there was no harm done." She folded her hands in her lap. "I came to ask you if you knew anyone here who could give me a translation of my great-whatever-grandmother's diary. It doesn't have to be to English, modern Greek would do fine."

Damian thought for a moment. "Yes, there is someone. A villager who taught ancient Greek in a high school in Ioannina before he retired, and he's also familiar with the customs and dialects of the area."

"Sounds perfect," Alexa said. "I'll be glad to pay him."

"I expect that won't be necessary, Alexa. He'd consider it a fascinating project. I'll talk to him tomorrow. Will that be soon enough?"

"Fine."

"Did you find anything interesting in the diary?" Damian asked.

"Only that there was some kind of feud between the Doukases and the Thetalous." She got up from the chair and walked toward the door.

She was obviously going. Damian searched his mind for an excuse to make her stay, to keep her there a little longer. Swallowing his frustration, he realized he couldn't even walk her back; he couldn't leave Lisandro, especially since the old man had been complaining of chest pains at supper.

"How about some coffee before you go? I was just planning to have some." He hadn't, but she didn't need to know that.

"Thank you, but I'd better get back. I don't want to take up more of your time. I'm sure you have things to do."

"At this hour?" He almost laughed. "Okay," he said, resigned. If she didn't want him, it was hopeless. It was hopeless, anyway; what could a successful Canadian investment broker have in common with a small-town Greek lawyer? No use reaching beyond his grasp.

With surprise he realized he'd never been tempted to, until now. He'd never met a woman with whom he wanted to take chances. Love, to him, was a myth, a dream that led only to disappointment and betrayal.

"See you tomorrow," he said. Oh, Alexa, he thought regretfully, when he realized from the hurt in her brown eyes that he'd spoken too harshly. Go away, it would never work for us.

"Good night, Damian," she said quietly, and walked away.

He followed her progress down the hill, keeping his eyes on her as she stepped through pools of light and disappeared into rivers of dark. When she turned the corner, he closed the door, his loneliness acute and painful.

BETTER THIS WAY, Alexa told herself as she hurried toward the square and the hotel. The tap-tapping of a cane drew her eyes to an old man walking ahead of her. His presence was reassuring somehow, after the almost-silent darkness earlier. She overtook him, and wished him a good evening as she passed. He stopped, saying nothing as he gazed at her from behind thick-lensed glasses.

Thinking he was hard of hearing, she repeated her greeting in a louder voice. Still, he said nothing. Shivering, she picked up her pace, conscious of the dark, unfathomable eyes on her until she was hidden by a curve in the path.

She entered the hotel, passing by the dining room, where several tables were occupied. She had dined earlier than local custom, but for the short time she'd be here, she didn't see the need to change her habits.

She thought of Damian, and the idea of leaving filled her with regret and a disquieting sensation that she was throwing away something that could prove of great value.

She had reached the foot of the stairs when she turned instead toward Poppy's office. She would study the diary a little more. Perhaps she could find some proof that her father was alive.

Halfway down the short hall that ran next to the kitchen, the sound of angry voices brought her to a stop.

"I won't do it." Poppy's voice, high pitched, desperate.

"You have to help me," a harsh male voice replied with biting menace. "You have to, or I won't be responsible for what happens to her."

Alexa just had time to flatten herself against the wall when Angelo came charging out of the office.

Chapter Five

Angelo didn't seem to notice her as she hid herself in the slight indentation created by the storage room door. He cut into the kitchen, setting the two-way door to swinging madly. Alexa caught it in time to see him go out the back exit.

She ran across the kitchen, ignoring the cook who stared at the open back door. Cautiously, Alexa poked her head around the doorway. Angelo ducked under the clothesline, pausing only when he reached the corner of the next building. The shadows were dense, but she could make out another man talking to him. The low keening of the wind around the hotel drowned out any possibility of hearing what they said.

Behind her, Alexa heard the clatter of pots as the cook went back to work. Abruptly, Angelo walked away. The man he'd been talking to stepped out into the open.

Were her eyes playing tricks on her in the uncertain light? The figure heading toward the square looked just like Kritikos, the man who'd spoken to her in Volos about her father.

She stepped out of the door, hoping to get a clearer look when he passed the streetlamp. But no, he skirted the edges of the lighted circle and disappeared down another path.

Even if she followed, she wasn't likely to catch up since there were any number of paths he could veer off to.

Going in, she closed the door. In the hall, she found Poppy, her eyes red-rimmed, her demeanor subdued.

"He's gone," Alexa said.

Poppy looked startled for a moment, then resigned. "I have to get to the front desk. Someone's waiting."

Alexa laid a hand on Poppy's arm. "Please, Poppy. It's important. I need to know what the man who was asking about a house looked like."

"Late fifties, probably." Poppy's brow creased in concentration. "Heavyset. He had a round face, a thin mustache and a small beard, like a professor. Except he didn't look like a professor. His eyes—they were hard, cold. I didn't like his eyes."

Neither did I, thought Alexa. It had to be Kritikos. The question was, had he followed her? Or had someone else manipulated his and her own trip to Elatos? Poppy shifted restlessly, and Alexa threw her a smile. "Thanks, Poppy. You've been very helpful. Oh, could I have a jug of water for my room later?"

"Of course," Poppy said. "There are always some in the kitchen fridge. Just help yourself."

Alexa's smile faded when Poppy left. She set her legs in motion, going toward the front door. It was time she had a talk with Angelo. That car parked by his house had to belong to Kritikos.

Outside, she scanned the square. The gray Escort was there, parked in front of an ouzeri, kitty-corner from the hotel. Kritikos was not visible. Only one die-hard shepherd clad in a black felt cape sat at an outside table. The rest of the patrons had been driven inside by the evening chill.

She was too angry to be nervous about the dark paths this time. Angelo's house showed a faint light through closed shutters. She banged on the door with her fist, nearly catching Angelo in the nose when he suddenly opened the door.

He looked at her with profound disfavor. "What do you want, Alexa?"

Some change from their earlier encounter. "I want to know what your game is."

He held the door wider, swinging his arm in an expansive gesture. "Come in, by all means." His mouth twisted in a parody of his usual charming smile. He laid his hand on her arm but she shook him off.

Angelo shrugged, closing the door. He led her toward the lighted room at the back of the house. Sand grated under her shoes. She saw that the room they crossed was empty, with a heap of fallen fireplace bricks on the crumbling hearth.

In the kitchen Angelo dragged out a chair for her, dumping a pile of magazines from it to the floor. The rusted sink held several days of soiled dishes, mercilessly illuminated by a single naked light bulb hanging from the ceiling. Through a doorway at one side of the room, she could see a bed, tumbled sheets dragging on the dusty floor.

"Sure, look down your nose," he said sarcastically. "If you hadn't left me, I wouldn't be living in this dump."

She'd thought herself immune but she couldn't suppress a little stab of guilt. Although why she should feel guilty, she didn't know. He was the one who'd broken their marriage vows, almost from the first day, she'd found out later. "You had a good job, Angelo. And your citizenship. Nobody chased you back here."

"And I had you," he said. "I want you back, Alexa. I want what's rightfully mine."

Blood beat painfully against Alexa's temples. "You got your settlement. Wasn't that enough?"

"Not nearly. I want you, Alexa."

Alexa jumped up from the chair. "After what you put me through, Angelo? You expect me to listen to this?"

Abruptly he changed tactics. "Alexa, please. Sit down. We can talk calmly. Like adults."

Eyeing him in distrust, she sat again, perched on the edge of the hard seat. She had to control the anger that seethed in her. In a shouting match he always won. No wonder. From what she'd heard lately, he must have gotten into many shouting matches in his youth as the town trouble-maker.

She swallowed, her throat dry. "Angelo, do you know a man named Pavlo Kritikos?"

A knowing smile crept over his face. He tilted his chair back on two legs, the back resting against the wall. She didn't trust the deceptively relaxed pose for a second.

"Did you send him to me in Volos with this wild story of my father being alive?"

"Yes," he said, without blinking an eye.

Her chair crashed to the floor as she leapt up. "You rat!" she screamed at him. "You rotten, lying bastard."

He remained where he was. "I didn't lie. Kritikos did. Only it wasn't exactly a lie. The story he told you is true except for a couple of things. We heard the story originally about a year ago."

Before her mother's death. Alexa opened and closed her mouth, shock making her speechless. "And you didn't tell me?" she ground out, the words rising on the last syllable. "Or my mother. She was still alive—"

"Why should I? There was nothing in it for me. And your mother had told me if I tried to see her, or you, she'd have me thrown in jail."

"You tried to kill me."

"I should have done it, too. I would have been long gone before they found your body on the mountain."

She clenched her fists. "Just tell me this, where is my father now?"

The corners of Angelo's mouth turned up. "How should I know? He may be dead now, for all I know. Apparently in the letter he said he was ill, wanted to make amends to those who'd helped him." His eyes narrowed and his smile became crafty. "I'd like to see those diaries. I know you have them."

"How do you know that?" Alexa asked, a cold sensation settling in her stomach.

"Easy. Poppy told me, only she wouldn't let me have a look at them."

So that was what the argument in the office had been about. It was high time Alexa put them in a safer place. Not that she didn't trust Poppy, but she knew Angelo to be a master of manipulation. He could go from charming to cruel in seconds, and poor Poppy wouldn't stand a chance against him.

"Not that the diaries were any secret," Angelo continued. "They've been talked about ever since the old house was torn down last spring. But they were in Ioannina until Lisandro came here. In case you're wondering why I came back to this benighted village, I wanted to dig into your family history. I figured it would give me a lead on the sword."

"The sword of Dimitrios?" What didn't he know? Alexa's throat felt dry and scratchy.

"That's the one. The one they say your father took."

"He didn't."

Angelo shrugged. "How would you know? You were a kid."

"And the diaries won't help you," Alexa stated. "I've already been through them both. What do you want with the sword, anyway?"

Tipping the chair forward onto its legs, Angelo reached out a hand and stroked it down Alexa's cheek. She flinched wildly away. He laughed. "Alexa, you're still as naive as you were years ago. But the story goes that the two families, yours and mine, made plenty of money from industries encouraged by the Turks before they were driven out. The proceeds were converted into diamonds, which are hidden in the hilt of the sword. I want those diamonds."

Greed. She might have known. "Angelo, you're dreaming. You surely don't think you're going to find the sword, do you, when they've been looking for it all these years? And even if you do, what makes you think the villagers are going to let you take the diamonds? *If* they're still there."

"You're going to help me. The sword rightfully belongs either to your family or mine. Which amounts to the same thing, since you're my wife."

She stared at him in disbelief. "Have you forgotten? I'm not your wife."

"A Canadian divorce doesn't count here."

"A church divorce does. Last year I got a church divorce."

"Then why haven't you changed your name back?" he said with a sneer.

"I was working on that, too. But then my mother died. You can bet that it will have top priority when I get home."

He tipped his chair back again. "Doesn't matter, anyway. You're here now. You're going to help me. First I want the diaries."

Alexa dragged in a deep breath, willing herself to be calm. "Angelo, I'm telling you, there's nothing in the diaries. My mother's doesn't mention the sword. The other diary does, but it's so obscure and vague, it's no use at all. Yes, both names are mentioned, Doukas and Thetalou, but it doesn't tell me anything. Besides, how would that help you find the sword now?"

His jaw set stubbornly. "There has to be something, some place where they traditionally kept the sword during times of war."

"I'm sure it's not in the book." Alexa moved away from the table. "And even if you do find it, it won't be easy to take it out of the country, if that's what you're planning. You know how sticky customs can be."

"Not if they don't know I have it."

"You've told me," Alexa said. "Aren't you worried that I'll go to the police?"

He laughed, throwing his head back as if it were a huge joke. "What would you tell them—you, an outsider? Both your parents took the coward's way out. And your father was a thief. You'd be lucky if the police gave you the time of day."

"My father was not a thief." She nearly choked on the words, wanting to smack the smile off his face. Only the nagging possibility that Angelo might know something else kept her from walking out.

"Tell me, Angelo," she said tightly, "where does your friend Kritikos come in? How did he know I was in Volos? And don't tell me that my aunt told him. That's what he said, but the fact is, she barely knows the man."

His chair hit the floor with a thump. "I told him you were coming."

"Did you, now? And how did you know, may I ask? And he's here now, isn't he? I saw the car. And I saw you talking with him behind the hotel this evening. You set me up, didn't you?"

"So?" he said coolly. His eyes narrowed to slits. "I guess it won't hurt if you know. I've been keeping an eye on you."

"You what?" she yelled, outraged. "You mean this past year, when I thought I was finally free of you, you had someone following me?"

He smirked, polishing the edge of his nails against his shirt. "Yes, I had you followed. I knew the minute you arrived in Greece. And I sent Kritikos to talk to you in Volos. I knew you'd come, out of curiosity about your father. I wanted you here."

Her heartbeat roared in her ears, filling her head with noise. For a moment she couldn't think. Then anger surged anew. "Why?" She forced the word out through clenched teeth.

"I figured if you came here, Lisandro would give you the diaries. If he'd had your address, I imagine he would have mailed them to you. That's why I didn't give it to him. As long as he had them, I might have a chance to look at them. If you hadn't come to Greece on your own, I would have written you. If you thought your father was alive, you'd have come. I've wanted those diamonds for a long time."

"How long a time?" Alexa said bleakly. "Was it all part of this plan that you came to Canada, met me and married me? If no one knew where we were, how did you find us?"

Angelo smiled complacently. "I didn't plan it from the beginning, no. But my mother knew Olympia was in Vancouver. After she died, I decided to go there. You were a really foxy lady. It wasn't a hardship to marry you."

"Thanks," Alexa said dryly.

"You're welcome," Angelo said coolly. "Anyway, my plan worked. Lisandro gave you the diaries."

"So that's why you were after Lisandro, to get the diaries."

"Partly. I think he knows something he's not telling."

"How could he? He wasn't here at the time, Damian said."

"He knows people who were. He knew Elias, your uncle, for one. Kritikos put it together."

"Where is Kritikos now?" Alexa asked.

"Down in the coffee shop, I guess. He's taken a room at the hotel since there's not much room here. He'll be handy to keep an eye on you."

Alexa walked across to the door. "It doesn't make any difference. I won't let you have the diaries." Her voice rose. "And I won't stand for you terrorizing that sick old man, and neither will Damian."

Angelo got up. He grabbed her upper arm and swung her around to face him. "Not sweet on him, are you, Alexa? He's a good-looking guy. But he's just a small-time lawyer. You're better off with me. Think about it, Alexa. A fortune in diamonds. You could help. You might be able to get something out of Lisandro through Damian."

She jerked her arm free. "You're crazy, Angelo. You'll never find the sword, not through me, not through anyone."

She ran from the house, going up one path and then another without paying any attention to direction. She stumbled over a tree root and realised the path she was on had dwindled to nothing and that there were no streetlamps in sight.

The hoot of an owl above her head startled her. It flew by, so close she felt the draft from the huge wings. Trees surrounded her, dark sentinels.

Think, she told herself. The village was in a valley. To get to the square one had to go downhill. She started down the path, stepping carefully to avoid slipping on the pine needles that littered the ground. Abruptly the forest cleared and she could see houses beside the path.

There were no lights. It suddenly dawned on her that the streetlamps were off.

She stood still and listened. Small animals rustled in the undergrowth. A stick snapped. Heart pounding, she turned her head from side to side, her eyes probing the gloom. Was that a shadow deeper than the others, someone watching her?

A night bird shrieked and she jumped, starting down the path. By the time she reached the hotel, she was running.

DAMIAN WOKE WITH A START. The room was cold, damp night air drifting through the open window. He heard nothing, yet the quality of the silence seemed sinister, as if an alien presence had passed through the familiar rooms.

Swinging his legs to the floor, he stepped into the short hall. Lisandro's door stood open as usual; the old man disliked closed spaces. Damian also kept his own door open, so that he would be able to hear if Lisandro called him in the night.

He heard nothing. It disturbed him. Often at night, Lisandro's breathing was labored. Better go and check for a moment, since he was up, anyway.

He glanced into the room, his eyes accustomed to the almost-total darkness. The window was also open, the shutters ajar as usual. The curtains swayed languidly.

The bed was empty, the turned-back sheets a faint, light blur. Damian's heartbeat went into overdrive.

Quickly he checked the bathroom. Deserted. Dread formed a heavy lump in his chest.

Where could Lisandro have gone at this time of night?

Going back into his own room, Damian pulled on a pair of jeans, yanking up the zipper with trembling hands. He had just reached the front door when it opened.

"Papa," he whispered, light-headed with relief.

Lisandro closed the door quietly behind him, setting his cane in the brass bucket that served as an umbrella stand. "I couldn't sleep. I went out a little. I'm sorry I disturbed you, Damian."

Damian frowned. Lisandro sounded strangely distracted. "Papa—"

Lisandro wrapped his arm around Damian's neck, as he had when Damian was a boy who needed affection. He kissed him on the cheek. "Go back to bed, son. We'll talk in the morning."

"Let me help you."

That the old man didn't object testified to his fatigue. Against his side, Damian could feel the tremors that shook Lisandro's body as he sat down on the bed. Turning on the bedside lamp, Damian stooped to take off Lisandro's shoes.

"Ouch." He popped his thumb into his mouth, sucking out the thorn that had pricked him. Dry thistle leaves, armed with hooked thorns, were caught between the soles and the uppers of Lisandro's shoes.

"Must have been quite a walk," he said casually while alarm bells clanged in his head. The nearest thistles grew around an abandoned house halfway to the square. Had Lisandro walked that far? Fear for the old man's safety tightened Damian's throat. He could have collapsed at any time, lain on the path until morning, when it would have been too late to help him.

"Papa, please," he said quietly, helping Lisandro out of the rest of his clothes, "next time, let me know when you're going out."

"Yes, Damian." Lisandro smiled gently as he lay back against the pillows. "You're a good boy."

Damian felt an unfamiliar stinging in his eyes. "Go to sleep now."

He waited a moment. Lisandro's eyes closed, and a soft snore issued from his parted lips.

Smiling, Damian moved away from the bed, hanging the clothes over a chair. He was about to turn off the light when he froze, staring at the massive chimneypiece.

He must have walked in and out of this room a thousand times, so accustomed to every detail of furniture and decor that it no longer registered on his conscious mind. But now, something was wrong.

One item only. Out of place.

The small curved knife that hung beneath the crossed swords was missing.

Chapter Six

She dreamed, nebulous, fragmented dreams that filled her with a nameless dread. She saw her mother with a worried expression, and Angelo telling her she would never be free of him. The picture in her mind changed. Kritikos stood before her, his eyes fierce and cold, his voice chanting, "Find the sword of Dimitrios. Find the sword of Dimitrios."

She woke, her heart pounding, the images and words as clear as if they'd been a movie projected on the ceiling.

It didn't make any sense.

Except her relief at finding herself in the hotel bed and not wandering through the village in her nightgown.

She lay back on the pillow, throwing her arm over her eyes to block out the rising sun. Angelo. What was she going to do about Angelo?

Nothing for now, she decided. Strictly speaking, he hadn't done anything illegal. And if she went to the police with some story about Angelo planning to smuggle diamonds, which he hadn't found yet, out of the country, they would laugh at her.

And Angelo would come across as perfectly sane and plausible. When the brakes had failed on her car after she'd left him, there had been no proof then, either. While she had gone to phone the police, a cruising tow truck had taken away her car, for illegal parking, no less, since the fender was crushed against a post in a tow-away zone. By the time she retrieved it the next day, the brakes worked perfectly. And Angelo had been there, turning on the charm for the female police constable, joking that his wife wasn't the best driver in the world.

Of course no one had checked into her driving record to find that she'd gotten her license at sixteen with a perfect score and hadn't had an accident or a ticket since.

She got out of bed, went into the bathroom and splashed cold water on her face. Her jaw set in determination, she looked in the mirror. Dark circles under her eyes lent her face a fragile appearance. She scowled at her reflection. A couple more nights like this and the villagers would think they were haunted by a sleepwalking ghoul.

Alexa met Poppy near the front desk when she went down. "Lovely morning again today," the girl said cheerfully, taking the empty water jug Alexa handed her. "I'll be right back with your breakfast." She swung away through the kitchen door.

Alexa stared after her. Poppy must have had a good night, in contrast to her own. There was no sign of the agitated young woman who'd been crying in the hall last evening.

Poppy brought her breakfast, eggs, toast and crisp bacon. Alexa's stomach growled. Poppy laughed merrily. "You are hungry, aren't you?"

She was, but she had to take care of another matter first. "Poppy, I heard you and Angelo arguing last night."

Poppy's cheeks turned pink, and she gave a small, embarrassed laugh. "It's all right now. It won't happen again. I've told him he can't come to the office when I'm working." She laid her hand on Alexa's. "Trust me, Alexa. I won't let him have the diaries. I know how important they are, a legacy from your mother and your father's ancestor."

Alexa gave a sigh of relief, grateful that Poppy had anticipated her request. "Thanks, Poppy. I appreciate that."

After breakfast, Alexa had just stepped out of the front door of the hotel when the church bell tolled. Not the familiar hourly ringing, but a deep, sonorous *bong, bong, bong.* A long-buried memory struggled to the surface. She was a child; she'd heard a bell, just like that, a measured clanging that had filled her with a visceral fear. Remnants of that fear raised the hairs on the back of her neck now.

She heard the faint creak of the door behind her. Poppy came out onto the step. "It's the funeral call," Poppy said, her eyes round and apprehensive. "Someone must have died in the night."

Alexa closed her eyes, her heart squeezing with pain. Please, God, don't let it be. Her voice wobbling, she said, "I hope it isn't Lisandro. He looked all right yesterday."

"Just what I was thinking," Poppy said soberly. "Damian has been quite worried that he could go any time. Alexa, please, go down and find out. I can't leave the hotel unattended."

Alexa hurried across the square toward the nearest coffee shop. The two old men sitting in the morning sun only shook their heads when she asked them. The ringing of the bell continued, reverberating from the surrounding mountains.

The yeasty scent of fresh bread and the clamour of voices poured out of the bakery as most of the town gathered to buy their daily supply. Alexa's knees went weak with relief as she spotted Damian among the shoppers.

Loaf in hand, he pushed his way out. Alexa had an urge to throw herself at him, an urge she checked just in time. "Lisandro is all right, is he?"

Damian's smile turned to puzzlement. "Yes. Why wouldn't he be?"

Alexa gnawed her lower lip, feeling marginally foolish. "The bells. Poppy said they mean someone died."

"No, Lisandro is fine this morning. I left him sitting in the rocker outside. Vassiliki is cleaning the house."

"You mean the lady I saw yesterday?"

"The dragon lady herself."

The bells echoed around them, beating into Alexa's head. She clapped her hands over her ears. "When will they stop?"

Damian took her arm. "Come along. We'll ask the priest what's happened."

They crossed the square, passing the bench where the old men sat. The one at the end, dressed in unrelieved black, his cane planted firmly between his knees, muttered something. Alexa paused, thinking he'd spoken to her. The sunlight flashed on his glasses, obscuring his expression. Before she could formulate a greeting, he stood up and walked toward the coffee shop.

Her brow creased with a troubled frown, she turned to Damian. "Who was he? I saw him last night, on the path, after I left your house."

"That's old Mitso." Damian smiled. "He's one of the local characters. Must be a hundred years old."

The melancholy tolling grew louder, then abruptly stopped. Silence jangled the air, filling gradually with the shouts of the fish seller and a truck's loudspeaker advertising onions for sale. Alexa was grateful for the support of Damian's hand as her legs trembled with released tension.

He looked down at her, seeing her pale face. "The bells, they really bothered you, didn't they?"

Distressed, Alexa raked her fingers through her hair. "I don't know why. Something about when I was a child. I just felt scared, like I wanted to hide in a dark closet somewhere."

"Your father's funeral, perhaps?" Damian suggested, his voice tender.

"I don't even know if he had a funeral."

"They would have had a memorial mass."

"Probably," she said, unconvinced. No memory at all surfaced, not even one of her and her mother fleeing the village. She'd been six; most children could remember events that happened before they were six, even as early as three or four.

She hadn't realized it before, but, except for vague impressions of stone houses and the green forests around Elatos, she didn't have any concrete memories of her childhood until their arrival in Canada. No wonder nothing looked familiar to her; it wasn't just the changes in the village, but some block in her own mind.

The church, dim and cool, enveloped her with a familiarity she eagerly embraced. Christ Pantocrator gazed down into a shimmer of rainbows as the sun streamed through a single stained glass window high on the wall behind the simple altar. East, of course. All Greek churches were oriented with the altar toward the east.

Crossing herself, she dropped a coin in the box and lit a candle, placing it on the stand that held several others. She stood for a moment, her lips moving in a silent prayer, a desperate request that the mystery around her father would be resolved, and soon.

"Good morning, Papa Apostoli." Beside her, Damian greeted the priest who appeared from a back room.

A thin, energetic man, he shook each of their hands. His fine dark eyes regarded Alexa seriously, with a troubled look she wondered at. She could not guess his age; it could have been anywhere from forty to seventy, his face framed by curly brown hair only lightly sprinkled with gray.

"The bells," Damian said. "We were wondering—"

The priest shook his head, his eyes strangely sorrowful as they rested on Alexa. "I'm sorry. I can't tell you. It's a police matter."

"A police matter?"

"I'm sorry. That's all I can say."

Unsettling thoughts churned in Alexa's head, not helped by the priest's cryptic answer. She lifted her eyes to his again, and a profound sadness seemed to communicate itself to her. He knew something. "Papa Apostoli, perhaps you can help me. I'm looking for my father, Dimitrios Doukas. I've been told he was alive as late as a year ago. Do you know anything about this?"

Damian turned to her, his brows knitted. "You're looking for your father? Is that why you came to Elatos?" His voice was toneless, as if he'd purged it of emotion.

"I meant to tell you, Damian," she quickly said. "Today." She turned back to the priest. "Can you help me? Were you here at the time he disappeared?"

Papa Apostoli crossed himself, bowing toward an icon depicting the stoning of Stephen. "I came later, but I know it was a time of great confusion. I'm afraid there's nothing I can add. I'm sorry."

Disappointed, Alexa turned away. Damian waited by the church door. She could tell by the rigidity of his body that he was angry. Mentally bracing herself, she followed him out.

"Why didn't you tell me you were looking for your father?" he said furiously. "Was it a deep, dark secret? I'll bet you told Angelo."

"I found out last night that Angelo used that story to get me here," Alexa said, striving for a reasonable tone. "And why should I have told you? I've known you for less than a day and a half."

"What does time matter? You can grow up with some people and not know them. With others, there's an instantaneous accord. I thought— Oh, never mind what I thought." He took a firmer grip on the loaf of bread he carried, inadvertently bending it in the middle, and headed off down the narrow street.

Alexa had to run to catch up. "Damian, wait."

"Why?" He didn't turn but he slowed his steps.

"Damian, I came here for the reasons I mentioned. And you knew I was a Doukas. I didn't lie to you."

"No, you just forgot to mention the most important reason you're here."

Alexa's fist tightened on her purse strap. For an instant she debated going back to the hotel, leaving him with his unjust anger. But she realized she might be cutting off her best source of information. She reined in her temper. "Damian, I came here hoping it would be simple, that someone would know about my father. Instead I find nothing's as it was, not the village, not the people. And I hear all these conflicting stories about the time he left. I didn't want to stir up old animosities. It's only now that I realize my father was generally well thought of, in spite of the stories."

Damian kept on walking. She nearly had to run to keep up. "Fine," he said flatly. "But you didn't even tell Lisandro, and he could have helped you."

Alexa stopped, grabbing Damian's arm, making him turn to face her. "How?" she asked urgently. "He wasn't here when my father left. Why should he know anything about him?"

"You'd be surprised what he knows. He didn't have to be here to know what went on, both then and later."

Chewing on her lower lip, Alexa hesitated. "Will he talk to me?" she asked diffidently.

"Why don't you ask him yourself, Alexa?" Damian shook off her hand and resumed walking.

"Thank you, I will," she muttered, glaring at his back in exasperation.

A boy of about ten came running down the path, almost crashing headlong into them. Damian put out his hand and steadied the boy, who immediately began dancing from one foot to the other in great agitation. "Mr. Damian, something has happened at Mr. Angelo's house. The police are there. A policemen from Ioannina, too. He just came."

Damian gripped the boy's shoulder. "What? What's going on?"

The child's eyes were bright with excitement. "I don't know. They wouldn't let me close to the house."

Sick dread sent a chill through Alexa, as if ice had entered her bones. Pushing past Damian, she ran up the path, heedless of fir branches whipping her face and shoulders.

Two police vehicles sat outside the chain-link fence, one a car from Ioannina. The other was the battered Land Rover she'd seen parked in front of the police station on the square. An officer, so young he looked like a boy dressed in his father's uniform, stood at the gate.

"Please, I have to go in," she gasped, fighting for breath.

"It's all right," Damian said, taking her arm in a firm hand. Dimly, she noticed he wasn't even breathing hard. "Let us by. You won't get into trouble."

The policeman's brow creased. "The man from Ioannina said to keep everybody out."

"I'll clear it with Spiro," Damian said, steering Alexa around the young man.

At the open door, he stopped. His breath stirred her hair as he bent close to her ear. "I don't know what we'll find in there. Do you want to wait out here until I see?"

She gulped air into lungs that felt starved. Her heart drummed loudly in her ears. "No, I can't wait. Something's happened to Angelo. I know it. Otherwise we'd hear him bellowing."

The bare bulb hanging from the living room ceiling spotlighted the scene as if it were a stage. Only it wasn't. Alexa pressed her hand against her stomach.

Angelo was dead. She knew it even before she saw the knife sticking up out of his chest.

For an instant the room turned gray and she swayed on her feet. She closed her eyes, rallying her strength, grateful for Damian behind her. He didn't touch her, but she felt his warmth, his concern, as if it were his hands caressing her chilled skin.

Spiro, the village constable, stood up from his position next to the body, disapproval in the set of his mouth as he saw them in the doorway. "Damian," he said by way of greeting. He turned to Alexa. "I'm sorry, Mrs. Thetalou. I understand Angelo was your husband. I'm afraid he's dead."

Not only dead but murdered. "Thank you," she said numbly, at a loss. Her strongest feeling at the moment was relief, and for that she felt guilty. Irrational tears sprang to her eyes. Angelo had been a human being, however flawed; he didn't deserve to be lying ignominiously on a stone floor with a knife in his chest.

Distraught, not really aware of what she was doing, she buried her face against Damian's shirt. He smelled of sun-dried cotton and fresh bread. Fresh bread? She gave a shaky laugh. He still held the loaf he'd bought earlier, battered and crumbling. "I'm sorry, Damian. The bread is ruined."

He ran his hand up under her hair, his fingers warm against her scalp. "Easy, Alexa. Don't fall apart now."

"Mrs. Thetalou, you were here last evening, weren't you?" said Spiro who had been watching them closely.

Heat stole into Alexa's cheeks; what must he be thinking? His impassive face told her nothing.

"Yes, I was here," she said, meeting his eyes squarely. "But he was very much alive when I left."

"I wasn't accusing you of anything," Spiro said mildly. "Only trying to establish time of death."

"I came here late in the evening." She pursed her lips, trying to remember. She'd gone to Damian's first, then back to the hotel. "It could have been ten or eleven o'clock. I'm not sure, exactly. I wasn't thinking about time."

"What were you thinking?"

A frisson of alarm chased over her skin. "Just that I needed to talk to Angelo."

"Why don't we go into the kitchen where we can sit down, madam," Spiro said smoothly.

Alexa swung her gaze over to Damian. He squeezed her hand. "It'll be all right, Alexa," he said. "Come over to our house when you're finished here. Will you need me, Spiro? I should be getting back to Lisandro."

"Go ahead," Spiro said. He permitted himself a small smile. "I know where you live if I want to ask you anything."

Alexa couldn't shake a feeling of abandonment when Damian left. As a distraction, she turned her attention back into the room. The policeman from Ioannina had apparently finished with the crime scene. He directed two assistants to load Angelo's body on a stretcher. They lifted him, leaving a chalk outline on the floor in front of the ruined fireplace.

"Madam." Spiro gestured toward the cluttered kitchen.

As if mesmerized, Alexa watched the two men carry Angelo past her. She raised her hand. It was shaking. "One moment." Her voice sounded like a stranger's. She pulled back the blanket, not sure what compelled her to gaze upon Angelo for the last time.

His face, handsome even in death, was frozen in a look of surprise. The black hair clung to his head, matted with blood. She dragged her eyes lower.

The knife. An icy heat washed through her body. She'd seen that knife. She shook her head, denying the thought with ruthless force. It was just not possible.

She shook her head and replaced the blanket.

Numb, she went into the kitchen and sat down on a hard chair, ironically the same one as last night.

Spiro sat down on the opposite side of the table, laying a notepad and pen in front of him.

"I've been told that you and Angelo quarreled last night," he said without inflection.

"By whom?" Alexa snapped defensively.

Spiro shrugged. "That's not important."

"Perhaps it is to me," Alexa said.

"Only if you have something to hide, madam."

Alexa forced a smile that felt like a grimace. "Why don't you call me Alexa. Since you're going to be asking me personal questions, it seems odd to have formality between us."

"Fine, Alexa." He smiled thinly. "A number of people heard you arguing. There are houses beyond this one. People were walking by. Your voices were raised."

"I used to be married to Angelo," Alexa said. "We raised our voices quite often during our marriage. It doesn't mean I killed him."

Spiro opened his notebook and jotted down several lines. "Mmm. Alexa, we're only questioning those who had contact with him. It would appear you were the last person who visited him."

"Except for his killer," Alexa retorted.

"Mmm," Spiro said again, writing in the notebook. "What did you argue about?"

Was he allowed to ask all these questions if she wasn't a suspect? Alexa wished she'd talked to Damian first. After all, he was a lawyer; he would know. "A personal matter. Several personal matters. I hadn't seen Angelo in quite some time." She attempted a nonchalant shrug. "You know how it is, catching up on old times."

Nothing could have prepared Alexa for Spiro's next question: "Is it true that you're here to look for your father who supposedly died more than twenty-five years ago?"

DAMIAN, HIS MIND in a turmoil, headed home at a pace barely short of a run. It was incredible that Angelo had been murdered in a town where the last violent act had been a wolf stealing a lamb from Papa Apostoli's backyard over a year ago.

Poor Alexa. She'd looked so white and drained, he wondered whether she'd still harbored feelings for Angelo. Of course, seeing your former husband dead would be a shock for any woman.

He shouldn't have left her. He should have stayed, but at the sight of the knife, terror had slammed into him, making him incapable of any other thought.

Lisandro.

No. "No!" He yelled the word aloud. The trees swallowed the sound. Lisandro was a gentle man. Oh, he could be tough if the situation warranted it, but he would never kill another human being.

Lisandro couldn't have killed Angelo. Damian sank down on a fallen log next to the path, the seed of doubt bitter in his heart. Lisandro had been out last night. Logic told Damian that Lisandro, with his weak heart, couldn't have gone as far as Angelo's house, but what if he had?

The evidence fit, no matter how repugnant the thought might be to Damian. The thistles stuck on Lisandro's shoes and socks—Angelo's unkempt yard was full of thistles.

But most damning of all was the knife. A knife that looked like the one missing from Lisandro's room was now buried to the hilt in Angelo's chest.

Chapter Seven

As soon as Spiro finished with his questions, Alexa hurried to Lisandro's house. Lisandro was in bed when she arrived. He barely opened his eyes when Damian led her into the room. The seriousness of his illness suddenly hit her. Hard.

His chest rose and fell with his labored breathing. The hand he lifted to greet her fell heavily to the bed. Dusky mauve smudges darkened the skin beneath his eyes, and the blue tinge in his lips was pronounced.

Alexa's eyes met Damian's worried look. He shook his head. "He seemed well this morning and now he's like this."

She glanced back at the bed, saw Lisandro's eyes closed. "Does he know about Angelo?"

"I don't know. He's too tired to talk. That might explain it, though, if someone came by and told him. It must be all over town by now."

"Yes, it must be. If not the truth, then a thousand rumors," Alexa said.

Damian moved over to the bed to draw the blanket closer around Lisandro who appeared to be sleeping. Alexa took advantage of the moment to glance at the chimneypiece. Two swords and a knife. Her knees went weak with relief. She'd been wrong.

She turned away, saw Damian looking at her, his eyes troubled, dark as a midnight sea. "He's sleeping."

They went into the kitchen, its pristine order a glaring contrast to the squalor of Angelo's.

"Was Spiro rough on you?" Damian asked gently, all traces of his anger outside the bakery gone.

"No. No, he wasn't," Alexa said, conscious of unfinished business between them. "Just doing his job."

"He didn't accuse you of killing Angelo, did he?"

Alexa frowned. "Not in so many words. But he did point out that I was apparently the last person to see Angelo alive and that a number of people overheard us quarreling last night."

Damian swore under his breath. "He's crazy if he thinks you killed him."

"Oh?" Alexa lifted one brow. "What makes you think I didn't? It was pretty obvious how we felt about each other."

Damian grinned at her, the darkness that dwelt behind his eyes momentarily gone. "You'd be more likely to have brained him with a chair in the middle of Poppy's dining room than sneak over to his house and stab him."

"What if we got into a fight?" Alexa said, playing devil's advocate. "Couldn't I have killed him in a fit of temper?"

"No, Alexa, I don't think you're capable of killing anyone."

Alexa dipped her head, embarrassed. "Thanks," she muttered. "Especially since you hardly know me."

His mouth compressed in displeasure. "We discussed that. I don't want to hear it again. What I want to hear about is this business of your father supposedly being alive. But first, can I pour you some coffee?"

She realized her stomach felt hollow. "Yes, please."

He pushed the crumbling loaf of bread aside and filled two mugs from the automatic coffeemaker. Alexa eyed the machine. "First time I've seen one of those in Greece."

"Lisandro likes gadgets." He set the coffee in front of her. "Milk? Sugar?"

"Sugar, no milk." She stirred the fragrant liquid, sipped and gave a satisfied sigh. "Okay, about my father." She paused, biting her lip. "Did you know that Spiro, the village constable, had heard I was looking for my father before I told anyone?"

"Wasn't I the first person you told?" Damian asked.

"You were, but Angelo knew why I was here. Spiro wouldn't tell me how he knew. Anyway, I was visiting my aunt, my mother's sister, in Volos last week. My mother had asked me to. Once her estate was settled, I took my holidays and came here."

"Your first trip to Greece?" He sat down opposite her at the table, his hands clasped around his mug.

"Yes." She trailed her fingertip around the rim of her cup. "My mother never came back, said there were too many painful memories she didn't want to relive. Sometimes I felt as if her life had started when she arrived in Canada, and the rest didn't happen."

Damian said nothing. She looked up to find him staring into space, his face drawn into harsh lines, his eyes dark and haunted. What was he thinking?

"It's sometimes easier to block out the past than to reconcile it with the present," he said softly, as if to himself. Which told her exactly nothing.

"I met a man in Volos last week," she said, seizing on the business at hand to avoid speculating about the ghosts of Damian's past. "Actually, he found me, which I thought odd at the time. He told me my father might be alive, that an Albanian who'd met my father years ago received a letter from him. If it's true, he was alive less than a year ago."

"Could you check this story?"

Alexa shook her head. "No, although my aunt knew the man. She didn't seem to like him, though, or trust him. The man told me I would find the answers to my questions in Elatos. He said that was all he knew."

"Or wanted to say?" Damian said sharply.

"Exactly. I couldn't let it go without investigating even the slimmest possibility. My mother wasn't only my mother, but my best friend, as well—I'd never criticize her for the decisions she made. I had a happy childhood. Still, I grew up without a father. You've no idea how unsettling that can be for a child at times."

Damian dragged in an audible breath. "Believe me, I know."

"Oh— I'm so sorry, Damian...how could I have forgotten?"

Alexa, moved with compassion, covered his hand with hers. He stiffened, as if he would pull away, but then he relaxed, clasping her fingers with his own.

"Please, continue," he said, his face shuttered.

"I rented a car and came to Elatos," she continued. "And here I met Angelo. Not the happiest surprise, I can tell you."

"You didn't know he was here?"

"How could I? The last time I'd seen him, about a year ago, he was still in Canada. He didn't say anything about coming to Greece, but he must have left soon after since people tell me he's been here that long. But that wasn't the most startling thing. Last night I saw Kritikos. Right outside the hotel."

"Kritikos?" Damian frowned.

"Pavlo Kritikos," Alexa declared. "He's the man who met me in Volos." She took a fortifying drink of her coffee. "Angelo sent him."

Damian looked baffled. "Angelo sent him? Sent him where?"

"To meet me in Volos. To tell me the story. To get me to come here."

"So the story wasn't true."

"According to Angelo, it is true. Only the timing was different from what Kritikos told me. The story came out at least eight months ago. That was one of the things Angelo and I argued about. If I'd known sooner I might have been able to contact my father before my mother died. Now it's too late."

"If he's alive, it might not be too late."

"For my mother, it is."

Damian nodded. "Yes, I guess so. I'm sorry."

"So am I," said Alexa seriously.

"Did you tell Spiro all this?"

"Yes. I didn't think it would make much difference. It was no secret how Angelo and I felt about each other, if anyone cared to check. What's one motive more or less?"

"How did Spiro react?"

Alexa looked at him, an ironic smile tilting up the corner of her mouth. "Is that the lawyer talking?"

Damian's expression lightened marginally. "I'm not a criminal lawyer. I work with contracts and land agreements and boring stuff like that."

"Spiro just kept making notes in his little book. And then he told me not to leave without letting him know."

"Are you planning to leave? If you did, no one would blame you."

She pulled back her hand, picked up her coffee cup. "No, I'm not leaving, not until I find the answers to all my questions. I need to find out what's happened to my father. And if they don't find Angelo's killer, I'll always be under suspicion."

Damian murmured a protest. "You don't know that you're a suspect now. Where did they take Angelo's body?"

"To Ioannina for an autopsy." Alexa shivered in remembered horror. "Once that's done, they'll bring him back here for a funeral and burial in the family plot." An unwelcome thought struck her. "I won't be expected to arrange it, will

I? I don't think he has any living relatives, so they may consider me next of kin."

"Even if they do, you don't have to deal with it, Alexa. Papa Apostoli can arrange everything. That's what's usually done in cases like this where there're no relatives."

Reaching across the table, Damian recaptured Alexa's hand, his thumb tracing soothing little patterns on the back of it, driving out the image of Angelo lying dead in his half-ruined house. "Alexa, tell me about Angelo."

She tried to jerk her hand away, but he held it. "What's to tell?" she said in a brittle tone. "He was my husband, we divorced, and now he's dead. End of story."

"Not the end of the story. It's only the beginning if Spiro decides you killed him."

Alexa's eyes widened. "He can't do that, can he?"

Damian shrugged. "From what you've told me, probably not, but people have been convicted on flimsy evidence in the past. You had opportunity and motive. That might be all they need."

Alexa sat for a moment, digesting this, knowing he was right. She fixed her eyes on his face, that narrow, dark face with its brooding eyes that seemed to embody the essence of the Greek spirit—complex, fierce, but also gentle. She could trust him; she was sure of it.

And if she stayed, there would soon be more than trust between them. Even now, a hot yearning coiled inside her as he softly stroked her hand. After leaving Angelo, she had stayed clear of men, suspicious of any relationships. With Damian, despite the air of secretiveness she sensed at times, she felt the awakening of sexual desire, a desire she'd thought Angelo had killed forever.

It was this that made her hesitate. If she told him about her relationship with Angelo, would she be diminished in Damian's eyes? As if he knew her thoughts, he smiled. "Trust me," he said, his voice deep as velvet. "Trust me."

Okay, she thought. She'd risk it. Collecting her thoughts, she drank the cold dregs of her coffee, grimacing at the bitter taste. "I met Angelo fifteen years ago. I was eighteen, in university, naive and idealistic. He'd recently arrived from Greece, an immigrant who came to my mother for a job in one of her restaurants. She gave him one—after all, he was from Elatos. He worked hard, I'll say that for him, learning English and the business. Within a year, she made him manager of one of the restaurants and we were married."

"With her approval," Damian said.

"Of course." Alexa nodded. "I wonder if part of it was nostalgia, though. Angelo coming from the last place we'd known Father. He talked about him, you know. And now I wonder how much was true and how much was carefully manufactured lies."

She took a deep breath. "The first year was perfect. I was in love, foolish creature I was then, completely besotted. The second year, when he opened his own restaurant, wasn't bad, except that he was seldom home. I was in my final semester of university, and I barely noticed. Then I graduated, got a job at a prominent brokerage house, and everything fell apart."

"He hit you." Not a question. Damian's voice was laced with contempt for a man who would beat a woman.

"Sometimes," she admitted, surprised she no longer felt pain or the vague guilt that often plagues victims. "But more often, the abuse was emotional. He was jealous of my work, jealous of the men I worked with. And his business started losing money because he spent so much time following me around, spying on me, that he was hardly ever there to take care of it."

"How long did you stay with him?" Damian asked.

"Five years. I tried to make it work. At least I was lucky. I didn't need to stay for financial reasons like so many women in bad marriages. Neither did we have children to complicate things. But it was still a harrowing time. Angelo fought the divorce, and it was three years before I had the final papers. He tried to get a large settlement—I realized one of the reasons he married me was because of my mother's success with her restaurants. He thought I was rich. We were comfortable, but most of the capital was tied up in the business. I finally gave him a sum of money to get him to leave me alone."

"A large sum?"

Alexa glanced at him sharply but his expression remained neutral. "Yes, a large sum. All I could raise at the time. Not enough to make him independent, but enough to provide a cushion if his restaurant went through rough times."

"Did that satisfy him?"

"No. He tried everything he could to get me back. First he used charm, and when that didn't work, the threats started. He ignored restraining orders, or he hired someone to do the harassing for him. But last year it stopped. Now I know why. He'd left Canada and come back to Elatos."

Damian nodded thoughtfully. "You didn't tell Spiro this whole story?"

"No, of course not. It has nothing to do with Angelo's killing."

"Unless Spiro thought it did. How does he know you weren't aware Angelo was here and had come to kill him, to keep him from harassing you."

Alexa gaped at him. Was he serious? If so, she'd made a big mistake in telling him about her marriage. "Are you going to report me to the police?"

Damian's brows flew up. "Now, why would I do that?"

"What you just said," she stammered. "Of course, it's absurd. If I'd known Angelo was here, this is the last place I would have come."

"I believe you, Alexa."

She let out her breath in a gust of relief. "I hope so, Damian, because it's true. I didn't—" The dreams she'd had, the ones she didn't remember—could she have been sleepwalking? What if she'd gone back to Angelo's house and killed him? But where would she have gotten the knife?

She'd seen such a knife in only two places, in the village museum and on Lisandro's chimneypiece. Neither one had been accessible to her.

Besides, she'd always thought the sleepwalking inconvenient but ultimately harmless. A person couldn't do anything while sleepwalking that they wouldn't do awake. For instance, she'd never stripped off her clothes and walked naked down the street. And usually she'd even put on a robe over her nightgown, proper and modest.

She couldn't have killed Angelo.

Couldn't she? Deep down inside her, at the time of the divorce when Angelo wouldn't leave her alone, she'd often thought he would be better off dead.

Was it possible the thought had become deed?

"I didn't kill him," she said, but to her own ears, the words sounded uncertain.

"Then who did?" Damian asked. "Any ideas?"

"No."

Her eyes rested on Damian's back as he poured another cup of coffee. The knife. Damian had had access to Lisandro's knife. And he'd made no secret of his anger when Angelo had demanded to see a dying man, regardless of that man's wishes.

Was Damian capable of murder? She remembered the stillness that had come over him in the restaurant, the feeling that under that stillness lay a dangerous power. She saw in him the instincts of the heroes who had fought to restore their Greek heritage. He might kill to protect those he loved.

No, this was crazy. She herself was a more likely suspect than Damian. Besides, the knife was not missing from Lisandro's room. And for all she knew, there might be half a dozen similar knives in the village.

"What are you thinking?" Damian sat down again after refilling her cup.

Alexa shook her head. "I don't know. It's all confused." She broke off, tempted to confess everything, the ugliness between her and Angelo, her own fears.

No, she couldn't tell him, not until she sorted it out in her own mind.

Damian's eyes rested on her, shadowed and brooding. She squirmed in her chair, knowing he couldn't guess her thoughts but uncomfortable nevertheless. "Did you see the man about translating the diary?"

Restless and distracted, he drummed his fingertips on the table. "I asked George and he'll do it. Do you have the diary with you?"

"No. It's locked in the safe in Poppy's office. Angelo wanted those diaries," she added thoughtfully. "I wonder if his friend Kritikos knew about them. Just in case he's in with Angelo on that, we'd better keep it a secret. I suppose your friend can be trusted?"

"He'll keep it to himself. Do you want me to come and pick up the diary later, say, after lunch? Vassiliki is coming back then, to stay with Lisandro."

"Fine." Alexa got up from her chair. An awkwardness seemed to have fallen between them, and she didn't know why. "Thanks for the coffee."

AFTER SHE LEFT, Damian remained sitting at the table. Where had Lisandro been last night? And where was the knife?

It had been gone in the night. He hadn't dreamed it, nor had he dreamed the thistles all over Lisandro's shoes, thistles like those growing in Angelo's yard. Of course, they grew elsewhere, too, but those places were just as far from the house.

The oddest thing was, in the morning, the knife was back. His gaze had gone first of all to the chimney when he'd entered Lisandro's room, and he'd seen it there.

Only later, with Lisandro rocking out on the stoop, had he taken a close look at it. Somehow the knife seemed subtly different. A trace of tarnish in the intricate design of the hilt. But he couldn't be sure. How much attention does one pay to a familiar object?

No, the murder weapon couldn't have been the Doukas knife.

That conclusion filled him with a tenuous relief.

How long had Lisandro been out of the house? Damian had only just fallen into a troubled sleep when he'd heard a sound, or whatever had awakened him. Damian had thought Lisandro's condition too serious to allow him to walk farther than the cow shed, but perhaps he had made it to Angelo's. Damian could walk the distance in ten minutes, but Lisandro probably would have needed nearly an hour to get there and back. In Damian's estimation, he hadn't been gone as long as that.

But he wasn't sure.

Which brought up another discrepancy. Lisandro had been out after midnight. Yet Angelo had been fully dressed. In the living room, not asleep in his bed. This seemed to indicate that he might have been killed earlier.

Not only that, it was absurd to think a man of Lisandro's age and ill health could overpower an able-bodied man, knock him down and stab him.

No, the murderer couldn't have been Lisandro.

Which left only Alexa, no matter how much the idea horrified him. With Lisandro sleeping, she could have taken the knife yesterday when he'd gone to the kitchen.

Killing Angelo with her own father's knife might have struck her as an odd kind of justice.

He wondered if she was aware of the seriousness of the feud between the Thetalous and the Doukases. Her comment that her mother had been friends with Angelo's mother wouldn't mean much because feuds rarely involved the women of the families. And it appeared that Olympia and Angelo's mother were drawn together in their mutual grief after losing their husbands.

He was almost certain that Alexa was innocent. But that little niggling doubt remained.

She had had motive and opportunity. And might well have availed herself of a handy weapon.

ALEXA, SUNKEN in her dismal thoughts, trudged back to the hotel. The day was again fine, warm but with a certain briskness to the air that hinted of autumn. Passing the police station, she noted that Spiro's big Land Rover was absent from its marked parking spot.

In front of the hotel, she eyed the rented car she'd driven to Elatos. She drew her finger through dust on the fender. She should wash it.

It suddenly struck her that the car stood lower than it had. She squatted down to look at the wheels. Both tires on the driver's side were flat. She walked to the other side, her movements stiff, her mind blank. The same. On the rear tire steel fibers protruded from the mangled rubber.

Slashed.

Someone had made very sure she couldn't leave Elatos.

Chapter Eight

The stultifying blankness fled from Alexa's mind, replaced by a burning anger. First Angelo and now this. Someone was responsible and someone was going to pay.

She clenched her fists, grimly organizing her thoughts.

Top priority was new tires, which she guessed were not readily available in Elatos, a village with a two-pump gas station. However, the car was rented; the agency was supposed to look after problems.

The police would have to be notified, as well. She glanced across the square. Still no sign of Spiro's Land Rover. Never mind. She would catch him later.

The dining room was deserted at this hour; Poppy was somewhere in the back to judge by the radio music coming down the hall. Alexa dug in her purse for coins, dropping them on the reception desk. She pulled the pay phone closer, flipping the switch on the attached meter, as Poppy had shown her the other day.

The call went through at once. After a brief discussion of liability, and the finer points of vandalism versus negligence, she extracted a promise from the agent that new tires would be sent, on the condition that Alexa file a report with the police.

She hung up the phone and stood for a moment, fingers pressed against her aching forehead.

"Are you all right?"

Alexa whirled around. Poppy stood behind her, a look of concern on her pretty face. "Oh, you startled me. Yes, I'm all right." She laughed shortly. "It's my car that isn't. You didn't see anyone hanging around it this morning, did you?"

Poppy wrinkled her brow. "No. I don't think so. But several people have been in and out."

"Then you've heard about Angelo."

An indefinable expression crossed Poppy's face. "Yes, I've heard." She looked at Alexa, a pink flush coloring her cheeks. "I'm sorry. After all, he was your husband."

Alexa nodded. "Thank you, Poppy," she said simply, not knowing what else to say. The thought crossed her mind that Poppy might be feeling relief that Angelo would no longer be coming by to bother her.

Did that give Poppy a motive? The incipient headache nagged at her temples. When a man no one liked was murdered, everyone who knew him could be looked upon as a suspect.

She felt Poppy's hand on her arm. "Alexa, can we go out and look at your car?"

Poppy turned pale when she saw the gaping holes in all four tires. "Of course the hotel will reimburse you. This is dreadful. First someone breaks into your room and now this."

"Don't worry about it, Poppy," Alexa said. "I've already phoned the rental agency. They're sending new tires, although it'll take a couple of days. It's not your fault." She looked around at the people walking across the square, the old men sitting in the sunlight, their canes between their knees. "It couldn't have happened this morning."

She raked her memory. How had the car looked in the night when she came in? Or this morning, when she'd gone out? She had to admit that she had barely glanced at it, and hadn't seen anything out of the ordinary. Yet the vandalism must have happened in the dark.

"The streetlights—were they out for a while last night?"

"Yes, they were," said Poppy. "The power was off for some time after midnight, to allow the electric company to change a transformer near the highway."

No wonder she'd lost her way coming from Angelo's house. And the square had been dark, as well. Slashing four tires with a large knife would have taken about five minutes, with little risk of being observed.

"We must report it to Spiro," Poppy added. "He's just come back."

"He didn't go to Ioannina with Angelo's body?"

Poppy clicked her tongue, tipping her head back in the Greek negative. "He's the senior officer. He sent the other officer with the Ioannina policemen. Do you want me to come with you, Alexa?"

"No, I can manage." Alexa gave Poppy a quick, abstracted smile. "I don't want to keep you from your work."

"You're sure?" Poppy's eyes were wide, and Alexa smiled again, knowing the girl was torn between duty and wanting to take part in this new drama.

Alexa gave her a little push toward the steps. "I'm sure. I'll come by afterward and tell you how it went."

THE POLICE STATION, a small, Spartan building, was saved from mediocrity by the beauty of the stonework that formed its walls. Inside, however, the decor was strictly utilitarian.

After the hard October sunlight, the foyer, furnished with two wooden benches, appeared dark and gloomy. Alexa's rubber-soled shoes squeaked on the polished wooden floor as she walked to the first office.

Spiro sat behind the desk, wire-framed reading glasses resting halfway down his nose. He looked surprised to see her. "Alexa, what can I do for you?" He gestured her to a chair.

Sitting down, she gave him a concise account of the damage to her car. He wrote down a few notes, then raised his head, at the same time laying his glasses on the desk.

"What time did you get back to the hotel?"

She hadn't noticed his eyes before. They were blue, a not uncommon color in Epirus, sharp and penetrating. She had the impression they missed little, and that he would certainly know if she were lying.

She was innocent, she reminded herself forcefully. "I'm not sure. I didn't look at my watch. But it could have been after midnight."

He frowned, gray brows bristling. "You said you spent about an hour or two with Angelo. It seems to have taken you a while to get back to the hotel. Where were you during that time?"

"I took a wrong turn and got lost." She shifted uncomfortably. "After I left Angelo, I was upset. I didn't pay attention to the time."

"So you have no idea what time you got back?"

"The streetlights were off. That's all I remember." In truth, she wasn't at all sure how long the lights had been out. Nor did she know if accuracy in the time span would help her or incriminate her.

"Mrs. Thetalou—Alexa—the power was off from about midnight to two o'clock," he said severely. "That leaves a wide stretch of time. Is it possible that you were sleepwalking and that's why you can't account for the time?"

She sucked in her breath. "How did you know about the sleepwalking?"

"You were seen on the hotel steps the first night you were here. Someone recognized the phenomenon."

Alexa realized she would be better off to level with him. "Maybe I did then, but I was wide awake when I left Angelo. And the square was dark when I got back. I assume it was during the power outage that someone had a chance to damage my car."

"Probably." Spiro steepled his fingers in front of his face. On his desk, the phone rang. "Excuse me. Yes?" he said into the receiver.

He listened for a moment. "Okay." Putting down the phone, he gazed thoughtfully at Alexa.

"You'll be pleased to know," he said at last, "that there were no fingerprints on the knife."

Alexa sagged in her chair, relief flooding her. But her euphoria lasted only for a moment before realization hit her. No fingerprints meant nothing. If she'd been the killer, she would have wiped the knife clean.

The same thing was going through Spiro's mind. "That means that the killer was wise, and that again we have no suspects, only questions. We should know more once the autopsy is done."

"You mean it's not completed?"

"No. Since it's a two-hour drive to Ioannina, there's hardly been time." He stood up, extending his hand to shake hers. "Alexa, I'll come by and see your car in a few moments. Wait for me at the hotel. And I'll let you know the results as soon as we have word on the autopsy."

DAMIAN WALKED INTO the hotel dining room in the early afternoon. Alexa sat at a corner table, head down as she picked desultorily at the spaghetti on her plate. Dejection was plain in every line of her body.

Sympathy gripped his heart. Was she mourning Angelo? To his surprise, anger followed hard on that thought. She couldn't mourn Angelo, not after what he'd been and the torment he'd put Alexa through.

She looked up when he sat down, her eyes troubled. "How is Lisandro?" she asked. "Any better?"

He lifted one shoulder and let it fall. "About the same. He's been asleep most of the morning. I managed to feed him some clear soup a little while ago but he's lost his appetite."

Alexa nodded, her thick hair falling forward to lie against one cheek. She'd hitched it up on her head with a couple of tortoiseshell combs, but they'd come loose, one of them dangling by a couple of teeth. Unable to stop himself, Damian reached across the table and pulled it out. "You were about to lose it," he explained at her questioning look.

She took the comb, pushed back her hair, and stabbed the teeth firmly through the springy waves. "I suppose you haven't heard what's happened," she said. "My tires were slashed."

"No!" An icy chill settled in his stomach. Something sinister had come to the quiet village.

"Yes." Alexa pushed away her almost-untouched plate. "They're sending out new ones."

"From the rental agency?" He signaled to Poppy to bring them coffee. Maybe the hot drink would drive away the cold foreboding inside him.

"Yes. Although they weren't very happy about it."

"What does Spiro say?"

Alexa shrugged. "He's writing a report for the agency representative. We figure it probably happened sometime during the night, when the power was off."

"The power was off?"

"From midnight to 2:00 a.m., Spiro said."

Damian did a quick calculation. He remembered turning on the light when Lisandro came back into the house. So it must have been after two, then. How much, he didn't know. "Do they have the results of the autopsy yet?"

Alexa shook her head. "And Spiro won't discuss it, although he did promise to let me know as soon as he hears."

Poppy set a tray on the table, laden with a sugar bowl, a cream pitcher and thick mugs rather than the usual thimbles of Greek coffee. "You didn't eat your lunch." She frowned as she picked up Alexa's plate. "Was there something wrong with it?"

"It was fine," Alexa assured her. "I wasn't hungry."

Poppy looked doubtful. "Can I get you something else?"

"No, thank you." Alexa colored in embarrassment.

Seeing her pink cheeks, Damian smiled to himself, thinking unexpectedly that she would probably blush shyly if he kissed her. In many ways, despite her disastrous marriage, she was naive and inexperienced in her relations to men.

"Damian, would you like anything to eat?" Poppy asked, jarring him out of a pleasant fantasy in which Alexa was pressed against him, wanting him, and he was luxuriating in the taste and scent of her.

"No, no, thank you, Poppy," he said absently, his eyes remaining on Alexa as she spooned sugar into her coffee and stirred it.

Poppy moved away, taking Alexa's plate. Damian added sugar and cream to his own coffee. "Alexa, how soon will you have the tires?"

She continued to stir her coffee, watching the dark swirls as if hypnotized. "A couple of days."

"So you're staying that long at least," he said, with a visceral satisfaction. Maybe they would have a chance to get to know each other better.

What did he want from her? The question had haunted him last night when, every time he closed his eyes, he saw the classic contours of her face and those deep brown eyes, as clear as forest pools. No matter what developed between them in the few days she would be here, he was afraid the memory of her would remain with him forever, emblazoned on his soul.

If only things were simple. If all his emotions weren't involved with Lisandro just now. If only she weren't a successful career woman from Canada who would be just as likely to move here as she would to the wilds of Africa....

What was the point of dreaming? Alexa wasn't interested in him. She would leave. She would forget him as soon as the plane took off from the Athens airport.

He brought his thoughts to an abrupt halt by gulping his coffee, searing the roof of his mouth in the process. "Damn." Hastily picking up the glass Poppy had left, he quenched the fire with cold water.

"Watch that coffee," he said. "It's hot." He glanced around the nearly empty room. "I don't see your friend Kritikos."

That snapped her attention away from stirring her coffee. "He's not my friend. Maybe he left town. I haven't seen his car all morning."

Damian frowned. "You say he was talking to Angelo behind the hotel last night. Did they look friendly, or were they arguing?"

Alexa bit her lip, picturing the scene. "I don't know. They stayed in the shadows while they were talking. I only recognized Kritikos when he passed under the streetlamp. But they must have been at least marginal friends, since Angelo admitted he got Kritikos to talk to me in Volos."

"Unless Kritikos has fish of his own to fry." Damian sipped gingerly from his coffee cup. "Maybe he and Angelo had a falling out since he came here."

Alexa perked up. She leaned forward, placing her arms on the table. "And maybe he killed him. I just remembered. When they moved Angelo's body, there was a lot of blood by the bricks where he was lying, under his head. I wonder if he could have fallen by accident, or if someone pushed him."

"You mean that the fall killed him, rather than the knife?" Damian looked skeptical. "Then why bother to stab him?"

"I don't know. Wasn't there an Agatha Christie story like that, where a lot of people stabbed a man because they all wanted part of his execution?"

"I vaguely remember it. And Angelo's manner and background didn't exactly win him friends, but it still seems farfetched. It was late at night. The house is near the edge of the village. What are the odds of someone stumbling on Angelo lying on the floor after his fall and then finding a knife to stab him?"

"Put like that," Alexa said, "it seems unlikely. But it does raise doubts about his death being murder. And Spiro isn't saying anything."

"Police procedure," Damian said. "They never discuss cases with civilians. Not even with lawyers."

Alexa's brow lifted. "I thought you didn't do criminal law."

"I don't, but I've friends who do."

"Well, I suppose we'll find out when the autopsy is done."

And maybe time of death, thought Damian, which might eliminate some of the suspects. He finished his coffee and pushed his chair back. "If you'll give me the diary, I'll take it over to George—the retired schoolmaster I mentioned before—so he can get a start on translating it."

She handed the diary to him, having earlier retrieved it from the safe. "I'll come with you," she said, getting up.

Damian shook his head. "It's better if I go alone. Angelo wanted that diary. Maybe Kritikos does as well, if they were in this together. If you suddenly call on someone you don't know, especially a retired teacher of classical Greek, and he happens to hear about it, he'll suspect that it's about the diary. I'd rather not take the chance."

"But what about you?"

"I know a lot of people in Elatos. It won't look odd if I go to his house, and I'll put the diary in my pocket so no one sees I'm carrying it."

He saw stubbornness in the set of her jaw, but she nodded. "All right."

ALEXA FOLLOWED DAMIAN out, debating with herself whether she was doing the right thing. How well did she know him? Maybe he was after the diary, too. No, that was absurd. The diary had been available to him for months; Damian could have interpreted it at any time. So could Lisandro, for that matter, which brought up the question of why he hadn't.

"Lisandro must have been curious about the sword," she said at the door. "Why didn't he check out the diary?"

"Probably because it rightfully belonged to you or your mother, not to him," Damian said evenly. "Lisandro is honorable to a fault. It's very likely he hasn't even read the diaries."

Alexa's misgivings subsided, although the unsettled feeling that had plagued her all day remained.

"I know he had someone checking to see if they could track down your mother's address," Damian added. "He was planning to send them to you."

"She wrote that she hid them, in case Father came back," Alexa said with a catch in her voice. "I don't understand why she never told me about them, though. All I can think is that she never allowed herself to give up hope that the report of Father's death was a dreadful mistake, that he would come back to find her diary."

"I'm sure she'd be pleased that you finally have it."

Outside, they found that the sunshine of the morning had vanished. Billowing clouds scudded across a darkening sky, driven by a fretful wind that lifted Alexa's hair. One of her combs clattered to the floor, and Damian picked it up, smiling faintly as he handed it to her.

"Better use something more sturdy to hold your hair," he said.

"I should get it cut. It's getting too long."

Damian looked horrified. "It's beautiful. It would be a crime to cut it." He curved his hand around her head. The vibrant strands of her hair clung to his fingers as if they loved his touch.

A fierce pleasure uncoiled inside Alexa's chest. Forgetting her uneasiness, she pressed her face to the front of his shirt. The homespun cotton smelled of lemon and sunshine. Damian set his fingers under her chin, tilting up her face. Mesmerized, she stared into his eyes, losing herself in the stormy, dark blue depths that burned with a tender fire.

"Alexa," he said, a breath of sound. Above the village, the wind roared like ocean surf in the pines, but Alexa heard only the pounding of her heart as he laid his mouth on hers. His lips were firm and warm. She shivered as his tongue caressed the sensitive skin of her lower lip.

Only for a moment. He withdrew, leaving her breathless and yearning for more. Yet part of her was grateful that he'd pushed no further. There was no chance of her staying. Why torture herself with tantalizing possibilities?

"I'll let you know when he's finished," Damian said in an even tone that almost fooled her.

Almost. But not quite. Before he turned away, she saw the pulse in his throat, beating as erratically as her own.

ALEXA REREAD her mother's diary, reliving the strong emotions that came through the rather formal wording. Her mother had been torn by indecision for days. It was only the approaching danger that finally made her leave, the danger to her child even more than to herself. "For Alexa. For her future."

Unshed tears pricked Alexa's eyes and dimmed her vision. She went to the window of her room, looking out over the square. It was deserted in the late afternoon, and dead leaves scuttled across the flagstones like mice running from a cat. The sky was a mass of leaden clouds, swollen with rain. Or snow.

A knock on the door brought her away from the window. Spiro stood there, his crested cap clasped under his elbow. "May I come in?" he asked politely.

Alexa pulled the door wider. "Please sit down."

He sat, formally upright in the armchair near the window. "I've heard from the coroner in Ioannina. Angelo died around midnight or perhaps a little later."

"What killed him?" Alexa felt as if her emotions had frozen.

"There are indications that he was still breathing when the knife entered his chest. But the wound on his head was severe enough that it's doubtful he would have lived until morning. Which means the case is inconclusive." He stood up, fitting his cap carefully on his head. "I'll be continuing the investigation. Again, please let me know if you decide to leave Elatos."

"I can't until I have new tires, anyway."

"There is a bus," Spiro reminded her.

"I know, but I won't leave the car. When will his body be released?"

"It's been released. It will be brought back here either tonight or tomorrow. Since he has no relatives, the burial will be next to his mother and father in the village cemetery. Papa Apostoli will look after the arrangements."

Alexa let out a breath of profound relief. "Thank you."

Spiro touched the bill of his cap. "Good day, Alexa."

When the door had closed behind him, Alexa covered her face with her hands. Nothing was resolved. Not Angelo's murder. Not her own confusion.

It suddenly hit her that Angelo was dead. It hadn't seemed real before, but the talk of the funeral had driven away the numbness in her brain.

Hot tears streamed down her cheeks. She swiped at them with her hand, but nothing would stem the flow. Stumbling across the room, she groped blindly in her purse for tissues. The purse fell off the desk. Lipstick, wallet and loose coins clattered to the floor and rolled toward the corners of the room.

Tears dripped on the backs of her hands and she helplessly braced them on the desk. This was so ridiculous, crying over Angelo. But she knew it wasn't only Angelo. It was Damian as well, his kindness, the emotion that spun a web between them, two lonely souls caught by destiny. A destiny that couldn't be fulfilled.

Feeling as if she were navigating under water, she turned on rubbery legs and made for the bathroom. Tearing off a length from the toilet roll, she mopped her face and sank down onto the floor to rest her face against the cool porcelain of the pedestal sink.

Gradually the tears diminished, leaving her wrung out, more exhausted than on the worst day of trading in a plummeting market. She dragged herself to her feet and crossed the room to her bed. The contents of her purse still lay on the floor but she didn't care.

Shivering, she rolled under the blankets and slept.

SHE AWOKE TO THE STEADY banging of a loose shutter against the building. Sitting up, she shook her head, raking her hair out of her face. An uncertain twilight dimmed the room, turning the furniture into indistinct shadows. She got up, slowly, shaky as an invalid.

Her reflection startled her, blotched skin and red-rimmed eyes surrounded by bruised circles. Grimacing, she splashed cold water on her face, the fuzziness leaving her brain as she toweled her skin dry. It must be dinnertime. As if cued, her stomach growled, unhappy no doubt about its missed lunch.

Next to the desk, she paused. Her purse lay on it. The sight of it triggered a memory. Hadn't she dropped it earlier, spilling everything in it?

She glanced toward the door. Was it locked? Going across the room, she tried the knob. Loose. Lost in her grief, she hadn't checked it after Spiro left. She'd fallen asleep, leaving the room accessible to anyone who wanted to enter.

Her mother's diary. Where had she put it? She checked the desk drawer. A writing pad, a pen and a couple of brochures extolling the beauties of Epirus. Bitter panic rose in her throat.

No, that wasn't where she'd put it. She rummaged in the tumbled bed, letting out a little cry of triumph as she extracted the diary from under the pillow. It hadn't been stolen despite her carelessness.

Her eyes fell back on her purse. Maybe she'd dreamed that she'd dropped it. Pulling it open, she looked inside. Everything seemed to be intact. She gave a self-derisory laugh. She must have been dreaming.

No, wait, her lipstick was missing. Down on her knees she scanned the far corners, finally spotting it under the bedside table, along with a couple of Canadian quarters.

Her blood chilled, she stared at the unlocked door, certain now. Someone had been in her room.

Chapter Nine

When Alexa left her room, Kritikos was standing in the hall, inserting his key in the door of the room directly across from hers. Alexa would have walked by him without speaking, but the man turned with an affable smile, his crooked tooth gleaming.

"Good evening, Alexa. I'm sorry I didn't get a chance to speak to you yesterday, but I was happy to see you completed the arduous journey here. Have you had any luck with locating your father?"

"I've talked to Angelo," Alexa said crisply. "Your version of the story differed somewhat from his. Why did you lie?"

Kritikos shrugged. "Only a small lie. Does it matter now?"

"It might have mattered to my mother, if we'd known sooner."

"But no one knows where your father is. I do hope you find him."

"Don't bother to lie anymore," Alexa said coldly. "I don't think you care one way or the other."

Kritikos's smile vanished. "Please, Alexa. You wound me. I'd like to see your father, talk about old times. Oh, and before I forget, please accept my condolences on the unfortunate demise of your husband."

"Thank you," Alexa said with as much graciousness as she could muster. The man made her skin crawl, the way he looked at her with those reptilian eyes. "Did you talk to Angelo last evening?"

She was gratified to see surprise jump briefly into his eyes before he masked it under downcast eyelids. "Why should I have seen Angelo last night?"

"I just wondered. Your car was parked in front of his house yesterday."

His brows lifted, but this time his expression was ambiguous. "He'd asked me to come and see him as soon as I arrived. And I thought he might know of a small house I could rent."

"You're planning an extended stay?" Alexa asked, keeping her tone neutral.

Kritikos seemed to take it at face value. "I haven't decided, since there appears to be no houses available. This hotel doesn't give one much privacy."

Alexa shrugged, playing along with the game she'd started. "It's a small town. People are curious about visitors."

Kritikos's mouth hardened. "Too curious for their own good," he said, his eyes on her. Then, as quickly, his mood altered, and he smiled again. "Would you allow me to join you for dinner?"

Alexa's first impulse was to refuse; sitting across the table from this man was sure to make her lose her appetite. But hard on that urge came the thought that further conversation might give her useful information. How much did he know? And why was he here? Had he followed her, or did he have his own agenda?

"I'd like that," she said, smiling even though it made her cheeks ache.

"Good." His broad grin was spoiled only by the hard glitter that stayed in his eyes. "I'll meet you downstairs in five or ten minutes. You go ahead and pick a table."

At the top of the stairs Alexa glanced back, but he'd already gone into his room and closed the door.

POPPY WRINKLED her brow in comical perplexity when she saw Kritikos joining Alexa at her table. Alexa tossed her a smile she hoped was nonchalant. Shrugging, Poppy resumed the helpful attitude of a good hostess and brought over the menus.

"Good evening, Alexa, Mr. Kritikos. I didn't know you were acquainted."

"We met in Volos," Alexa said. "Mr. Kritikos knows my aunt."

Poppy handed him a menu. "Have you found a house, Mr. Kritikos?"

The corner of his mouth turned down. "Not so far. I'm afraid I'll be your guest for a while longer."

"So what do you do for a living, Mr. Kritikos?" Alexa asked after they had given their orders.

"Please, no mister. My name is simply Kritikos." He gestured with his hand, a diamond pinky ring flashing. "I'm a businessman. I have properties in Volos and in Athens. I'm thinking of buying something out here, for summer vacations, but I want to get the feel of the place first."

Alexa toyed with her fork, drawing little grooves on the tablecloth. "How long had you known Angelo?"

He stared past her, into the middle distance. "I knew Angelo's father, when Angelo was a child," he said after a long pause. "I only met Angelo again a year ago, when he returned to Greece. We didn't know each other well, except to reminisce about his father."

Simple and straightforward, on the surface. Why did she feel he wasn't telling the whole truth? Probably because she knew he'd lied to her before. And his eyes—even when they met hers, there was so little emotion in them she had a sensation of looking into a water-filled well. Of course, logic told her he wasn't obligated to tell her anything; nor did she have to believe anything he did say.

Curbing her frustration, she began to eat the salad Poppy set before her.

"I understand you lived here as a child," Kritikos said.

"Only for a short time, when I was six."

"You must have known Angelo then. You were children together."

"Hardly." Alexa took a slice of fresh bread and buttered it. "He was eight years older than I, so he was almost a teenager when I was a child. My mother knew his mother, though."

Kritikos applied himself to his own salad, chewing thoughtfully, his eyes on the window, where the cloudy dusk had given way to darkness. "Angelo was very broken up over your divorce," he said unexpectedly.

"Was he?" Alexa's voice was flat, hiding her disbelief. "Angry, perhaps, but he didn't show any regret around me."

"That was why he returned to Greece. It made him uncomfortable to live in the same city with the woman he still loved."

Alexa stared at him. "Still loved?" she echoed, rashly perhaps, but what did it matter now that Angelo was dead, unable to hurt her again? "Kritikos, I don't think Angelo ever loved me. I don't think he was capable of an honest emotion that wasn't directed at himself."

"You're very bitter." His eyes wandered over her, curiously flat.

"Wouldn't you be?" she retorted. "He only married me for the money he thought I had. Whatever regard he had for me died quickly when he found I had none of my own, that my mother's was tied up in her restaurants. By that time, I'd found out he'd been continuously unfaithful to me, and I wanted out of the marriage."

"Alexa."

She jumped when she heard Spiro's voice behind her. Her back to the door and her attention on Kritikos, she hadn't seen him come in. She wondered how much he'd overheard. What she'd just said coupled with the argument that she'd had with Angelo last night might be enough to convince him to arrest her.

Half turning in the chair, she faced him. Out of uniform, dressed in a casual sweater and twill pants, Spiro appeared less official.

"Alexa, I came to tell you that Angelo's body is now in the church. Perhaps you'd like to speak to Papa Apostoli later." He gave her a weary smile. "Although if you don't want to be involved, I'm sure he would understand."

"No," Alexa said, suddenly wanting to get the whole thing over with. Once Angelo was laid to rest, she could put their disastrous relationship behind her. "I'll see him. As soon as I finish eating."

She forced herself to eat the food on her plate, although she couldn't have said afterward how it tasted. Kritikos kept a brooding silence across from her. This had been a bad idea from the first; she should have known he was too cagey to give away anything he didn't want her to know. And what he *had* told her was probably a lie. She'd learned nothing for all her efforts.

She pushed aside her plate, declining dessert even when Poppy tempted her with a description of fresh baklava. She laid money on the table, but Kritikos immediately scooped it up and forced it into her hand. "No. When I eat with a lady, I pay."

She wanted to argue for the sake of pride, then gave it up. He'd lied to her; she figured he owed her. "Thanks," she said, rising from her chair. "If you'll excuse me."

He also got up. "Of course. Again, my condolences."

THE CHURCH DOOR CREAKED faintly as Alexa closed it. Flickering candlelight sent her shadow grotesquely up the side wall. She inhaled the scent of incense and beeswax.

The simple pine casket rested on a stand between the two cantors' lecterns, the cover lying loosely on it. Burning candles at its head sent fragrant smoke drifting toward the dome.

Papa Apostoli knelt at the altar, praying quietly. At the sound of Alexa's footsteps, he got up, genuflecting toward the icons on the elaborately carved iconostasis. He turned and came toward her. "Ah, Mrs. Thetalou. It was good of you to come. Would you like to see him? I can remove the cover."

Alexa shuddered. "No. That's all right." She'd seen enough this morning at the murder site.

She stood next to the casket, bowing her head in a brief prayer, feeling nothing. She lit the candles she'd picked up at the door, adding them to the stand.

Papa Apostoli waited at the back of the church. "The funeral will be at eleven in the morning," he told her.

Alexa pulled several bills from her purse. "How much would it be for your services?"

He looked faintly embarrassed, but she could see from the threadbare edges of the sleeves on his black robe that times were obviously tough. He named a figure that she felt sure was far too low.

She counted out the money, added several thousand drachmas on top of it, and pressed the bills into his hand.

"It's too much," he protested.

"Give what you don't use to the church," Alexa said. She stopped and kissed the back of his hand, the form of respect she'd learned as a child. "Thank you. Good night."

"Go with God, my child."

THUNDER RUMBLED ACROSS the mountain peaks as Damian reached for the latch on the shutters. Outside the window, tree branches tossed in the wind.

Damian pulled the shutters closed, securing them for the night. The marmalade cat purred softly. Damian bent and scratched his ears. The cat rose on his hind legs, begging to be picked up. "Not now, cat," Damian murmured. Usually the creature was out prowling at this hour, near midnight, but he didn't like wind or rain; it looked as if they would see plenty of both before morning.

He closed the other shutters, locked the front door and went down the hall to Lisandro's room. The cat followed, padding on silent white paws.

To Damian's surprise, Lisandro was awake, sitting up in bed, after sleeping all evening. "Papa, you're feeling better."

"A little." Lisandro's voice was weak, but he murmured his pleasure when the cat jumped up on the bed and settled in his lap. "Damian, we have to talk."

Damian frowned. "Are you sure you're up to it? You'll feel better in the morning."

"You must go to Angelo's funeral in the morning. I also should, but I don't think I'll be able to."

Vassiliki had been by earlier, telling them the funeral notices were posted in the square, that the mass for Angelo would be held tomorrow at eleven.

Sinking down onto the rocker next to the bed, Damian patted Lisandro's hand. "I'll go, if it's important to you. Alexa will be glad of the support. I don't imagine there will be a crowd."

"You might be surprised." Lisandro laughed shortly. "Angelo's father was well known in this area. They'll come out of curiosity. And possibly to make sure the troublemaker has a proper send-off."

Damian hid his surprise. It wasn't like Lisandro to use sarcasm. "What do you know of Angelo's father? They say he died over twenty-five years ago, long before you came to Elatos."

Lisandro's mouth set in a thin line, his fingers clenching in the cat's heavy coat. "Doesn't matter. I know, that's all." He turned his head to look at Damian, his eyes softening. "You like Alexa, don't you?"

More than was good for his peace of mind, Damian thought bleakly. "I like her."

"Then take care of her." Lisandro left off stroking the cat and clasped Damian's hand in a firm grip. "She may be in danger."

"From Angelo's killer?" he blurted without thinking.

"Who is Angelo's killer?" Lisandro said obliquely.

Thunder rumbled again, far away. In this room the shutters were still open, since Lisandro often slept badly and liked to be able to look at the stars. Not that he would see them tonight, hidden by the dense clouds.

As if to underscore his thought, rain began to whisper on the glass, a gentle sibilance that grew to a steady drumming as the wind picked up.

"I had a visitor this morning," Lisandro said presently.

Was that what had upset Lisandro, forcing him back to his bed? "Wasn't Vassiliki here?" Damian asked, displeasure making his voice sharp.

"I sent her to the store. We'd heard by then that Angelo was dead." The old man rubbed his chest, as if to erase his pain. Damian had seen the gesture a thousand times in the past year and it no longer alarmed him. "A man who drove a dusty Ford Escort from Volos came here."

Kritikos. "What did he want?"

"Nothing. At first." Lisandro clenched and unclenched his fist, flexing stiff joints. "He asked about renting a house. He reminded me of someone, or perhaps I'd met him before, long ago. It worried me that I couldn't remember. You don't happen to know his name, do you?"

"Kritikos, Alexa said. He knows her aunt in Volos."

The color drained out of Lisandro's face, leaving the skin taut and gray. "Kritikos?" he whispered, his voice a frail thread of sound. "No. It can't be." He choked on the words, his chin sinking to his chest.

Alarmed, Damian pulled his chair closer, picking up the glass from the bedside stand and offering him a drink. Lisandro shook his head. "It's all right. I'll be okay."

Setting down the glass, Damian wrapped his arm around Lisandro's shoulders, grimly aware of the fragile bones barely covered with flesh. The old man was wasting away, but he'd had emotional and spiritual peace. Now even that was gone. "Who is this Kritikos?" Damian demanded.

Lisandro's color had improved marginally, although the gaunt look remained around his eyes. "I'm not sure. But I can't take any chances. Especially with Alexa. You say she met him in Volos?"

"And he knew Angelo. Alexa saw them talking last night."

Lisandro compressed his lips. "So." He paused, apparently needing a moment to digest this. "Did he kill Angelo?"

"I'm not sure the police even questioned him. He wasn't around all day, which is kind of odd since the roads out of here are not the sort you go for a drive on without a destination. I'll mention it to Spiro, if Alexa hasn't done so. But there seems to be no motive in his case."

"You're saying that Alexa had a motive, aren't you, Damian?" Lisandro shook off his weariness and Damian could see a ghost of his former strength in the sharp speculation in his eyes.

"If bitterness and anger are a motive," Damian said reluctantly, "yes, Alexa had a motive. But by the same token, so did Poppy. Angelo was always bothering her. He was certainly no saint. But I don't believe Alexa killed him."

Lisandro's eyes twinkled. "At last, a woman you respect. She would be good for you, Damian. Don't let her get away."

Amused, Damian patted Lisandro's shoulder. "I think she might have something to say about that."

"Love can overcome the barriers."

"Maybe," Damian said, gently sardonic. "But probably not distance, since she lives thousands of kilometers away."

"You'll have to convince her to stay." Lisandro's face grew still, his thoughts turning inward. "I had a little girl once," he said almost inaudibly. "I missed her growing up. I've regretted it a million times, even though it was all for the best. I didn't need someone like Kritikos to remind me about the past."

"So you did know him."

Lisandro frowned. "I'm not sure. One's memory can play tricks. But I knew men like him. Men who never let the past die. Men to whom vengeance is life's blood. Damian, you learned to trust me. If you'd known what I'd been, you might have preferred the streets to the dubious sanctuary I offered you."

"You offered me a home," Damian insisted, baffled by the old man's words. He'd never wondered about Lisandro's past, never questioned where he'd lived or what he'd done before Damian came into his life eighteen years ago.

Lisandro smiled, a sad, wistful smile that had Damian wondering what he was thinking. "You've been a good son, Damian, loyal, loving. I hope you won't think badly of me when you learn of my past."

Damian's eyes stung. He held Lisandro's hand in his, feeling the tremor beneath the blue-veined skin. "It doesn't matter, Papa. Let the past stay where it is, in the past. Believe me, whatever you've done won't change how I feel about you."

Lisandro groped for a handkerchief under his pillow and blew his nose. Tucking it away, he ran his hand over the cat's fur. The cat responded by purring loudly, his eyes closing in ecstasy. "Having you in my life has been my greatest pleasure, almost making up for the past," Lisandro said quietly. "But you have to know the past now. I want you to know the truth, not a distorted version. You have to protect Alexa."

Damian's heart lurched in his chest. "What do you mean, protect Alexa?" he asked, keeping his voice steady with an effort.

"She may be in danger."

"Angelo threatened her, but he's dead. Who else would harm her?"

"Kritikos," Lisandro said starkly. "Something he said. It's been bothering me all day. He mentioned very casually that Alexa often walks alone, almost as if he were talking to himself. He said a woman alone should be more careful, that danger could come from anywhere. I'm afraid, Damian. I have to tell you the story, so you'll know."

Damian settled back in the chair. "Okay. I'm listening."

For a long moment Lisandro stared into space. Finally he spoke, in a voice that was strong and fraught with emotion. "April 21, 1967."

The day the sky fell in on Greek democracy. To Damian, a child at the time, it hadn't meant much, only that there were tanks in the streets, soldiers to avoid as well as police. But it hadn't changed his hand-to-mouth existence, the scrappy life he lived. His mother had been alive then, but the unsettled events only increased the parade of men through the squalid little Ioannina flat they called home, and he spent little time there.

"I was a lawyer in Athens at the time," Lisandro continued. "There were rumors for months, but it was still a surprise that morning when the tanks filled the streets and we learned that there had been a military coup of the government. I had connections with politicians considered enemies of the state. Therefore, I was quickly under scrutiny. I could have been arrested at any time."

A log fell on the hearth, making Damian jump. He got up to push it into place, stoking the embers until flames licked up around the wood he added. The fire crackled in counterpoint to the whisper of the rain.

"I took my family to Elatos, but I couldn't stay here," Lisandro said. "I had to go back to Athens a number of times. Here in Elatos I clashed with Angelo's father. He was one of the few in this area who supported the Junta, and he did his best to promote it. He knew my feelings. In the late summer he was murdered. I was the prime suspect, not that the secret police needed an excuse to arrest anyone. I made preparations to leave for Albania."

"Wasn't that border closed?" Damian asked, both horrified and fascinated.

Lisandro shrugged. "Not if you know mountain trails. I wanted to stay as close to home as possible. In the summer of 1967 we still had the hope that the situation would go back to normal."

"Which didn't happen for seven years," Damian said.

"Exactly." Lisandro cleared his throat. Damian helped him take a drink from the glass of water at his side. "My brother followed me, although he wasn't in danger, being a simple shepherd. He came to warn me that there was a contract out on my life. For the killing of Angelo's father and a number of other cooked-up charges, someone had ordered my death. I couldn't go back, and my wife might well have been in danger as well, since the Junta had no compunction about using relatives to blackmail their enemies into giving themselves up.

"My wife also left Greece. I never saw her or my little girl again. I can only be thankful that they did well over the years."

"Where?" Damian asked, his mind working. It couldn't be what he was thinking. No, it was too wild a coincidence.

Or was it? Was it all part of an elaborate plan?

Lisandro rubbed the scar on his cheek. "You'll know in a moment. But first I have to tell you one more thing. This Kritikos may be someone from the past. Even years later, some of the Junta were obsessed with revenge. You know that only a few of the leaders were ever punished. After the famous trials, a lot of what happened during those seven years was just conveniently forgotten. No country wants its dirty laundry hung out for the world to see, and we were no exception. I thought I was safe, under a new name, a moderately successful businessman who led a quiet life. My old identity had died with me."

"So you came back." What had Alexa told him? He should have asked her for details.

"My new surname—Cosmos," Lisandro said musingly. "You never questioned it because it is a legitimate name. But I took it because it means people. I was nobody anymore, and everybody. I liked the irony of it."

Damian sat up straighter. "What about Kritikos? Is his name real?"

Lisandro gave a rusty laugh. "Another irony, probably. The Junta leaders were from Crete—Kritikos is what we call Cretans. I wonder what this man was to them."

"I'll run a check on him. I'll give a friend of mine in the Ioannina police a call in the morning."

"I don't know if it will do you any good. He's bound to have an airtight cover."

"But if you don't recognize this man or his name, what makes you think he's here for any reason but what he says?" Damian asked.

"His connection to Angelo, partly. But more important, he lured Alexa here with the story that her father is alive."

"Don't you believe what he told Alexa?"

"It hardly matters," Lisandro said. "He may have made it up, hoping that it would flush out her father, if he's alive."

"And is he?" Damian asked, holding his breath but already certain of the answer.

Lisandro looked straight at him, his eyes infinitely sorrowful. "Yes, Damian, my son. He's alive. I am Dimitrios Doukas, Alexa's father."

Chapter Ten

A wrenching pain twisted in Damian's heart. "Alexa will be so happy," he said, but even as he spoke he knew it wouldn't be that simple. A secret that had remained buried for twenty-seven years wasn't going to emerge into the light of day without major repercussions. One man had already died, and there was reason to believe it was because of this secret.

He wasn't surprised when Lisandro shook his head. A tear slid down the weathered face, disappearing into the jagged scar. "We can't let her know. We must not let anyone know—but especially not Alexa. It would place her in grave danger if Kritikos is after me. He must not be allowed to use Alexa as a weapon against me."

"A weapon? Isn't that a little extreme?"

Lisandro swept his fingers down the scar, his mouth thinning to a grim line. "You're too young to remember, but these people are ruthless. He would not hesitate to use her, and then he would kill her, too, as casually as one slaps a mosquito."

Shaken by the intensity of Lisandro's statement and his obvious distress, Damian clenched his hands on his knees. "This man, Kritikos—you're convinced the danger will come from him?"

Lisandro's eyes narrowed and he gazed toward the fireplace. Embers snapped, sending sparks up the chimney. The scent of burning pine drifted around the room. "From him or someone who's working with him," he said slowly. "Don't forget what he said about Alexa walking alone. And we can't ignore his connection with Angelo, and now Angelo is dead, murdered. This story about the Albanian—yes, I did send money to the man last year, when I first learned of my illness. I wanted to clear up all my debts. But I'm not sure whether I believe that Angelo or Kritikos just happened to run into this man. The man was a lawyer—it's unlikely he would come to Greece as a refugee. They might have searched for him. And that would have been complicated, which indicates they had a compelling reason to do so."

Damian nodded. "The report that you were dead—was that manufactured to cover your disappearance?"

"No. After I left, my brother, Elias, met me near the Albanian border and we crossed together, using mountain passes no one except a few shepherds knew about. There we met more political refugees. The truck we rode on was ambushed by bandits. The driver was killed, and the truck, out of control, rolled into a ravine. It exploded, but some of us managed to jump free."

His eyes fell closed, lines of strain deepening beside his mouth. After a moment, he pulled himself together and continued. "In the morning we ran into a border patrol who took us prisoner. That was when I noticed Elias wasn't with us. Apparently he had escaped the crash, but he assumed I was killed since I'd been inside the truck rather than on the back of it. This was confirmed a couple of days later when he managed to find one of the men who'd been injured in a clinic nearby. The man was also sure I'd been killed, so Elias had to assume the worst. He went back to Greece and told Olympia."

Damian let out the breath he hadn't been aware of holding. "What about the story Kritikos told Alexa in Volos? That you stayed with a family."

"That was true. They didn't keep us prisoner long, preferring that we found work, of which there was plenty, since most of us were educated. I rented a room in the lawyer's house. His family was very kind to me."

"And you stayed for ten years."

"Is that what Kritikos said?" Lisandro asked, frowning. "It was less than eight years, only until the Junta lost its power. I'd been back in Greece about a year when I met you."

"And you found Elias again?" Damian asked.

"Yes. The political climate was still uncertain and there were many who held on to a desire for revenge. I couldn't take any chances, so I assumed a new identity. Only Elias knew it. Of course, without proper documentation I couldn't leave Greece. And I felt it was too dangerous to contact my family. I did the best I could. There was enough money in the accounts in Canada for Olympia and Alexa to live on if they were careful. But I soon heard that Olympia hadn't relied on that. She'd become a successful businesswoman on her own. They had adjusted. I couldn't destroy that when I could never be sure the revenge threats—"

"Threats?" Damian cut in.

"Yes, son. There were threats. I found out through discreet inquiries that someone from the old regime, one of the many who'd never been convicted, had sworn to kill me. It was safer to remain unknown." His voice broke. "Not that I haven't regretted it, but I feel as strongly now as I did then that it was the right course to take."

Damian sat silently beside the bed, hearing the rasp in Lisandro's breathing and the splash of rain against the window. What would he have done in a similar situation? He didn't know; danger, while part of his childhood, had seemed an adventure, not a threat to his life.

To abandon his family must have been a heartbreaking decision for Lisandro to make. The fact that he had done it jolted Damian. Damian had always looked to Lisandro as the epitome of stability, in direct contrast to his own mother, who had left him, a child, to the mercies of the streets while she went off with her latest lover.

Lisandro spoke again, his voice low and filled with pain. "Damian, I hope this doesn't hurt what we've been for each other. Please believe me, you took the place of the family I lost. Always. I couldn't be with them, and I knew it. You came into my life at a time when I was at the breaking point, wondering if I could go on. You truly gave me a reason to live."

Damian knew he had to say something. To remain silent would be an insult to Lisandro. "You saved my life, Papa." The words seemed trite to him, an inadequate indication of the emotion crowding his heart. He got up and knelt by the bed, gathering Lisandro's frail body into his arms. "I resented the discipline at first but I learned to love you, when I thought I was incapable of love. Without you, I would have ended up in jail or lying unmourned in the morgue."

He lifted his head to find Lisandro's eyes closed, his scarred face wet with tears. Gently, he smoothed the old man's hair, laying him back on the pillow. "Sleep now. We'll talk more in the morning."

"Would you bring me one of my pills, Damian?" Lisandro whispered, his fingers opening and closing convulsively on his chest. "Just one, with a glass of milk."

Damian warmed the milk and brought it into the bedroom. Finishing it, Lisandro lay back with a sigh. "Good night, son. Thank you for understanding."

But had he understood? Damian asked himself as he sat by the bed long after Lisandro's quiet snores told him he was asleep. Tonight Lisandro had laid bare his soul, revealing weaknesses Damian hadn't been aware of. Leaving one's family, for whatever reason, was not something to dismiss lightly.

The cat, tail raised, glided into the room, stopping at Damian's feet. He meowed inquiringly and set his front paws against Damian's leg. Damian smiled and picked him up, welcoming the warmth and softness cradled close to him. So simple, to be a cat—no painful introspection and, at least for this cat, no loneliness.

The wind moaned fitfully around the house. The clock in the kitchen chimed once. Damian didn't stir, couldn't bring himself to take his disordered thoughts to bed in the next room.

No, he decided finally, gazing across at the peacefully sleeping man, Lisandro hadn't been wrong. Not entirely right, perhaps, but certainly not wrong, either. He'd provided for his family, given them an escape route and insured their safety. He'd done all he could.

The cat's purring soothed him, making him think he might be able to sleep, after all. The fire had died down; he should get up and add wood to it.

HALF IN A DOZE, Damian jumped when sharp claws dug into his leg. As if shot from a catapult, the cat flung himself to the floor and scrabbled out of the room, leaving the rug in disarray behind him. A moment later Damian heard him yowling at the door.

Damian ran down the hall. Frantic, the cat clawed at the door, leaving long white scratches in the wood. Damian frowned. "You hate rain, and you want to go out?" he muttered. He drew the bolt, unlatching the lock.

A gust of rain hit him in the face when he pulled the door open. The cat skidded to a stop on the step, bouncing against a pair of bare feet coated with slimy brown mud.

"Alexa!" Damian choked on the word.

He drew her quickly inside the hall, pushing the door closed against the wind. The cat dashed past him, into the kitchen.

Alexa was soaked to the skin, her hair hanging in rat's tails around her face. Pine needles and little twigs were caught in the tangled ends. A thin cotton nightgown clung to her, revealing the lithe contours of her body, her nipples pebbled in the cold air. Damian glanced down. The hem was muddy around her ankles, the material shredded, as though she'd been dragged through a hedge.

She shivered, and he dragged his gaze back up to her face. His blood chilled when he saw her eyes. They were blank and unseeing, as if someone had emptied her soul.

"Alexa," he said again. He took her arm and she came with him into the bathroom, walking with a frightening docility. She seemed utterly unaware of him or of her surroundings.

Damian grabbed a bath towel and wrapped it around her. He planted another on her head, making a rough turban. Reaching around her, he turned on the bath taps, running the water slightly hotter than comfortable to his hand.

When the bath was half full, he dropped the towels and lifted Alexa into the water, nightgown and all. Other than a faint gasp, she gave no indication that she felt the hot water, and her eyes remained fixed on some point beyond him.

He knelt beside the tub, rubbing her bare feet, cleaning away the mud and restoring the icy skin to pink warmth. "Alexa," he said quietly, "speak to me."

The cat came in, his amber eyes curious. He rubbed his nose against Damian's hand, as if in apology. "Not now," Damian murmured, turning back to Alexa.

Sleepwalking. It suddenly hit him. Alexa was sleepwalking. He searched through his mind. What did he know of the strange phenomenon? That the person's state of being and awareness wasn't much different from normal sleep.

That, contrary to the old belief, it was all right to wake sleepwalkers, if necessary.

He gazed down at Alexa. Her eyes had closed, and he drew a breath of relief. She appeared to be in a normal sleep now. He had a curiously potent conviction that what he'd seen before was outside the bounds of sleepwalking. Was it possible that she'd been drugged? That fixed stare into nothingness, the tension in her body and the unreachable void in her mind hadn't looked natural.

Gently he shook her, calling her name. "Alexa, wake up." Her head lolled back against the end of the tub, and he hurriedly pushed a rolled towel under her neck. The mud from her feet and gown had settled to the bottom of the tub. He opened the drain, letting it run out, at the same time turning the tap back on to keep the water temperature constant.

Color returned to her cheeks, and suddenly she opened her eyes. "Damian." Her voice sounded hoarse, the word slurred. She sat up, making the water splash over the side. "Wh—what am I doing here?"

He grinned, unable to contain his relief. "I might ask you the same, walking around in a storm barefoot and half dressed."

She looked down at herself, and the pink in her cheeks became crimson. Her chin sank to her chest and a tear leaked from under her closed eyelids. "It's so stupid. I even put a chair in front of the door."

"You've had this problem before," Damian said.

Lifting her head, she met his gaze, her brown eyes dark and troubled. The pupils appeared normal, making Damian doubt his drug theory. He dismissed it as farfetched, anyway. She was hardly the sort to have taken anything voluntarily, and it was unlikely that someone would have had the opportunity to slip something into her food or drinks. "Since I was small," she admitted. "Particularly when I'm stressed." She clenched one fist, punching her raised knee, still covered by the wet nightgown. "I hate it. One day I'm going to find myself walking off a cliff or out a window."

"Not likely," Damian said. "I've heard that sleepwalkers can't do anything while asleep that they wouldn't do awake. I believe it's even been used as a defense in a criminal case." He handed her a couple of towels. "Can you get yourself out of there, or do you want help?"

For the first time since she'd appeared on the doorstep, awareness of her as a woman overcame his anxiety. Her breasts were small, high mounds under the soaked cotton, the upper curve just showing above the lace-trimmed neckline. Suddenly Damian's palms itched to touch them, to find out if the flush on her cheeks would deepen if he lowered the gown and tasted her with his mouth.

Reining in his thoughts, he shoved his hands into his pockets and backed up to the door. "Call me if you need me."

"I will, Damian. Thanks." He was sure he heard a smile in her voice but didn't trust himself to stick around to see if it was true.

He was in the kitchen warming some milk when she came out, wearing his robe, which she'd found hanging behind the bathroom door. She'd had to roll up the sleeves, but otherwise the fit wasn't bad.

"If you could lend me something to wear, I'll get back to the hotel," she said, her eyes skittering nervously around the room.

"Better if you stay for the rest of the night," Damian said. "You can have my bed. I'll be fine here." He gestured at a cot, normally used for extra seating, in the corner of the room.

He poured milk into a glass, adding sugar and stirring it. He set it on the table in front of her. "Here. It'll make you feel better and help you sleep."

She made a face, looking almost normal again except for the haunted shadows in her eyes. "I don't like warm milk, probably because my mother gave it to me for breakfast every morning when I was a kid."

Pushing the glass closer, he smiled. "Drink it, anyway. And tell me what happened."

Her eyes, dark as chocolate, swam with tears. "I don't know what happened. I only remember having strange dreams. Weird, mixed-up dreams. At one point it felt as if I was floating through the air, in a dark tunnel with a light at the end. Then it was cold, and I heard music, like in a parade, and people yelling, and guns."

"Were you frightened?" Damian asked.

She shook her head. "I'm not sure. After the music and the noise stopped, I felt even colder and I could see a fire in the distance and I walked toward it. Then I woke up in your bathtub."

"You scared me," Damian said, hiding his worry behind an even tone and a calm demeanor. "You were completely out of it when I found you outside. The cat led me to the door, by the way."

"I'll have to thank him." The lightness of her words was at odds with the perplexity creasing her brow. "How is Lisandro?"

Faced with her, the enormity of the secret he shared with Lisandro slammed into him, stealing his breath. He swallowed, willing himself not to show the emotion churning in his stomach. "He's sleeping. I gave him a pill for pain, which is also a sedative. He won't wake before morning."

"Then he doesn't know I'm here."

"No." Some of the chill left Damian's body as he realized they were effectively alone together. He looked at her, his blood heating even as sympathy tugged at his heart.

Her wet hair was combed severely back, mercilessly exposing the classic lines of her face. She was beautiful; without a shred of makeup, she was the most beautiful woman he'd ever seen. He could see himself kissing that lush pink mouth, running his tongue over the porcelain skin covering her cheekbones.

What would she do if he touched her, if he opened his mouth over the little hollow between her collarbones, where he could see her pulse beating?

Sternly, he shook himself. He had no right, no right at all. "Drink your milk," he said gruffly.

She drained the glass, grimacing, and limped over to the sink to rinse it. *Limped?* Damian got up and went toward her. "Do your feet hurt? I should have checked them. Those rocky paths are dangerous without shoes."

Placing his hands at her waist, he hoisted her up onto the counter. He picked up each of her feet in turn, running his fingers gently over the soles. She wiggled her toes, squirming. "Ticklish, are you?" he asked.

"Only a little. Ouch, it hurts there, by my middle toe."

He examined the spot, finding a small cut in the soft underside of her toe, probably from a rock. Then he noticed the tiny black pinpoint marks on her arch. He checked the other foot again, seeing the same marks. "Do these hurt?"

She jerked her foot back at the firm stroke of his hand. "Yes. Prickles."

"You've stepped in thistles or some kind of briars," Damian said. "The points are imbedded in the skin."

"Can you get them out?"

"Not easily. But they'll work themselves out in a day or two."

"Thistles," Alexa said. "Is it possible I've been to Angelo's house?" She gnawed on her bottom lip, stilling its trembling. Wrapping her arms around her middle, she hugged herself as if a chill wind had blown through the kitchen. "Back to the scene of the crime."

"You've committed no crime." Damian's voice rang harshly over the drum of rain on the window.

"Then why would I go to Angelo's house?"

Damian stroked her ankle, savoring the smooth silk of her skin. "Maybe you didn't." His mind flashed back to the condition of Lisandro's shoes yesterday morning, the conclusion he'd jumped to and then tried to deny. "There are thistles everywhere. And those marks might be pricks from evergreen needles."

She closed her eyes for a moment, her expression a study in misery. "I don't know anymore. It's horrible to have this feeling of being out of control. I must have walked through the woods somewhere, too. My nightgown was ragged at the bottom and my hair was full of sticks. I'd better get back."

She slid from the counter, wincing as she landed on the sore toe. "Please, Alexa," Damian said, laying his hands on her shoulders. "Stay here. You can't go out in that storm."

As if she hadn't noticed the wind and weather beating around the house, she cocked her head. "I heard voices, in the storm, eerie voices coming from the trees." Her voice was low, giving a singsong rhythm to the words. Damian stared at her, taking in the pallor of her face, the blank sightlessness back in her eyes.

"Alexa," he said.

She blinked, the vacant look receding. "I'm all right, Damian. I just remembered something else, what the voices said. Where is the sword of Dimitrios, just like in my mother's diary."

A new fear sent an icy chill up Damian's spine. "Are you sure you were dreaming? Or was someone there?"

She shook her head. "I don't know. I just don't know."

"Well, that settles it," he said firmly. "You're not going out there tonight." He took her elbow and steered her into his room, turning down the bed and tucking the quilt around her. He brushed his fingertip over her nose, not trusting himself to come any closer. "Sleep. We'll talk in the morning."

ALEXA WOKE SHORTLY after dawn, groggy and disoriented. She raked back her tangled hair and rubbed at her gritty eyes, squinting against the light. Where was she, and why was the lamp on when she could see it was daylight?

Her gaze fell on the dresser, the hairbrush lying there next to a flat brown wallet. Damian's room. Scattered memories of the past night flooded into her mind. Had he really put her into a bathtub full of hot water? Her tattered nightgown, dry and clean now, hung over a chair. On the end of the bed lay a thick sweatshirt, heavy wool socks and a pair of faded jeans.

What had happened before she'd found herself in the bathtub? She searched through her mind, finding little more than confusion and an impression of walking through cold rain among trees that hemmed her in and spoke with strange voices.

She tightened the belt of the terry robe she wore, Damian's robe, she guessed. Unlatching the window, she released the handle of the shutters, folding the panels to each side of the recessed opening. A brisk wind that held a suggestion of snow tugged at her hair. She leaned out. The rain had stopped, leaving behind a blue sky in which scudding clouds played hide and seek with the sun.

Somewhere in the house a door banged and she heard a whistle, followed by the plaintive moo of a cow. Scrambling into the clothes, which fit surprisingly well, she left the room, hopping first on one foot and then on the other as she pulled on the wool socks. In the bathroom she made quick work of washing her face and giving her teeth a cursory scrub with her fingertip.

She found Damian in a little shed behind the house, perched on a one-legged stool, his forehead against the cow she'd nearly run into the first day. Milk foamed into a bucket clasped between his knees.

The cow turned her head inquisitively at Alexa's approach, a long tuft of grass hanging from her mouth.

"Morning, Alexa," Damian said without looking up. "I'll be done in a minute."

She hunched down beside him. "How'd you learn to milk a cow?"

"I had to. The owner of this cow is away for a few weeks. He's always kept her here so he asked me to milk her twice a day while he's gone. There's really nothing to it, just a rhythmic squeezing. And she's very gentle, only kicked me once when I was learning."

Alexa laughed, lifting her head to scan the sky when she heard the lonely cry of an eagle. She could see it pinpointed against a patch of blue as it scanned the earth for a careless rabbit or mouse. She shivered, the terror of half-remembered nightmares crowding into her mind.

Nightmares or reality?

"Damian, what happened last night?"

He gave a final tug and stood up, setting the pail and stool aside. Giving the cow a pat on the side, he led her through the open gate of the pen, fastening it securely once she was inside. "And don't go wandering," he admonished her.

Damian picked up the pail of milk and slung his other arm across Alexa's shoulders. "All I know is that you showed up on our doorstep in the middle of the storm. As for the sounds you heard, I don't know whether you dreamed them or not. We heard nothing, but the storm would have drowned it out, anyway. You don't remember anything, then?"

Her mouth turned down. "I usually don't, when I've been sleepwalking. But this morning I did remember something. Someone came into my room and carried me to Angelo's house."

Chapter Eleven

Lisandro opened his eyes when Damian entered his room. Checking his pulse, Damian found it steady and strong. "Will you be all right while I take Alexa to the hotel?" he asked. "I'll be back in half an hour at the most."

"Alexa? She's here? This early?"

"That late," Damian said wryly. "She came after you fell asleep." He debated whether he should tell Lisandro how she had appeared in the storm, then decided he'd better. The incident puzzled and alarmed him, especially after Alexa's statement a few minutes ago. And it would remind Lisandro to remain alert.

Briefly he sketched the events of the night. Lisandro nodded, his face somber. "And where is she now?"

"In the kitchen, taking care of the milk." He searched the old man's face. "Do you want to see her?"

Lisandro hesitated, clearly uncomfortable. "No. Perhaps it would be better to wait until later. After the funeral."

Oh, yes, the funeral. Damian swallowed the bad taste in his mouth. "Okay," he said. "I'll be back shortly, and Vassiliki will be here to stay with you during the funeral."

"YOU SAY YOU LOCKED your door with the bolt and put a chair in front of it," Damian said as he and Alexa walked toward the hotel. "You don't mind if I take a look at your room, do you?"

Alexa frowned, picking her way around a puddle in a low spot on the path. "Go ahead. But what do you expect to find?"

The grin he threw her seemed forced, and the uneasiness that had been dogging Alexa since she got up grew. "I'll know when I see it," he said.

Kritikos sat in the dining room, his table covered with the remains of a substantial breakfast. He waved as he spotted Damian and Alexa; his brows lifted knowingly. Alexa's empty stomach lurched. Although Damian had offered her breakfast, she'd felt too jittery to risk eating. Now she was glad she hadn't.

"Good morning," she said politely, leading Damian up the stairs. She could only be grateful that Poppy hadn't been in sight, although she was sure the whole village would know in an hour that she had apparently spent the night at Damian's.

As expected, her room door stood open, the curtain swaying in the draft from the slightly raised window. Not enough of a draft to slam the door, evidently.

Without touching anything, Damian examined the frame. No marks of any kind that could indicate forced entry; however, the flimsy lock could be opened easily without a key. A hairpin or a small screwdriver could spring the simple mechanism in seconds. He should know; he'd used the method to get into abandoned buildings often enough during his childhood. Even into his own house when his mother had forgotten and shut him out.

In contrast, the sturdy dead bolt on the inside of the door would be difficult for an intruder to tamper with. Closing the door, Damian shot the bolt, then yanked at the handle. The bolt held, with no indication of slack in the screws holding it in place.

"The chair," Alexa said suddenly. "It's back in its normal place by the wardrobe."

"You might have moved it yourself when you left the room."

Alexa sighed. "Yes, I suppose so. I moved objects heavier than that when I was a kid. It seems as if I had a compulsion to get out. Except this time I'm sure someone was here. Maybe it doesn't make sense, but I just feel someone was with me wherever I went during the night."

Damian laid his hands on her shoulders, looking into her troubled eyes. "Alexa, I believe you, but there's nothing here to indicate it. I think we'd better talk to Poppy, though. Ask her if she's been up here this morning. Or if she saw anyone around last night."

Poppy, clearing off Kritikos's table, could not shed any light on the mystery. "Mr. Kritikos came in at about eleven, not long after the storm began. I was at the desk and wished him a good evening. He went upstairs and I heard his door close. After that, I didn't see or hear anything. The storm might have covered any sounds, but this is an old building, full of creaks. I'm so used to hearing its noises that I think I'd recognize an unusual one. I heard nothing."

"And you haven't been in Alexa's room this morning?"

Poppy frowned, clearly baffled by the line of questioning. "No, why would I? Alexa, you missed breakfast," she added as that had just occurred to her.

"I missed more than breakfast," Alexa muttered.

She glanced toward the windows through which the church tower was just visible. As if on cue, the bells began to toll the monotonous funeral cadence.

"Poppy, will you be attending Angelo's funeral?" Damian asked.

A strange look crossed Poppy's face. She lifted the stacked plates, cutlery rattling. "Probably. If I get through here in time." She was halfway to the kitchen when she turned her head. "It should be quite a spectacle, even more so than they say his father's funeral was."

A SPECTACLE? Alexa asked herself later as she stood next to Angelo's casket in the incense-scented church. She glanced around. Not unless one counted a sheer mass of people a spectacle. It seemed the entire population of Elatos had turned out, crowding around the priest and raising the temperature inside the small building to uncomfortable levels.

Sweat trickled coldly down Alexa's sides, under the sweater she wore. She lifted the heavy hair off her neck; her skin felt clammy and sticky.

Beside her, Damian smiled briefly, as if to tell her it would soon be over and she'd be able to breathe again.

The mass ended and the six pallbearers, recruited by Papa Apostoli, lifted the coffin onto their shoulders. The people moved aside to let them through, then pushed their way out the door to follow them to the cemetery.

The grave had been dug; picks and shovels lying next to it testified to the difficulty of carving such a hole in the rocky ground. Alexa stared into the rectangular pit, her mind blank, as it had been since she'd entered the church. Even the most perfunctory prayer was beyond her.

The priest swung his censer, intoning a blessing that was barely audible over the roar of the wind in the pines. The fragrant smoke stung Alexa's nostrils, and she was suddenly spun back six months to her mother's funeral. Tears filled her eyes, spilling over and running down her cheeks. Impatiently, she wiped them away with the wadded tissue in her hand.

She was acutely conscious of Damian standing beside her, of the concern in his eyes. She shook her head slightly, forcing her attention back to the priest's words.

The formal Greek was difficult to follow, especially when vagrant gusts of wind snatched away the words. At her back, the crowd stirred, murmuring. She tilted her head toward Damian. "What did he say?"

Frowning, Damian stuffed his hands into his pockets and hunched his shoulders. "It's an old funeral saying, not used much now. 'The earth that fed you now will eat you.' "

Alexa shuddered, her skin crawling. She was silent as Damian and the others echoed Papa Apostoli's final, drawn-out amen.

The priest came over and took her hand, murmuring condolences. He turned to speak to Damian as Kritikos, whom Alexa hadn't noticed until this moment, came forward and shook her hand. "I'm so sorry, Alexa. If there's anything I can do, please let me know."

His hand felt soft, as if he'd never worked, and unpleasantly moist. Revulsion crept through her. "Thank you," she whispered, wanting to jerk back her hand. After an interminable moment, he let go. Surreptitiously she wiped her palm on her skirt but the clammy dampness lingered.

No one else spoke to her, not even Poppy who stood on the opposite side of the grave, her face pinched with cold or sorrow, Alexa couldn't decide which. Skirting the mound of earth, the girl threw the yellow chrysanthemum she held onto the coffin, where it lay in bright contrast to the spray of white lilies Papa Apostoli had produced from somewhere. She looked at Alexa and smiled, an odd conspiratorial smile, as if she and Alexa had been partners in— In what? Angelo's death?

Baffled, Alexa mentally chewed over the thought, watching Poppy walk away, her black coat flapping.

The crowd was beginning to disperse as people separated into smaller groups. Their voices remained low, subdued—no Greek ever shouted in a cemetery; it was a sacred place. And at night, a scary place, even when one was an educated adult.

The grave diggers picked up their hammers, preparing to secure the lid of the coffin. Before they could pound in the protruding nails, a disturbance rippled through the crowd, voices rising.

A small man, leaning heavily on a cane, pushed his way forward. Alexa's eyes widened. Old Mitso, the man who'd stared at her in the square yesterday morning.

He walked up to the coffin. "Open it. I want to see the devil's spawn."

Alexa heard someone gasp behind her. A woman nearby crossed herself and wailed a couple of notes that sounded like a dirge. Or simply a cry of despair.

"Open it, I said!" Mitso's voice carried clearly over the wind.

The two men looked at each other, then at the priest, who stood as if in a trance, speechless. Shrugging, one of them slid the lid to the side. Mitso bent over his cane, gazing into Angelo's still face.

Silence. No one seemed to breathe. Even the wind had died momentarily.

Mitso straightened. His dark eyes flashed behind the thick glasses as he surveyed the people around him. He turned back to Angelo and spat in his face. "I curse you," he shouted. "You and your father. May you burn in hell for a thousand eternities."

Too shocked to move, not one person stopped him as he crossed the cemetery and disappeared into the woods.

One of the grave diggers broke the silence with a nervous laugh. He tapped his temple. Alexa could imagine him saying, "Old Mitso, finally gone over the edge," to his companion as they replaced the lid and tapped down the nails.

The villagers filed out into the street in subdued silence. Damian took Alexa's hand in his, and she curled her fingers around it, wishing she could warm the rest of her body as easily. Her knees shook and she was racked with an inner tremor she couldn't control. The edges of her vision turned gray and her head seemed as light as a bubble. She swayed, closing her eyes as blackness rushed to overtake her.

Damian must have sensed something wrong. He stopped, pulling her out of the wind next to the row of cypresses that guarded the cemetery. "Alexa, what's wrong? Your face—you're all white."

She felt as if every drop of blood in her body had drained out and seeped into the stony earth. "Something—" Her voice broke. Clearing her throat, she tried again. "Something about this place. I don't remember anything, but I've been here before."

"You lived here," Damian said gently.

"No, no." She shook her head impatiently. "It's something else. I don't understand it. It's as if everything that's happened since I came here is trying to tell me something. But I don't know what."

Damian wrapped his arms around her. For an instant, she resisted, but it didn't seem worth fighting. She relaxed, her body aligning with his, finding him a perfect fit. The fresh-air scent of him filled her, driving out the despair and the debilitating melancholy assailing her.

Sanctuary. She drifted peacefully, wishing she were lying down so that she could sleep until this nightmare was over.

"Alexa." Damian's voice jarred her back to the present. "Alexa, let's go. It's cold out here, and I'll bet you haven't eaten a thing all day."

She pulled away reluctantly, startled to realize it was true. Maybe that was why she'd had the dizzy spell, because she hadn't eaten. "Poppy should have something ready to eat," she said, pleased that her voice sounded normal despite the turmoil in her mind.

"You don't have to go back to the hotel yet," Damian said. "Lisandro hasn't been well and he'd like to see you again. We'll eat with him. Vassiliki is there, so I'm sure she's cooked lunch."

The old man, Mitso—why had he cursed Angelo? As far as Alexa knew, Angelo hadn't lived in Elatos for nearly twenty years. According to Poppy, he'd gone to Athens after his mother's death, and from there emigrated to Canada. Whatever wrongs he'd committed in his youth surely didn't rate that all-consuming curse.

"I'd like to talk to Mitso," she said suddenly. "Do you know where he lives?"

Damian stopped on the path, turning to face her, his hands coming up to clasp her shoulders. Alexa could see the worry that darkened his eyes to black. "Are you sure that's a good idea? From what I've heard, Mitso is unpredictable. This morning's incident proves it."

"What can a hundred-year-old man do to me?" Alexa said stoutly, although a shiver walked up her spine as she recalled the venom in the old man's voice at the grave. "I can find him at the square sooner or later. After all, we saw him yesterday. But the questions I need to ask him aren't the sort I want to air in front of half the village. Where does he live?"

Damian's shoulders sagged and he resumed walking. "Okay, I'll take you." He scanned the sky, which was becoming increasingly cloudy although the wind had died. "This afternoon? It's about a half hour walk." He eyed her feet. "You'll have to change your shoes."

"No problem," Alexa said. As an independent woman, perhaps she should have resented his insistence on going with her. But she wasn't stupid. For all she knew, Mitso's house was guarded by one of those fearsome, wolflike sheepdogs she'd read about.

"MITSO IS MORE THAN a little strange," Lisandro said after they'd eaten the lunch Vassiliki had prepared. He sat, propped up by pillows, in his bed. To Alexa, he didn't look well at all. Deep mauve tinted the slack skin around his eyes, and his hands trembled as he lifted his coffee cup to his mouth.

However, from the first moment she'd entered his room, she'd understood that he wanted no pity, no reference to his deteriorating health at all.

"Do you know him?" she asked.

Lisandro shook his head. "No, but everyone in Elatos knows his story, how in 1948, guerrillas raped his wife and daughters and then slaughtered them before his eyes. He refused to betray his friends who fought for freedom and justice. Rather than kill him, they left him to endure that diabolical punishment, the knowledge that he'd put his country ahead of his family, that he would live each day with that ghastly memory."

Alexa closed her eyes, unable to bear the pain in Lisandro's. So many wars. So much betrayal and death. Not for the first time Alexa asked herself if she shouldn't deny her heritage when it seemed written in blood and vengeance. But, as always, she remembered her mother's words, that for each unspeakable horror, there was more than one act of heroism. Good and evil—the battle between those opposing forces was never so evident as in Greek history.

She felt Damian's hands on her shoulders, warm and reassuring, his callused thumbs making little circles next to her spine. She leaned back, grateful for his presence, the strength that he seemed to lend her whenever she needed it. Angelo had never been there....

No, she didn't want to think of Angelo. She wanted to submerge herself in Damian, feel more than the gentle touch of his hands. She wanted to feel his heat, feel that he wanted her.

Startled, she realized she wanted him, too. Wanted him in the most primal sense, a woman with a man, naked together.

She couldn't have him, of course. At this moment, Lisandro was there, although he lay against his pillows, his eyes closed, lines of profound weariness etched in his face.

And later...she shook her head. No, she could never have Damian. She was far too aware of the emotions that ran deeply in them both. To admit to their feelings when their time together would last at most a couple of days more would make the pain unbearable when they parted.

No, it was better this way. Safer.

"Mitso's mind was never the same after that," Lisandro said in a dreamy voice. "He was harmless, of course. That's why what happened today surprises me. I wonder..."

Alexa pulled free of Damian's hands and leaned forward, taking Lisandro's hand in hers. "Please, Lisandro, tell me about Angelo's father. He was killed, wasn't he?"

For a long moment Lisandro said nothing. An errant gust of wind moaned around the house, as if to remind them that there was a world outside this room. "He was a spy for the military government," Lisandro said in a harsh whisper that rasped against Alexa's nerves. "He was found early one morning, just outside the village, with a bullet in his head. The gun was his own and lay nearby, but it was clearly not suicide. It was an execution."

"And my father and the sword disappeared around the same time."

"Yes."

"So the two events were connected."

Lisandro dragged in a long breath. "Perhaps. There is speculation to that effect."

Alexa hesitated, searching for the right words. When she spoke, she felt as if the question was ripped from her soul. "Is it possible that my father killed him?"

Damian stiffened. Although he was no longer touching her with his hands, she sensed the tension in him as if it lived in her own body. No one breathed, and then Lisandro broke the silence with a single word.

"No."

A cold hand gripped Alexa's heart. Lisandro wouldn't lie; she was convinced of it. Yet an undercurrent in his tone, a inexplicable quality of falseness, told her he wasn't telling her the whole story.

"Lisandro, please," she pleaded, tightening her fingers around his.

For a second he responded, then his hand grew lax, sliding away from hers. "Odd thing about Constantine's death. He was also stabbed numerous times in the chest. The knife wasn't found."

Another knife, the blade gleaming. Alexa shivered and closed her eyes, trying in vain to grasp the fleeing image. Was it memory or nightmare? "Lisandro—"

Raising heavy eyelids, he looked at her. "No more, Alexa. Not today."

Biting her lip in frustration, Alexa let Damian lead her from the room. At the door, she cast a glance back to the old man sleeping on the bed. This wasn't the end. She would get to the bottom of it.

He knew. And she had to persuade him to tell.

Whatever it was.

However painful it might be.

Chapter Twelve

The forest closed around them, enveloping them in a shroud of green. Heavy clouds, pregnant with rain, obscured the sun, and lightning stitched across the jagged peaks looming in the distance. Alexa wrapped her arms around her middle, glad she'd worn her heavy raincoat.

She slanted a glance at Damian's profile. He looked preoccupied, remote, as if he'd removed himself from her presence into a world deep inside himself. She knew he was unhappy about this expedition. As far as he was concerned, she could have waited until Mitso came to the square.

But Alexa couldn't stifle her sense of urgency. Of all the people in the village, Mitso was the most likely to know the real story of when her father had left. If anyone else knew it, they weren't talking.

Last night, after dinner, and this morning, before the funeral, she'd made inquiries, but no one had any answers. They were kind, but either evaded her questions or denied knowing what had happened. "I'm sorry. I grew up in Ioannina. I didn't know your father." She heard it over and over again.

And, surprisingly, many insisted, "The past is over." It was a sentiment Alexa had thought contrary to the Greek spirit. The lesson she'd learned at her mother's knee was that the past lived forever, and forever affected the present and the future. Only a fool turned his back on the past.

"Is it possible that Poppy also went to see Angelo that night?" Alexa asked, voicing a question that had flitted in and out of her mind a number of times since the funeral. "She had a very strange look on her face before she left the grave site."

Damian shrugged. "Angelo was interested in her, but I don't think she had a reason to kill him."

"Maybe not," Alexa persisted. "But suppose he tried to make a move on her and she pushed him away. He falls and hits his head. She's scared and runs out. Someone else comes along, sees an opportunity, and stabs him."

A surge of disappointment ran through her when Damian failed to look impressed. "I seriously doubt if Poppy would kill a man simply because he was bothering her. Don't worry, Alexa. Spiro will find Angelo's killer, if he can be found. He may look like an average provincial policeman, but he's shrewd and observant. And he probably has more evidence than he lets on."

"Which is why he hasn't arrested me, I suppose," Alexa said gloomily.

They were in deep forest again, walking beside a little creek that murmured musically over mossy stones. Alexa fought to concentrate on the cheerful gurgle rather than on the foreboding that pressed cold hands along her spine. The green darkness of the trees crowded in on her. Her breath hitched in her dry throat, and she paused, gazing up at the pewter clouds hovering in the treetops.

"Alexa, what's wrong?" Damian asked. He waited for her to catch up, then took her hand in his.

She welcomed the hard heat of his palm against her icy fingers, but it did nothing to chase the chill from her bones. As Damian stared at her, she replied, "What do you mean?" Her face was white, her eyes huge and dark, like black holes against the porcelain skin. She was afraid, but he couldn't figure out why.

Alexa's hair swung around her shoulders as she gazed fearfully into the trees. "I don't know. I feel I know this place, but I can't remember." She clenched her fist painfully around his fingers. "*Why* can't I remember?"

"If it's important, you'll remember eventually." Inwardly, Damian cursed his helplessness. He couldn't shake the suspicion that something traumatic had happened during her childhood, something so horrific her mind had blocked it out. He tugged at her hand. "Come along. We're almost there. Let's get this over with before we get caught in the rain."

They turned a corner in the path and the cabin stood before them, a small, sturdy building of rock walls capped by a slate roof. Trees grew around it, a couple of thick, ancient oaks and a wind-twisted pine. Nothing indicated that anyone lived there, not even a pretense of a garden.

"Mitso?" Damian called.

Not a sound. Not even an echo as the dense trees absorbed his voice.

"He's not here," Alexa whispered.

"He has to be."

They moved closer. They'd almost reached the door when a snarl of rage stopped them dead. A mound of black fur hurled itself around the corner of the house and catapulted into Alexa's legs. She clutched Damian's wool sweater, barely saving herself from crashing to the ground.

Another growl drew her eyes to the creature crouched on the doorstep, fur bristling. It was the biggest black cat she'd ever seen in her life. The animal's green eyes blazed with hostility, sharp white teeth displayed around a scarlet mouth bared in another snarl. It snapped its jaws shut and hissed at them.

"Nice kitty," Damian said in a cajoling tone, extending his hand. The cat's paw slashed at him, leaving a livid scratch on the back of his hand. "Not nice kitty," he amended with clenched teeth as he stared at his hand, startled to see blood.

The cat gave a loud, triumphant yowl. Abruptly the door opened. "What's going on here?" The cat scooted inside as the wizened little man poked his head around the doorframe. Thick brows like twin furry caterpillars knitted together. "What do you want, daughter of Doukas?"

No more cowering. This man had the answers, if anybody did. Alexa gathered her resolve and stiffened her backbone. She stepped up to the door, gratified to see that she was almost a head taller than Mitso. A physical and psychological advantage.

"My name is Alexa," she said evenly. "I need to talk to you. You're the only one who remembers."

Alexa entered and sat down on one of the cane-seated chairs around the scrubbed wooden kitchen table, pushing another toward Damian. She glanced around the room. A painted iron bed covered by a faded quilt occupied one corner. Across from it, a television set stood on top of a wooden dresser. The area where they sat was the kitchen, complete with sink and a couple of cupboards. All of it was impeccably neat and clean, including the packed earth floor under their feet.

Watching them, Mitso sat down in a worn leather chair by the table, exhaling gustily. He snapped his fingers at the cat who jumped up onto his lap, an enormous heap of black fur staring suspiciously at the visitors.

Alexa laced her fingers together on the table. "Now then, what do you know about my father? And about Angelo's father."

Mitso gave a cackling laugh, exposing his three remaining front teeth. "Direct, aren't you, missy? And smart, like your father."

"Please, *Barba* Mitso," Alexa pleaded, using the Greek term of respect for an elderly man. "I didn't come to cause you difficulty. If I could have gotten the answers from someone else, I wouldn't have bothered you."

Mitso, his eyes glittering, said nothing. Abruptly he transferred his inimical glare to Damian. "And what do you want from Mitso, Mr. Ioannina Lawyer? Never had much use for lawyers. Take your money and only give you double talk in return. Not good value at all."

Alexa was beginning to wonder if old Mitso was as crazy as everyone thought. Unfriendly he might be, but most of what he said made sense; it was not the rambling of someone who'd lost his mental faculties.

"I'm here to help Alexa," Damian said quietly.

"Sweet on her, are you?" Mitso's expression softened. "I remember how it was, when you're young and the sap's running." His voice rose to an anguished wail. "They killed her, slit her throat like an animal's. And murdered my babies, too."

The cat, startled, leapt to the floor and streaked out the door. Mitso stared after him, his mouth snapping closed. A tear seeped from the corner of his eye and ran down his wrinkled cheek.

"I'm so sorry," Alexa said, near tears herself. "I'm so sorry."

"They came back," Mitso said. "They came back, the murdering thieves. Constantine brought them."

Constantine? Angelo's father?

"Constantine promised them the sword, but when they came, it was gone. And Constantine was dead. They were going to kill us all. But I stopped them. Once. Constantine lay in the woods, his blood leaking into the ground. Not the first time. Greek soil is soaked with blood, that's why it's red. Dimitrios had to leave. They were coming for him."

Alexa's nails bit into her palms, drawing blood. Dimly she noticed the pain, but it was minor compared to the agony beating in her heart. "Who was coming for him, Mitso, who?"

"The young men. The soldiers." Mitso shook his head. "I don't remember. It's so long ago. My sweet Evangelia, my little girl, lying in the square, her body torn apart. I was a coward. I should have died for her." Wrapping his arms around his waist, he rocked back and forth in the chair. "They came and killed the men, for Constantine. I couldn't stop them when they came back. But nothing could bring back his cursed life. Nothing could take away the blood."

"Who killed Constantine?" Damian asked.

"Dimitrios did, of course. And we all thanked him and helped him get away. Then we paid, but it was worth it."

Nausea rose in Alexa's throat. She ducked her head down on her knees, waiting for the sickness to pass, the sickness she was afraid would never leave her. "Where is he now?" She forced the words out, slowly and evenly, while inside she screamed, *No, no, it can't be.*

"He didn't come back," Mitso said. His voice broke. "He broke his promise. He didn't come back. And the little girl went away, too."

"Little girl? What little girl?"

"The little girl with sunshine hair." Mitso reached out a gnarled hand and touched Alexa's hair. "Hair like this. The little girl cried and cried but her mother took her away."

"Was the little girl me?" Alexa asked tensely.

"You?" The old man's eyes looked at her blankly. "I don't know. Maybe she was my Evangelia." Mitso closed his eyes, a long keening cry rising up from his sunken chest. "No, not my Evangelia. I saw her dead. The little girl was alive. She was crying. All night she cried, and in the morning she was gone."

His voice dropped to a hoarse whisper. "She was gone. Everything is gone. Gone. Gone. Gone." He rocked in the chair, back and forth, back and forth.

Alexa knew they wouldn't get any more information as the old man wandered, lost and alone, into the past. "Who killed Angelo?"

Mitso looked at her, his eyes suddenly lucid. "The devil killed Angelo. He came in the door and killed him. But he didn't find the sword. And he didn't find Dimitrios."

Damian leaned forward urgently. "Where is the sword? And where is Dimitrios?"

Mitso began to rock again. "Gone. All gone. Gone."

Damian took Alexa's arm and gently drew her to her feet. Around them the word echoed from the bare stone walls. *Gone, gone, gone.* "Come, Alexa, there's nothing we can do."

She let him take her outside. The black cat ran past them into the house where, after a moment, Mitso fell silent. Alexa followed Damian into the forest, her body stiff, as if rigor mortis had set in. "Will he be all right?" Her teeth chattered so badly she could barely talk.

"I think so," Damian assured her. "While you went up to change your shoes at the hotel, I asked Poppy what she knew of Mitso. She told me he has spells when he seems all right, and then for no reason he goes off into the past. But as far as day-to-day living goes, he manages very well. Now that I've seen his house, I believe it. So I expect he'll be okay."

The path was too narrow for them to walk side by side. Alexa trudged behind Damian, her mind working over what Mitso had told them, trying to sort out his story.

The forest gloom lightened as a ray of sun broke through the clouds. A sign? Alexa wondered, momentarily distracted. If she could cut through and highlight the truths in Mitso's garbled version of the events of the past forty-five years, she might find some of the answers she was looking for.

Her father had killed Constantine, and as a result had to flee for his life. On the surface, it was plausible. But it didn't match her limited memory of the man, nor correlate with her mother's fondly expressed reminiscences.

"I don't believe it."

Damian turned. "What don't you believe?"

"That my father killed Constantine, executed him in cold blood. Mitso is confused, or he doesn't remember."

"Or he misinterpreted what he saw," Damian suggested. "And what about the little girl?"

"Yeah, that too." Alexa chewed on her lower lip. "Am I the little girl, or is he mixing me up with his daughter? He had more than one daughter, didn't he?"

"Three, I believe. And they were in their teens at the time of their death. Hardly little girls, although Mitso might still have thought of them that way."

"Would Lisandro know, do you think?"

Damian frowned, his eyes clouded. "I don't know. He's been so weak the last couple of days, I hate to bring all this up again."

"Again?" Alexa asked.

Damian cursed his slip. "We were just talking one night. Last night, as a matter of fact."

Alexa laid her hand on Damian's arm. "It's me, isn't it? My questions made him think of the past, disturbed him." She closed her eyes. "Lisandro, Mitso, Angelo—it's all a mess. I shouldn't have come here."

Damian wrapped his arms around her. "Then I wouldn't have met you," he said without thinking, seduced by the scent of roses that clung to her hair.

Momentarily she stiffened, then relaxed, her body a sweet, light pressure against his. "Is that important?" she asked, her voice muffled by his sweater.

He hugged her fiercely to him. "Yes, it's important."

"But I'll be leaving soon," she said in a forlorn little voice that tore at his heart and told him much more than he was sure she intended.

"I know. I can't even ask you to stay."

Why not? she cried in her heart. Just ask me and we'll work something out. But she asked herself, could she live with him if he never learned to truly trust and love her? In

Alexa's mind, love and trust were two halves of the same entity. One couldn't exist without the other. And Damian might not be capable of either.

She shivered as a cloud covered the sun. Gently she drew herself out of his arms. "We'd better go. Before it rains."

SHE WAS RIGHT, of course, to put a distance between them. Damian knew it, but that didn't make it easier for him to let her go. He wanted her, at least one night with her, since forever was impossible.

But now an even greater barrier separated them. If he made love with her and then she found out he'd known Lisandro was her father and had kept it from her, there would be hell to pay. She would never forgive him. The fact that he agreed with Lisandro that she was in danger wouldn't make any difference to her. Witness her confrontation with Angelo, a man she had reason to be wary of. Even now, she wasn't afraid, despite having her tires slashed and believing that someone had taken her out into the storm last night. No, she was far too reckless. He had to protect her, and that meant keeping Lisandro's secret.

As for Kritikos, why, she'd even been foolhardy enough to have dinner with the man last night. Baiting the tiger?

No, he—they—had to keep her safe. And that meant keeping the secret so that no one suspected the relationship between her and Lisandro. No matter what it did to Damian's chances with her.

The realization that he was capable of self-sacrifice astounded him. During his childhood and youth, he'd had to put himself and his survival first, leaving no room for the luxury of caring about someone else. He owed Lisandro, probably his life, but certainly his success. But that wasn't why he felt this urgent need to protect him. He loved Lisandro.

He stopped dead on the path. Alexa walked two steps past him before she noticed. Turning, she eyed him so oddly that he wondered what his face told her. "Damian, what is it?"

He shook his head, smiling ruefully. "Nothing." For a wild moment he was tempted to share his stunning discovery with her, but that would lead to complications he knew he wasn't ready to handle.

Tucking her hand into the crook of his elbow, he walked beside her toward the square. His heart felt suddenly lighter, his dark soul more at ease.

He'd thought himself too hard, too cynical, too suspicious, of other people's motives to ever feel love. But he'd trusted Lisandro even after he had a choice not to. He'd stayed with Lisandro even after the old man had told him he was free to live his own life. And Damian had never considered it a burden; quite the contrary, the years with Lisandro had been the best of his life, and though it pained him to know Lisandro was dying, he wouldn't have traded those years for anything.

Maybe he *could* love Alexa.

But then bleak reality hit him. *Why should she love him?*

THE RAIN LASHED icy whips across her face; the wind moaned her name. *Alexa... Alexa.*

She fumbled for the door handle. The handle turned but the door was swollen in the wet night, jammed in the frame. She pushed on it, and it leapt away from her, throwing her headlong onto a hard stone floor. Struggling to her knees, she crept into the room.

A man lay on the floor, blood pooled under his head. She gripped the knife in her hand, the ornate carved hilt digging into her palm. She raised it over her head.

Brought it down. Felt the jar in her wrist and elbow as it slid into flesh and bone. Heard the sickening gurgle of blood in a dying man's throat.

The man's eyes opened, staring at her. Accusing. "Why, Alexa? Why?" The voice rattled, became sibilant with a hiss of air... then silence.

She lay down next to the body, uncaring that her clothes were wet and the floor cold and dusty. She had done it; now she could sleep.

Forever.

THUNDER CRASHED OVERHEAD. Alexa jerked upright in bed.

In bed?

She glanced around the hotel room, abruptly illuminated by lightning. Another burst of thunder rolled across the sky.

She clapped her hands over her ears, her eyes skittering round the room. Was that a shadow in the corner?

Lightning flashed again, too brief to give substance to her fear. A shadow, nothing else, probably a trick of the uncertain light. Alexa closed her eyes, then opened them again, her arm snaking across to the lamp.

She pushed the simple switch. Nothing. Another power failure. Not surprising, judging from the fury of the storm outside.

From the corner of her eye she saw the shadow move, then vanish. She allowed herself a self-deprecating laugh. A night filled with nightmares and she saw things in her locked room. The chair she'd jammed under the doorknob was still in place.

IN THE MORNING she went down early, pleased to see the day was fine, with that almost painful clarity of air that follows a storm. Poppy brought her a menu.

"Thank you, Poppy. It's a lovely morning, isn't it? And the power's back on."

"The power?" Poppy looked mystified. "The power wasn't off."

"Not during the storm?" Alexa asked, a little niggle of anxiety surfacing. "I tried my lamp and it didn't go on."

"Must be the bulb."

Alexa shook her head. "It worked this morning. Are you sure the power wasn't off?"

"Positive," Poppy said. "The electric clock in my office was not even a minute off." She turned away. "Let me get your coffee."

"Wait." Alexa caught Poppy's hand. "About Angelo—"

"Angelo is dead," Poppy said flatly, her gaze falling away instead of meeting Alexa's. "You're probably wondering why I was at the funeral. I felt guilty. He was a troublemaker and I wanted him dead and then he was. I wondered if you didn't feel something like that, too, since he'd been making trouble for you."

"Maybe," Alexa said reluctantly. "How close were you and Angelo?"

"Does it matter?" Poppy shrugged. "I suppose it's no use hiding it. He said he wanted to marry me, months ago. But he kept putting off setting the date. I finally realized he was only taking advantage of me, so I told him it was over, I didn't want to see him anymore." She shrugged again. "He didn't take rejection very well."

"Don't I know it," Alexa said with heartfelt sincerity. "Thanks, Poppy. I appreciate your honesty."

Poppy smiled. "It's okay." She looked beyond Alexa toward the door. "Good morning, Damian. You're early."

"Good morning, Poppy," he said quietly. He pulled out a chair and sat down. "Alexa, how are you this morning? The storm didn't keep you awake, did it?"

"I woke up." Alexa frowned. "Poppy says the power wasn't off, but my lamp didn't work. I thought I saw a shadow in my room but maybe I was dreaming."

"Let's have look at your room. Poppy, could you make me two eggs, bacon and toast, please? Alexa?"

"Same for me, Poppy." Alexa allowed herself to be dragged up the stairs in Damian's wake. "Shh," she cautioned as his shoes thumped on the hall floor. "You'll wake up Kritikos."

"We don't want to do that, do we?" he muttered. Drumming his fingertips on the doorframe, he waited while she unlocked the door. Inside, he checked the dead bolt, finding it intact.

"I had a chair under the doorknob," Alexa said. "It was still there in the morning."

Damian strode across to the window. She'd left it slightly ajar to freshen the room, and he pulled it wider. The little balcony outside was too narrow to hold more than a single chair. Damian stepped out onto it, staring across at the one next door, separated from it by a wooden rail.

"Someone's been here," he said. "See the footprints? Muddy footprints." He came back inside and picked up one of her sneakers. "Different tread. Probably crepe soles, not a carved tread like yours."

"That explains the shadow, then," Alexa said, conscious of relief. "Someone was outside on the balcony and the lightning made the shadow."

"He was in the room," Damian said, his voice harsh with anger. "Didn't you lock the window?"

"Of course I locked it. But the only way onto that balcony is through the room next door, which is empty."

Damian turned, a metal object in his hand. "Here's your window latch. It was loosened. Anyone could open it from the outside." He stooped to examine the space behind the night table next to the bed. "Same muddy footprints. And mud on the lamp plug. Your lamp didn't work because the intruder unplugged it. And later plugged it in again." He picked up her nightshirt from the bed, grinning briefly at the screen print on the front: I Don't Do Mornings. "Were you wearing this last night?"

"What?" She looked at the shirt, then at Damian, her eyes wide. "No. I was wearing a long cotton nightgown." Frantically, she turned over the bed covers, dislodging the pillows. Going over to the wardrobe, she groped in the bottom of it, sifting through the clothes that needed laundering. No nightgown. "It's not here," she said in a fractured whisper, her heartbeat choking her.

"Don't panic, Alexa. Maybe you were sleepwalking, out on the balcony. Maybe you took it off yourself when it got wet in the rain."

"Then where is it?"

Damian had no answer, although he had a look in the bathroom.

"It's not there, either, is it?" Alexa stood in the middle of the room, an icy lump forming in her stomach. Had her nightmare been a dream? Or had it been a recall of the night Angelo died?

Had she killed Angelo while she was sleepwalking?

Chapter Thirteen

"You're staying at our house tonight. It's not safe here anymore."

Too numb to take in Damian's words, Alexa hugged her arms around her waist. She felt so cold, so empty.

"I killed him." The whisper hung in the air, suspended on the shaft of dust motes that slanted from the window.

"Whom did you kill?" Damian demanded harshly. "Angelo? Don't be daft. Don't you remember what I told you? Sleepwalking is like hypnosis—you can't go against your principles."

Her eyes met his, dark with shock. "You don't understand. I wanted him dead many times during our divorce proceedings." Her breath shuddered from her lungs. "I stabbed him. I took the knife and felt it go into his body."

"Not likely. How did you get the knife?"

She shook her head from side to side, sliding to the floor and kneeling there to sway like a reed in the wind. "From your house. From Lisandro's room."

"No, you didn't," Damian stated, praying it was the truth. Half of him was certain she was incapable of killing anyone. Yet the other, cynical half squirmed uncomfortably, reminding him that human beings were often untrustworthy and deceitful. "You had no opportunity. You were either with Lisandro or with me."

"I could have slipped it into my purse the first day I visited Lisandro."

"No, it was there after you left. I saw it."

"Some other knife, then."

"Like from the village museum? Not a chance. It's always locked if nobody's there." He knelt on the floor beside her, gathering her into his arms. "Alexa," he said gently, "someone has been coming into your room and doing these things. I don't know why, but you're not safe here. Come with me now. Lisandro would be so happy to have you in our house where he can see you."

He longed to tell her why, but knew he couldn't. Now, more than ever, he had to keep Lisandro's identity to himself. Until they sorted this out. If Alexa's tormentor was also after Lisandro, as Lisandro feared, his next step would be to use Alexa to get to him.

He gave her a little shake when his strongest instinct was to tuck her into bed and stand guard while she slept. Then he would join her and make love to her until neither of them could think straight.

Tantalizing as this scenario was, he pushed it into the back of his mind. He took her cold hand in his and brought her to her feet. "Come on. Breakfast first, and then we'll take your things over to the house."

KRITIKOS SAT AT THE FAR side of the dining room when they came down. He lifted his hand in greeting, and Alexa forced a smile in return. She ate quickly despite her lack of appetite, and discovered she felt better with her stomach full.

"I'm going to talk to more of the villagers," she said to Damian as she drank a second cup of milk-laced coffee.

"I need to stay with Lisandro today," Damian said regretfully.

She couldn't help feeling a twinge of disappointment. She buried it under renewed determination. "Of course you do," she said. "I'll be fine on my own."

"As long as it's daylight and you stay where there are people. But be careful. I don't think you're in any danger from the villagers, but watch for strangers." Was it an accident that his gaze flicked across to Kritikos at that moment?

Kritikos got up and walked toward the door, favoring them with a distant nod as he passed.

"I wonder why he's still here," Alexa said.

"Wasn't he looking for a property to buy?"

"That's what he said."

Damian frowned. "Then why did Stavros complain to me about how slow business was only yesterday? He's the only real estate agent in Elatos, and if he wants to buy property, Kritikos would have to go to him."

"Well, I never did think he was telling the truth," Alexa declared. "He looks you straight in the eye but his words always sound evasive. As if he has something to hide."

"And you had dinner with this man?" Damian's brows lifted.

Alexa smiled sheepishly. "Snooping. But it didn't do any good. The only thing I found out was that he once lived here, as a child. And that he grew up on Crete. Not very useful, I'm afraid."

Lisandro's enemies also came from Crete. It looked to Damian that Lisandro wasn't far off base in his assessment of Kritikos.

"Be careful of him," Damian said, wishing he could keep her at his side all day and all night, keep her safe. But he didn't suggest it, knowing that he couldn't even put his warning in stronger terms than he had. She was sharp; if he said any more she would demand to know every detail, particularly those he couldn't tell her.

THE TIRES FOR Alexa's car hadn't arrived on the morning bus, nor were they on a truck of dry goods for the village shops that arrived shortly after. Alexa accepted the delay philosophically. She wasn't ready to leave yet.

Since yesterday's questioning of the villagers had proved unproductive, she decided to tackle it from a different angle today. Some of the old men who sat in the square each day might have known her father. And then there was Stavros, the real estate agent.

Approaching the old men was awkward, almost a breach of village etiquette. They kept to themselves, whether they sat on the park bench or at the coffee shop.

Stavros would be easier; she would start with him.

Damian pointed out the real estate office, wedged in a lane beside the church. He squeezed her hand, dropping a quick kiss on her mouth, before turning and striding off in the opposite direction.

Bemused, Alexa touched her fingers to her lips. A tingle remained, long after he was out of sight. An old woman, dressed in black, smiled at her, winking one rheumy eye. Papa Apostoli, his black robe flapping, wished her a good morning. He too gave her a knowing smile, and didn't seem to expect a reply.

Realizing she was making a spectacle of herself—Damian's fault—Alexa set her feet in motion, walking briskly down to the real estate office.

STAVROS NIKOPOULOS, the hand-written sign in the window proclaimed. Alexa pushed open the door. The waiting area was littered with old magazines and books of house plans. From the office in the rear, she could hear a man talking on the phone.

She'd barely settled into a chair when he came out, a balding man of about forty. "May I help you, Mrs. Thetalou?"

By now everyone must know her name. And her purpose in the village. No matter, it saved time and explanations. "I'd like to talk to you, Mr. Nikopoulos, if you have time."

"All the time in the world, madam." He swung his arm to encompass the shabby office. "As you can see, this isn't New York."

"Or Vancouver," she said dryly. "Where at times, houses are bought and sold several times in one year."

"Is that so? Maybe I should consider emigrating." He pulled out a chair in the inner office, gesturing for her to sit down. Seating himself behind the desk, he waited for her to state her business.

Alexa fidgeted, not sure where to start. "The land Lisandro has his house on, were you involved in selling it to him?"

"No, I was not. Lisandro came here with proper documentation that he had bought the land from Elias Doukas, who by then had died. He came to me for planning approval, which was readily given, since a new house on the lot would be an improvement over the heap of mud and bricks that was there then. Your parents' old house, I believe?"

"Yes." Alexa nodded. "I don't suppose you remember them."

Stavros tipped his head up and clicked his tongue. "No. Any real estate dealing they had would have been with my uncle. Unfortunately he died some years ago, and I took over the business."

"Did your uncle ever talk about Dimitrios Doukas?"

"He was sympathetic to him, if that's what you're wondering. He didn't think he walked off with the sword."

"What about the death of Constantine Thetalou?"

"Your father-in-law?"

"Not really, since I only met Angelo years later."

Stavros pursed his lips and steepled his fingers in front of his face. "Constantine's death was a good thing at a bad time. He was disliked in Elatos because he favored the dictatorship, even approved of their brutality, but in the end, because of his death, the brutality came here. Do you know that most of the men of Elatos were killed in that winter after Doukas left? As retaliation for Constantine's murder. And those who survived, they just want to forget what happened. Can you blame them? For a time, the women, the widows of those killed, shunned all contact with the survivors, calling them cowards."

Alex felt the blood drain from her face. "That is shocking."

"Yes, shocking but understandable." Stavros stood up and placed his hands flat on the desk. "Mrs. Thetalou, you grew up in Canada. You can't know how unforgiving we Greeks can be in tragedy. Why don't you give it up? Leave the past alone and get on with your life."

Alexa stood up, too. "I can't. I have to find my father."

Stavros shrugged, spreading his hands. "I feel for you, but I think you're looking in the wrong place. Try Vital Statistics in Ioannina."

"I did. They have nothing on him, only a date of birth, here in Elatos. Same as the records in the village office, which also shows he died in 1967. There's a grave marker in the cemetery, where I'm sure he's not buried because his body was not returned to Greece. Tell me, Mr. Nikopoulos, did my father grow up here?"

Stavros perched his hip on the corner of the desk. "I believe so. But he would have attended high school in Ioannina since we've never had one here. And he went to university in Athens, then lived in Canada for a time. He practiced law in Athens later. He didn't come back to Elatos until the troubles started, when you were a small child."

"How do you know all this?" Alexa asked curiously. "You were a child yourself."

"I was, but anything to do with Doukas was food for gossip, since a Doukas was one of the founders of Elatos. And Dimitrios was especially interesting when he showed up with a beautiful wife who was not from here. Your mother did very well in Canada, didn't she?"

"Very well. But she would have been happier to remain a simple housewife if only my father had been with her." She put out her hand to shake his. "Thank you, Mr. Nikopoulos. You've been very helpful."

"Not much, I'm afraid. I hope you find out what's happened to him."

Did he? Alexa wondered gloomily as she stepped out onto the street. Did anybody? She was beginning to realize what she was up against. No one wanted to remember, much less talk about, that infamous piece of Greek history.

And if her father was still alive, he had another, secure identity that no one knew.

Disappointment gnawed at her. There were still the old men to question, but she no longer had any hope they would help her. If her father lived, he hadn't returned to Elatos.

Instead of returning to the square, she turned the opposite way and headed toward the birch grove. The day remained sunny, although a cold wind cut through her heavy sweater and swung her skirt against her legs. A brisk walk would clear her head.

She came to the fork in the path, where a left turn would take her to the birch grove. She glanced at her watch. How much time had passed? An hour since she'd left Damian?

She recalled their conversation in her hotel room. Distraught as she'd been, the last part of their conversation had barely registered in her mind. He'd warned her to be careful. She frowned. In spite of everything that had happened to her, what she could remember at least, she hadn't been harmed.

So far.

Had it been her imagination or was there a deeper meaning behind Damian's warning? Did he feel the incidents would escalate?

Taking the left fork, she hurried toward Lisandro's house, remembering belatedly that her clothes were still at the hotel. She would have to go back and pack them.

"MY DEAR GIRL, you came to see me." Struggling up from his chair, Lisandro greeted her with a broad smile as Alexa entered his room.

Alexa smiled. "You look well today."

And he did—there was an almost healthy color to his skin, his eyes were lively and inquisitive. She grasped his shoulders, frail and distressingly bony under her hands, and kissed his cheek. Sitting down, he patted a chair next to his. "Sit, sit."

A fire crackled on the hearth. Alexa extended her cold hands toward the flames, amused to note that the window, as usual, stood open a crack.

"Damian says you'll be staying here."

Alexa looked closely at Lisandro's face. No sign of worry. "Did he explain why?" she asked cautiously.

"Your tires were slashed and it appears someone was out on your balcony. Isn't that enough?" He took her hand in his and held it with wiry strength, the cat in his lap purring under their linked fingers. "And Damian doesn't like Kritikos, the way he looks at you." Lisandro laughed. "I never thought I'd see the day, but I suspect you've conquered Damian's heart."

Alexa's own heart fluttered oddly. Had she? "I doubt that any woman could capture Damian's heart," she said uncomfortably.

"He's grown very fond of you, my dear." Lisandro leaned toward her, his smile vanishing. "Damian's spent too much of his life closed away from people. Self-preservation, you know. I can't blame him. He had a dreadful childhood. But I think you can make him realize all women aren't like his mother. I think you can teach him to love."

A lofty ambition, Alexa thought wryly. She doubted anyone could teach Damian something he didn't want to learn. And she would be gone in a few days, taking with her only a memory of a man with dark, haunted eyes, who'd all too quickly entered and exited her life. She wondered if he knew just how deeply he'd touched her.

To her relief, Damian, his hands washed and his hair slicked back with water, came in, saving her from replying. He tilted up her face, a finger under her chin. "You look flushed. Is it too warm in here?"

"No, it's just fine."

"You saw Mitso?" Lisandro asked.

Alexa nodded. "Yes, yesterday afternoon."

"Did he tell you about Angelo's father?"

"Some, but toward the end, he seemed confused." Briefly she related what Mitso had told them. As she talked she was disconcertingly aware of Damian, leaning back against the windowsill, the worn jeans molding his strong thighs and hugging his lean waist. His arms, crossed over his chest, were tanned and sprinkled with soft black curls. She remembered how hard they'd felt under her hands, and heat coiled in her abdomen.

Sternly she rebuked her imagination. She'd never been so conscious of a man's physical presence, and she wondered if she were in a second adolescence, driven by raging hormones.

"Alexa."

Lisandro's low voice drew her attention away from Damian. But before she swung her gaze around, she saw the small, smug grin that curved his mouth.

Sexy. He'd kissed her only once or twice, and it probably hadn't meant anything, but she could still feel the heat.

"Alexa." Lisandro had asked her a question, and she hadn't a clue what.

"I'm sorry. I was woolgathering."

He grinned complacently. "Can't say I blame you. Alexa, you say Mitso told you Dimitrios Doukas killed Constantine?"

"Yes, but I know it isn't true."

"You know it isn't true?" Completely serious, Lisandro stared at her. "How do you know it isn't true?"

"Why, you told me yourself that Dimitrios didn't kill Constantine."

"Yes, I remember." A note of impatience came into his voice. "But how do you know I told the truth? No one would blame you for believing Mitso, who apparently was there while I was not. What is truth, anyway? Everyone you talk to has his own version of the truth."

Was it her imagination, or did Damian stiffen? "I remember enough of my father to know he wasn't a murderer."

Damian spoke, his face inscrutable. "I thought you had no memory of when you lived here."

"I don't, of the village. I do remember that my father was a gentle man who used to tell me stories. I used to sit on his knee and rub my chin against his beard. It was dark blond and very soft, like fur."

Her brows knitted. "That's odd. I hadn't remembered that before, that he had a beard."

"And beards were uncommon in Greece at that time," Damian said. "They were associated with priests. Very few other men had them."

"My father did. Which strengthens the possibility that he did come back to Greece. Without the beard, even those who'd known him before probably wouldn't have recognized him. Especially after nearly ten years had gone by." Her shoulders slumped. "I won't ever find him."

"Unless he finds you," Lisandro said gently. He took her hand, rubbing it between his own. "Alexa, have patience. It will all work out."

"How?" she asked, her eyes wide. "Do you know something you're not telling me? Please, Lisandro, if there's anything you know—"

Lisandro shook his head, his eyes kind. "Patience, Alexa. When do you have to be back at work in Vancouver?"

"I took a leave of absence. I can take as long as I need."

"And money isn't a problem?"

She gave a short laugh. "Not at all. I've been pretty lucky with investments, thanks to some of the people I work with. If I don't work for a while, I'll hardly slide into poverty."

"Good." Lisandro's tone carried a wealth of satisfaction. "So you can stay awhile. Indulge an old man."

"What about your mother's restaurants?" Damian asked. "Didn't you inherit them?"

"Actually, that's one of the things that made Angelo bitter. I wasn't the heiress he thought. Long before her death, my mother had already designated that since I had a stable career and didn't need the money, the restaurants would be sold and the profits used to set up a charitable foundation. Angelo only found this out when we were divorcing."

"What did he do?"

A steely note laced Damian's words. He was very close to anger, Alexa realized. If she told him the truth, he would go over that edge, and she didn't want him to upset Lisandro.

"You wouldn't want to know," she quipped. She knew from the way Lisandro's hand tightened on hers that he wasn't fooled by her facetious tone. Neither was Damian, to judge by the scowl that knitted his brow.

"So Angelo could have planned to get even with you," Damian said flatly.

"He could have," she agreed. "But why would he? He had nothing to gain. And what's the point of speculating now? He's dead and it's over."

"It's not over until his killer is found," Damian said grimly.

Vassiliki came in and announced she was ready to go home and that lunch was on the table. But as they ate the sumptuous meal of grilled lamb and a salad made of tender new lettuce, Alexa couldn't shake off her uneasiness. Angelo might be dead but someone was still after her.

Kritikos?

As an acquaintance of Angelo's, he was the likeliest suspect. And he was only across the hall from her at the hotel, in possession of a key which likely could open any door in the building, including that of the room next door to hers.

The only thing he seemed to lack was a motive. Just because she didn't trust him and those flat, dead eyes of his made her skin crawl, it didn't mean he was a criminal.

AFTER LUNCH, Alexa helped Damian clear the table. Lisandro went into his room to take a nap, leaving the two of them in the kitchen to wash the dishes.

Her hands up to the wrists in soapy water, Alexa waited for the questions from Damian. All through the meal she had been aware of his eyes on her, the words unspoken as long as Lisandro was with them. He dropped the last of the cutlery into the drawer and slammed it shut. Alexa made a business of rinsing the sink and hanging the dishcloth over the edge of the counter.

She stood there, staring out of the window at the pine trees swaying in the wind above the house, their roar dimmed by the surge of adrenaline in her own body as she braced herself for Damian's questions.

Damian said nothing, but she could feel his eyes boring into her back. Finally she could stand it no longer. "Okay, spit it out. What do you want to ask, not that any of what went on between Angelo and me is your business?"

"I know," he said, deceptively mildly. "But I'm going to ask, anyway. What did Angelo do when he found out there was no money and that you wanted a divorce?"

She turned, her gaze coming up to collide with his. "He tried to kill me."

Damian paled, looking shaken, although he must have expected something like that. "Are you sure?"

"Sure?" she asked flippantly. "Of course I'm sure. The first time he tried, my brakes failed. When the police checked the next day, they found nothing wrong with the brakes. So that was inconclusive. The other time wasn't. He took me to a remote area and threatened me with a knife. He said that no one would suspect murder, especially if the body was in a burned-out car. He kept me there for hours. I don't know what made him change his mind. Maybe the fact that my mother would send the police after him if anything happened to me."

"Didn't you prosecute him?" His voice was completely calm, she noted with the detachment she'd learned to activate whenever she thought of Angelo's dark side. But then she looked down at his hands, gripping the back of a chair. The knuckles were white, the tendons distended like ropes. If they had been around Angelo's neck—

"Prosecute him?" she echoed. "You're a lawyer. You must know how it would have gone. My word against his. No proof of any kind. The best I could do was get a restraining order, but still he phoned at night and left messages on my car. Even after I changed cars. It was uncanny how he always seemed to know where I was."

"The police?" he said tonelessly, his face blank.

"They took fingerprints when my car had a crude word sprayed on it, but they didn't catch him. Threats are hardly a priority when there is robbery, drug dealing and murder going around."

Alexa picked up the jacket she'd left on a chair. "Look, Damian, it's over. I'm going down to the hotel to get my things. That is, if you still want me here."

He blinked, focusing on her as if he hadn't seen her before. His eyes softened. "Of course I want you here. I want you to be safe." He touched the skin beneath her eyes with one finger. "You're losing too much sleep."

"Not the first time," she said stoutly. "I'm used to it."

He laid his hands on her shoulders, and for a moment she thought he was going to kiss her. The thought made her knees weak and set up a yearning in her heart. Stop, she commanded her errant emotions. Don't fall in love with him. He may have even darker traits than Angelo. And he doesn't believe in love.

Damian leaned forward. She waited, breathless, her lips parted. Then he made a harsh sound and lifted his head, merely pulling her tightly against him for a disappointingly brief instant. "Be careful, Alexa. Be careful."

THE WIND BUFFETED her as she walked down the path. Shivering, she pulled her jacket closer around her throat. Dead leaves scuttled along the path with a sound like furtive footsteps. The impression was so real that at one point she whirled around, certain someone was following her.

A bush swayed beside the path. She laughed at her fancies. Only the wind. More than one bush was swaying, the pines roaring like a high surf.

She encountered no one on her way to her room. Everything appeared as she'd left it, including the unmade bed. With no other guests booked, Poppy could wait until she left. In fact, she'd told Alexa she'd miss her but agreed that she'd be safer with Damian and Lisandro. Alexa had been expecting a spate of apologies, but Poppy was briskly philosophical, only extracting a promise that Alexa would come and see her before she left Elatos.

"Of course I will," Alexa had said. "My car will be here, anyway, until the tires come."

Alexa dragged the suitcase from the top shelf of the wardrobe. In doing so she must have dislodged something caught behind the case. A cloth flopped down onto her head. Dropping the suitcase, she clawed at the stiff material obscuring her vision, finally pulling it free.

A low cry escaped her as she saw what it was. Her nightgown, still damp and covered with mud.

Stifling a scream, she ran from the room.

Chapter Fourteen

"Alexa!" Poppy called to her as she ran down the stairs and toward the front door.

"Not now, Poppy." Alexa managed to choke out the words from a clogged throat. The door slammed in her wake and she dashed blindly across the square. She passed the church and plunged down a wooded path leading out of the village.

She felt numb, her legs automatically propelling her down the rocky path. For once she didn't notice the isolation, nor the green gloom and the sinister rustling in the forest.

Gradually, feeling returned to her brain. Fear surged up, setting her heart hammering in her chest. She quelled it firmly. Fear paralysed. Anger would be more useful, fed by the same adrenaline as the fear but under her control.

After Damian's sensible reassurance and the evidence of the locked door, she had been almost ready to dismiss last night's disturbed sleep as nightmares. Vivid nightmares, but not reality.

The damp nightgown slapped her in the face with the truth. She had been wandering somewhere. And she didn't know how she'd gotten out of the room. At home, she'd unlocked doors but never relocked them upon her return.

The window. Was it possible that she had climbed over the rail, onto the adjoining balcony, and gone out through the other room? And left the muddy footprints they'd seen?

That didn't make sense, either. The footprints were not the pattern of her shoe soles, not to mention that her shoes hadn't been wet. And why would she have unplugged her own lamp?

Slow down, she told herself, getting a grip on her headlong speculations. Someone had been in her room and had likely entered through the window, easily and silently because of the defective latch. The footprints practically proved it. This brought up the possibility that the same person had taken her from the room. Hadn't she mentioned to Damian that she felt she'd been carried?

She was, in common with many sleepwalkers, extremely receptive to suggestion. She knew this from what her mother had told her about her childhood, and from research on the subject she'd done since. She could have been taken to another place, even walking there herself if the suggestion was strong enough. Later she'd returned to the room, exchanged the gown for the T-shirt she'd woken up in, and gone back to bed, recalling nothing in the morning.

Which meant that someone was taking advantage of her sleepwalking for his or her own purposes.

The only other possibility was that she really was going crazy.

A new idea hit her. What if someone were trying to make her think she was going crazy? She shook her head. Too absurd. What could be gained by tormenting her so? The whole thing made no sense.

She resumed walking, her footsteps silent on the pine-needle-strewn path. Glancing back, she suddenly realized how far she'd come. The fork that led to Mitso's house must be just ahead.

She stopped. Around her the woods were hushed, the wind momentarily at rest. A shudder ran up her spine and she broke out in an icy sweat. The eerie silence seemed ominous, as if the earth held its breath. Not even the black-and-white magpies, so noisy earlier, scolded one another.

Without warning, a man bumped her from behind. Two men. Before she could scream for help or make a run for it, one of the men held her arms while the other whipped a rough sack over her head. She inhaled, coughing as her throat filled with moldy dust.

The man gripping her wrists was too strong for her to break his hold. She knew it in the first split second. She let her body go limp, hoping to catch him off guard. No luck. His fingers tightened and she gasped in pain. She breathed in quick, shallow pants, the suffocating folds of the sack choking the scream in her throat.

She could hear them arguing, in a language she didn't understand. An image flashed into her mind of the two refugees she'd seen on the road the first day. She recalled the lurid stories her aunt had told her. Was she being kidnapped, held for ransom?

For a mad moment, she wanted to laugh, probably would have except for the lack of air. Who would pay a ransom? No one knew where she was except her aunt and the car rental company. Neither of them would rescue her. Her aunt was too poor to pay for her return, and the car rental company wouldn't care, as long as they eventually got the car back. They could even collect the rental fee out of the enormous deposit she'd left with them. She could disappear and no one would know for days.

Except Damian. He was expecting her back at the house. When she didn't return, he would know something was wrong.

She renewed her struggles, bringing her foot around to stomp on the man's instep. He yelled in pain and his hands slackened their grip. She jerked one hand loose, swinging it up and catching him on the nose. He let go. She almost fell, but recovered and gathered herself to run.

Too late. The other man pushed her to the ground, where she lay, gasping and winded. She heard a third voice, saying something in Greek she couldn't quite make out, the tone harsh and angry. The man who'd knocked her down braced his hands on her shoulders and pushed her head against the hard earth. The rough pattern of the sack ground itself into her skin.

She heard the newcomer's voice again. For some reason it seemed familiar but the sack muted the sounds around her. She lay still, trapped beneath the weight of the man sitting on her back, pine needles prickling through her sweater and jacket.

Her sleeve was roughly wrenched up, her arm twisted painfully behind her back. A sharp pain stung her shoulder. A hypodermic.

She tensed her muscles, heaving herself up under the man. Then a numbing heaviness crept into her limbs. A woolly gray shroud descended and enveloped her brain.

COLD. SHE WAS SO COLD. Her teeth chattered together with a constant clicking. Clenching them tightly, she listened. The wind soughed through the pines, a gentle murmur.

She opened her eyes, cautiously probing the darkness. Nothing. Not a glimmer of light. How had she gotten here, wherever here was? She turned her head, realizing that she was on a cot that rocked slightly when she moved. The pillow felt hard but smooth under her cheek.

Memory rushed back. Two men had grabbed her on the path, put a sack over her head. She raised her hands; they were free. The sack was also gone; her cheek burned slightly as she ran her fingers over it. She remembered the man pushing her down, the rough sack and the pine needles that had poked through it.

The room she was in felt small and was apparently windowless. She smelled damp earth, not the potpourri Poppy used to scent the hotel rooms. Her throat ached when she swallowed.

From somewhere outside the room she heard the rising and falling cadence of voices, too distant for her to discern words.

Slowly she sat up, testing her limbs. She seemed unhurt but her muscles were oddly lax, lacking in strength. She felt the same bone-deep fatigue she'd suffered after a twenty-kilometer race she'd once run in high school.

Drugged. She'd been pricked by a needle, wielded by the third man who'd joined the two who jumped her. The spot high on her arm felt tender to her exploring fingertips.

She stood up. Her stomach heaved distressingly. She closed her eyes, seeing a swirl of colored dots. The room seemed to spin under her feet.

Steadying herself with a hand against the nearest wall, she walked around her prison. As she had guessed, the room was small. A window just over her head had been boarded up; opposite the cot, the only piece of furniture, she discovered a door. She couldn't tell if it gave access to another part of the house, or if it led outside. No light showed beneath it, although her fingers discovered there was a crack between the wooden panels and the hard earth floor.

She crept back to the bed and sat down, her fingers raking through her disheveled hair.

Damian. Damian must be looking for her by now. She groaned softly. Where would he begin? The village houses were widely scattered and the surrounding mountains consisted of acres of nothing but rock and trees.

Oh, why had she run off willy-nilly from the hotel instead of going straight to the police?

A scraping sound outside the door arrested her despairing thoughts. A key in the lock. A moment later the door swung inward, with little effect on the total blackness in the room. She saw the outline of a man, silhouetted against a marginally lighter background, before the door was shut once more. The darkness closed around her.

The man thrust a glass into her hands. Droplets of water condensed on her palm. She licked her lips, summoning saliva into her dry mouth.

The man must have sensed her inaction. "Drink," he said in Greek in a muffled voice she couldn't identify.

Still she hesitated, her throat reminding her of its raw dryness as she swallowed. What if they'd drugged the water?

"Drink, or I'll pour it down your throat." The words were indistinct, slurring together. Or distorted by an accent. A heavy hand tightened on her shoulder.

Given no choice and realizing dehydration would make her weaker, she held the glass to her mouth and drank. To her relief, the water tasted normal, sweet and cold from the village spring. The cool liquid soothed her parched throat, and she swallowed the rest of it, draining the glass.

"Eat this." The man thrust a chunk of bread into her hands. Her stomach responded with an indelicate growl, and she remembered that her last meal had been lunch with Lisandro and Damian. It must be after dinner now, although the darkness made it impossible to guess the time.

That was what was missing. Her watch. Even in the dark she would have been able to activate its tiny light and see the time. The watch was no longer around her wrist; either she'd lost it or her captors had removed it.

She dutifully bit into the bread, pleased to find it was a sandwich stuffed with cheese.

The man had moved away, to stand near the door. Invisible in the darkness, his presence remained an ominous entity in the small room.

She finished the sandwich and debated whether she could rush past him. He hadn't locked the door; she'd heard no key after he'd entered the room. If she took him by surprise, she might be able to get away.

On the chance that his night vision was sharper than hers, she pretended she was still eating the bread. Her mind worked over possibilities, some of which struck her as ridiculous. She almost laughed aloud, an odd euphoria bubbling over her nerve endings. She no longer felt afraid; if she could get the door open she could just fly over the trees, through the night, and reach Damian's house.

"Damian," she whispered. "Damian."

"Did you say something?" The man's low voice drifted over her.

"I'd like to go to the bathroom." She didn't need to, but it seemed like a way to get outside.

"In a minute. You can't go out right now."

Her hands flopped into her lap, and she stared at them, even though she couldn't see. Why did they feel so heavy? Why did her head feel so light, her ears buzzing?

She lay down, closing her eyes. She felt the touch of the man's fingers on her wrist, soft fingers, not a man who worked outdoors. Not like Damian.

Damian...

The last sound she heard was a grunt of satisfaction from the man. Oblivion claimed her.

WHERE IS THE SWORD of Dimitrios? The words echoed in her head. She struggled to sit up but her entire body seemed glued to the cot.

Where is the sword of Dimitrios? The words echoed with a hollow ringing in the room. Deep, eerie, as if the sound originated from a great distance, not only of space, but of time.

"Little girl, tell me. Where is the sword of Dimitrios?" This time the sound was close, spoken by an oddly familiar muffled voice.

"I don't know." She thought she screamed the words but no sound came out. Only the continuous echo rebounded in her skull: *Where is the sword of Dimitrios?*

Cold seeped into her body and snapped the frayed threads of willpower. "Go away," she muttered. "Leave me alone."

She lay on the floor, dirt packing under her nails as she groped in the darkness with one hand. No one came. The night was filled with the question: Where is the sword of Dimitrios?

And she didn't know the answer.

"WHERE IS ALEXA?" Voice raised in desperation, Damian leaned across the hotel counter to summon Poppy.

Poppy came around the corner and stared at him. He knew he must look a sight, his hair standing on end, his eyes wild. She would think he was crazy. He forced his voice down, forced himself to breathe deeply and slowly. "Poppy, where's Alexa?"

The girl frowned. "Isn't she back yet? Have you checked her room?"

"She's not there. And what do you mean, back? She was going to pack and then I was coming to pick up her suitcase to take it to our place. Why would she go out?"

Poppy began to twist the dust cloth she held between her hands. "I don't know. She came in. I heard her go upstairs. About five minutes later she came down again. She was almost running and her face was white. I called to her but I guess she didn't hear me. She ran out the door."

"And you haven't seen her since."

"No. But she could have come in when I was busy in the office or the kitchen."

"Her suitcase is on the floor. She hasn't started to pack."

Tears gathered in Poppy's eyes. "I knew I should have gone after her. She looked terrified. Her eyes—the look in them scared me." She covered her face with her hands. "Nothing has gone right since she came. I'm sure it isn't her fault, but someone doesn't want her here."

Damian went still. Slowly and deliberately he took hold of Poppy's wrists and pulled her hands away from her face.

Tears streaked her cheeks, making red blotches on her pale skin. "What do you mean, Poppy?" He steadied his hands, hard put to keep from shaking her. "Do you know something you're not telling me? And even if you won't tell me, why haven't you talked to Spiro?"

Poppy shook her head, hiccupping as she mopped at the tears with an inadequate handkerchief. "There's nothing to tell Spiro. You don't go to the police just because you don't like the way a man looks at you, or you wonder why he's talking to certain people."

"Who, Poppy? What man?"

"The man staying here, Kritikos. I saw him talking to a couple of strangers last night, out by the cemetery. I went to put some flowers on my father's grave and I saw them."

"Did they see you?"

"I don't think so. I waited near the gate until they left."

"What did these strangers look like?"

"Like all those refugees, skinny and unshaven, with ragged, out-of-date clothes."

"You're sure they were Albanians?"

"I don't know. They looked as if they were, but they could have been from Ioannina or any place."

"You didn't hear what they said?"

She stared at him with wide eyes. "Damian, I told you, they were too far away. And I didn't want them to see me. I don't like the way that man Kritikos looks at me." She shuddered. "Those cold, empty eyes, as if he has no soul."

"He looks at everyone that way, Poppy. Where was Kritikos when Alexa ran out?"

"Not here," Poppy said positively. "He went out in his car this morning."

Damian squeezed her shoulder. "Wait here. I'm going to have another look at Alexa's room."

Upstairs he learned nothing new. The wardrobe door stood open. Alexa's suitcase lay on the floor. He picked it up and put it on the unmade bed. The bathroom was tidy.

The towels hung on their rods. Alexa's makeup bag was zipped and sitting on the edge of the sink.

He went back into the bedroom. An object he hadn't noticed before protruded from under the tumbled blankets. He pushed them aside, revealing Alexa's purse, the brown leather shoulder bag she took everywhere.

She'd expected to come back. It told him that much, but little else.

He went down the stairs and found Poppy red-eyed but composed, offering a watery smile to a couple of dinner patrons coming in the door. "Has Kritikos been back since this morning?" he asked, not sure what he was getting at. Anxiety churned in his gut. The more complete a picture he formed, the better his chances of guessing where Alexa might be.

"Yes. He came in about an hour ago, stayed about ten minutes, and left again. In his car."

Damian nodded. Not much there. The man seemed to spend a lot of time driving around. "Thanks, Poppy. Could you let me know the minute she gets in, if she comes back?"

"Yes, of course, Damian." Her voice wavered, but she steadied it bravely and went to hand menus to the couple in the restaurant.

SPIRO SAT AT HIS DESK, working on a seemingly endless supply of paperwork. Damian didn't know the man well. Other than at the scene of Angelo's death, he'd only greeted him in the square once or twice.

Spiro looked up as Damian came in. He laid his reading glasses on the papers with every indication that he welcomed the interruption. "What can I do for you, Damian?" He gestured toward a chair.

Damian sat down. "I may be getting upset over nothing, but I can't find Alexa."

Spiro put on the reading glasses again, positioning a yellow legal pad and making a note on it. "How long has she been missing?"

He was taking him seriously. Damian let out a long breath of relief, but beneath it, his panic burgeoned anew. Until this moment, he'd thought his terror at discovering her gone might be a product of his own imagination. "Since about three this afternoon. Maybe half past. Poppy says she looked upset when she left."

Spiro looked up from his notepad, pursing his lips. "How do you know she hasn't simply gone for a walk? By all accounts, she's been doing a lot of that lately. At night as well as during the day."

"She's not sleepwalking in the middle of the afternoon," Damian said, giving Spiro a severe look. "And I don't think she's gone for a simple walk. Number one, she left her purse behind. That doesn't mean much, of course. But she was supposed to be there waiting for me to pick up her suitcase. She hadn't even packed yet."

"Maybe she changed her mind," Spiro suggested pragmatically.

"She would have told me."

Spiro folded his hands before him on the desk. "Look, Damian, she's a grown woman. She looks as if she can take care of herself. Maybe she had a message about her missing father and ran out to follow it up."

"How?" Damian lifted his brow skeptically. "There are no telephones in the rooms and Poppy received no message to relay to Alexa." He clenched his fist, pounding it against his knee. "Something's happened to her. She wouldn't behave this irresponsibly." Not after his warning.

Or would she? She'd had dinner with Kritikos, the man who'd told her that her father was alive. It suddenly occurred to Damian that she might have gone off with the man somewhere, playing amateur detective. The thought made his blood run cold.

Damn it, he should have been more specific in his warning, no matter what questions it brought. By now Kritikos would know of her friendship with Lisandro. If he had a long-standing plan of revenge, he would be more than willing to use Alexa as a pawn.

"Damian, she's an adult," Spiro said with an air of patience he must have honed on other distraught citizens.

"I know." Damian clawed his fingers through his hair. "And she's impulsive, courageous and inclined to move before she thinks. You don't know what this man Kritikos is up to, do you?"

"Kritikos? You mean the heavyset man who's staying at the inn?" Spiro shook his head. "I talked to him about Angelo's death, but he says he wasn't at Angelo's house that evening. He could have been lying, but there's no way of knowing. As far as I know, he hasn't broken any laws."

Nor had Damian's contact in Ioannina come up with any information on the man so far. Frustration set his teeth on edge.

"Okay," he said, exhaling gustily. "I guess you're not ready to send out a search party for Alexa."

"I'm sorry, Damian. I know how you must feel, but it's too soon, especially since there's no proof she's in trouble."

"Not yet," Damian said grimly. "Would you let me know if you see Kritikos or his car?"

Spiro stared at him, his eyes sharp with speculation. "Okay."

Damian shivered as he stepped outside. Pewter gray clouds churned across the sky, portending another storm. He strode down the street, past the shuttered shops, to the cemetery. He gazed across the little meadow with its neat gravestones, gray granite or white marble.

On impulse he stepped inside the cemetery, going to the enclosed area that held the graves of war heroes. There were a lot of them, crowded together, left in place rather than disinterred after three years as was the custom. He readily found the stone for Dimitrios Doukas: Died 1967, Resting in the Arms of God. A couple of rows over, he found another with the same name, died 1916, probably that of Alexa's great-grandfather.

Going back to the newer section he scanned the names. Many had died in 1967 and 1968. He remembered what Lisandro had told him, that after 1968 Elatos had become a virtual ghost town, only to be revitalized during the past ten years.

He was halfway back to the cemetery gate when it struck him. The name Constantine Thetalou was missing. He retraced his steps to Angelo's grave, in the regular section of the cemetery. It was easy to find, the fresh earth pounded into mud by the recent rains. There it was, next to Angelo's, Constantine Thetalou, died 1967. He stood for a moment, frowning. Interesting, that; Constantine apparently hadn't rated a hero's burial but had rated a permanent resting place.

However, this wasn't finding Alexa. Briskly he walked past the church, taking the right fork in the path, then veering to the left until he reached the birch grove. Birds sang sleepily in the trees as the sun set in a blaze of tangerine and crimson. No sign of Alexa.

He covered every path in the village, including the most obscure shortcuts, asked everyone he encountered, even knocking on several doors. No one had seen her.

Finally, near midnight, he returned home to find Vassiliki dozing in a chair by the kitchen stove, and Lisandro asleep. He sent Vassiliki home and went to check on Lisandro a final time.

The old man awoke. "I waited and waited for Alexa," Lisandro said querulously. "Is she with you?"

Damian shook his head. "She decided to stay at the hotel one more night." He felt guilty about the lie, but he couldn't bear to upset Lisandro. Let him have a good night's sleep. If Alexa didn't turn up tomorrow...fear chilled him.

He patted Lisandro's shoulder, giving him a quick kiss on the cheek, a gesture of affection it had taken him years to be comfortable with. "She'll be here tomorrow."

She'd better be, he vowed fervently. Or he would tear this place apart to find her.

Chapter Fifteen

Sick with worry, Damian spent the night pacing back and forth in his room. At three, he went out, after checking that Lisandro was sleeping and that his breathing was easy.

Carefully locking the door behind him, Damian jogged down to the square. The police station was dark and deserted, a yellow light bulb glowing over the door.

The hotel lobby was a cavern of dim shadows, lit by a fluorescent tube behind the counter. Damian tiptoed up the stairs. Hope surged for an instant when he saw Alexa's door was closed. But it plunged when he found it unlocked, pushed it open and saw nothing had changed from the afternoon.

Across the hall, he paused before Kritikos's room. Stealthily he tried the doorknob. Locked. No way of telling whether the man was there or not.

He went back outside, scanning the vehicles parked at the edge of the square. A gray Escort stood next to Alexa's Renault. He didn't know Kritikos's license number, but the sticker on the back advertised a Volos Ford dealership. Had to be the man's car. Which meant that he was very likely asleep upstairs, and not somewhere torturing Alexa.

Damian walked home, taking a circuitous route. Nothing disturbed the peace of the night except an owl hooting softly in the trees.

Lisandro still slept. Damian went to his own room, hoping against hope that Alexa might after all be sleeping in his bed and that this was all a nightmare. No such luck. His knees gave way and he sank down onto the edge of the bed, holding his head in despair, his eyes burning.

Desperately, he prayed for morning. It would be light and by then the police would listen to him and organize a search. He would find her.

Toward dawn he must have dozed off, half sitting, half lying, on his bed. A loud yowl from the cat outside the open window shot him to his feet.

He opened the front door. The cat slipped by inside, ephemeral as orange mist. The world was shrouded in gray, a dense fog that clung to the ground, leaving the trees poking their sharp tops through it, as if they floated in midair. The sun was only a glimmer behind the mountains.

A white cloth lay on the steps. Damian picked it up, running the cotton through his hands. A nightgown, stained with mud. Hadn't he seen a cotton gown like it in Alexa's room the other day, when he'd checked the locks?

Perplexed, he moved to the end of the step, wondering if the cat had dragged the garment home or if someone had dropped it there, startling the cat. Nothing moved, although the mist made it hard to see beyond twenty feet.

He turned back, then saw a note attached to the door. His heart leapt in his chest. From Alexa?

When he unfolded the paper, he saw that the writing was spidery, ragged and uncertain, and the words were in Greek.

The little girl was there.

Mitso

Little girl? What little girl? And where had she been?

Unless he meant Alexa. At Mitso's age it was easy to become confused, and Alexa might have seemed like a little girl to him.

New hope flared in him. Maybe she had gone to talk to Mitso since he appeared to be the only person in Elatos who might have known her father. And maybe she had decided for some reason to spend the night.

It was farfetched, he admitted, but any lead was better than nothing.

Quickly he went back inside the house. He touched Lisandro's shoulder, waking him with a quiet word. "Lisandro, I have to go out for a little while. Will you be all right?"

Lisandro looked confused but he nodded. "You'll be back soon, my boy? And you'll bring Alexa?"

Damian's heart turned over at the longing in the old man's voice. "Soon," he promised. "Soon."

MIST SWIRLED AROUND his ankles as he strode up the path leading to Mitso's house. The small gray building was almost hidden in the fog. The sun had risen to gild the tops of the peaks in the distance but Damian barely noticed.

The door was unlocked. Damian knocked lightly as he pushed it inward. "Mitso?" he called softly, not wanting to startle the old man.

He stepped inside without waiting for a reply, bracing himself for an assault by the attack cat. The single room felt cold and clammy, damp in the early morning chill. No fire burned in the stove. Nor did the cat guard the hearth.

Damian moved farther into the room, and his heart stopped. Alexa lay in a heap on the floor, half hidden by the large leather chair. "Alexa!" He sank to his knees beside her, his hand going to her throat to check her pulse.

She was alive. He closed his eyes. Thank you, God. Thank you.

Under his fingers, her heartbeat was slow but steady and strong. Her skin, however, felt cold; the mud-stained jeans, sweater and jacket she wore little protection against the near-freezing night.

He gathered her up into his arms, carrying her to the bed. Where was Mitso? The thought made little impression as his concern for Alexa took precedence. He turned back the quilt and bundled Alexa under it, tucking it around her. She cried out, as if in fright. Damian's mouth tightened as he saw the red scrapes on her cheek, the clear tracks from tears in the mud smeared on her face. She whimpered again, stirring restlessly. He stroked the matted hair back from her face, and she settled, breathing deeply in sleep.

A drugged sleep? That thought faded too, as he headed for the little bathroom at the back of the house to find a towel to clean her face.

The bathroom door stood ajar, but when he pushed on it, it refused to move. Something caught behind it, perhaps towels fallen from their rod, Damian surmised. He set his shoulder against it and heaved. The door moved far enough for him to reach around it.

He poked his head into the room and groaned at his second shocking discovery of the morning. Mitso lay on his back on the tile floor, and Damian knew there was no use checking for his pulse. The old man was dead, his eyes open and fixed. Beside him the cat crouched menacingly, snarling in a futile attempt to protect his master.

Damian shuddered, keeping a wary eye on the cat. He knelt beside the body, running his fingers over the man's eyelids to close them. As he had expected, the wrinkled skin was flaccid and cold.

Damian settled back on his heels. He would have to get Spiro and a doctor up here, not just for Mitso but perhaps for Alexa, as well. He wasn't sure whether he should wake her or just let her sleep.

The mellow tinkle of sheep bells brought him to his feet. He ran to the door. A shepherd, Kosta, he thought his name was, herded a flock of sheep and goats across the small clearing. "Kosta," he called.

Kosta raised his hand, giving some kind of signal to his black-and-white dog. The dog circled to the front of the flock, stopping the lead ewe, who gazed at him dumbly and began to nibble on a bush.

Hoisting his thick black cape higher on his shoulders, Kosta walked up to Damian. At the bottom of the step he stopped and leaned on his staff. "Has something happened to Mitso?" he asked.

"I'm afraid he's dead," Damian said. "There's a woman here. She may be ill. Is there any way you can get Spiro and the doctor up here?"

Kosta nodded. "I can send my grandson. He's with me today." Thrusting two fingers between his teeth, he gave a shrill whistle. The last of the flock emerged from the mist, followed by a small boy who carried a replica of his grandfather's shepherd's staff.

Kosta explained the situation with a few words. The boy nodded, turned and ran down the path, as surefooted on the uneven surface as one of the goats.

"A woman, you say? That Canadian woman was around yesterday," Kosta offered.

Damian lifted his head, every sense on the alert. "When?"

"Oh, I don't know." Kosta stared at the sky, clearing now that the sun warmed the air. "Late afternoon, maybe. She was walking on a path in the woods. Over there." He swung his arm to the right. "I thought it wasn't a good place for a woman to be walking alone, but she's a foreigner." He shrugged negligently, with the implication that foreigners often engaged in explicable foolhardiness.

Damian ground his teeth, valiantly hiding his frustration. "Did you see anyone else?"

"I just said she was alone," the shepherd said testily, exhaling pungent blue smoke from a cigarette he'd rolled and lit as he spoke. "But a while later, I thought I heard voices."

"And you didn't go to check it out?" Damian demanded incredulously. "You didn't see anyone?"

"How could I? I was too far away, on the other side of a deep ravine. You know there's a ravine in that section of forest?" he added as if Damian were a slow-witted child.

Damian sighed. "Yes, I know. Look, can you tell Spiro to come right in when he arrives? I'll be waiting inside. I have to check on Alexa."

The shepherd gave a cackling laugh. "At least you won't have to check on Mitso, eh?"

Damian's gaze sharpened. "You knew Mitso, I suppose."

"I knew him. He shouted at me every time I took my flock past here. But I had as much right as he to walk on this land. It's the only way up to the high mountain meadows."

Damian had one more question. "Did you know Constantine Thetalou and Dimitrios Doukas?"

To his disappointment, Kosta shook his head. "Not me. A few months after they died, the village was almost empty. Only a few old women spent the winter, those whose husbands were killed. It was at least five years before anyone else returned, and then only a few at a time, mostly relatives of former residents. I lived over near Ioannina and only came here when the free grazing land became scarce there."

"Okay," Damian said. "Thanks."

In the house, he found that Alexa had become more restless. Her hair lay tangled on the pillow, the quilt hanging half off the bed. She moaned softly as he touched the purple bruise on her cheek. Her wrists had faint abrasions as well, he noticed.

Had she been tied? Anger surged within him, hot and bitter. His hands clenched into fists. He would find the person who had done this to her and make him sorry he'd been born.

The sound of voices outside brought him to the door. Spiro and the doctor whom Damian knew from his occasional visits to Lisandro stood talking to Kosta. They shook his hand and headed for the house.

"You found her, then," Spiro said.

"I found her." Damian nodded grimly. "But she seems in a deep sleep. I think she was abducted, possibly drugged."

"Let's have a look, shall we?" the doctor suggested in a kind voice that soothed some of Damian's anxiety.

He checked her over, testing for broken bones through her clothes, looking down her throat and shining a light into her eyes. Through it all Alexa slept, although from time to time she gave frightened cries, tossing her head back and forth, as if she were trying to escape a nightmare or a person who terrified her.

"Has she been drugged?" Damian asked, unable to keep silent any longer.

"Possibly. The pupils are slightly dilated. But the heavy sleep could be nothing more than a reaction to a bad fright. The best thing is just to leave her until she wakes naturally."

Spiro came back from his examination of Mitso's body. "He's dead, all right. Looks like a heart attack. No signs of outward injury." He glanced at Alexa's wan face, which was all of her that showed above the quilt. "Do you suppose she found him, perhaps in the evening, and she didn't want to walk back in the dark?"

Damian shook his head. "I doubt it." Flipping back the corner of the blanket, he lifted Alexa's wrist. "I think she was tied up."

Staring at the red scratches etched into the tender skin, Spiro let out a low whistle. "Certainly looks that way." He laid his hand on Damian's arm. "Want to have a look outside while the doc's busy with Mitso?"

The flock was gone, the earth behind the house pockmarked with little triangular hoofprints, both fresh and old. At the back, nearly hidden by trees, stood a small stone building with a corrugated metal roof. "A storage shed?" Damian mused aloud.

"Could be." Spiro walked up to the door, pushing it open.

A cot stood against the wall, barely visible in the shadowed interior. The boarded-up window on an adjacent wall shut out any glimmer of daylight. Damian stooped to pick up an object from the pillow. He showed it to Spiro. "One of her hair clips. This is where they kept her."

Spiro took the clip and turned it over in his hand. "No indication that anyone forced her here."

Damian stared at him in disbelief. "Didn't Kosta tell you? He saw her alone and then he heard voices. Doesn't that tell you anything?"

"It tells me," said Spiro in a pragmatic policeman's voice, "that someone saw her and talked to her. Maybe. Actually, you should know by now that voices carry far in the quiet woods. The voices he heard might have had nothing to do with Alexa."

"Maybe not," Damian conceded. "But how did she get the marks on her wrists?"

"They could be scratches from shrubbery."

"You think she walked up here, stayed all night, fell into a deep sleep on a cold earth floor, all on her own?" Damian asked furiously.

"Take it easy, Damian. I didn't say that. I'm only suggesting there are other explanations." He laid a placating hand on Damian's arm. "Let's see if she's awake. We'll ask her."

The doctor checked Alexa's heartbeat once more. "Sounds better now," he pronounced. "I think you can try to wake her, but don't be concerned if she seems confused at first."

He closed his bag. "I'll be back soon. We'll need the stretcher from the car to carry Mitso down."

"That's how you got here so fast," Damian said, his eyes on Alexa's pale face.

"We drove as far as we could," Spiro replied. "We made it to the bottom of that last hill."

There wouldn't be room for all of them in the car, though, Damian realized, sitting on the edge of the bed. He touched Alexa's cheek. "Alexa, wake up."

She muttered something, slurred words he didn't understand. Then, clearly, she said, "I don't know. I tell you, I don't remember."

"Remember what, Alexa?" Damian said softly.

THE PATH WAS NARROW, a rocky causeway across a bottomless ravine. Monsters lived down there; she could hear their hungry snarls. They were lurking in the gloom, waiting for her to trip off the path. If she fell, their claws would tear her apart. She would never find the sunshine again.

The sound of his voice came dimly to her, hope materializing out of the shadowy mist. She had to find him, to let him show her the way to safety. He wouldn't let her fall.

"Alexa," she heard him say.

SHE OPENED HER EYES, seeing nothing but Damian's face, his deep blue eyes. The naked emotion in them shocked her, set new panic fluttering in her chest.

Something had happened. Something terrible. Damian would not look like that, lost and despairing unless—

Lisandro!

"Lisandro?" She choked out the word, her throat raw and scratchy.

Damian gave a strangled laugh. "Trust you to think of Lisandro first. Alexa, he's all right. You're the one we've been worried about."

Safe. She was safe, with Damian's arms wrapped around her. But no, his arms were too tight, his grip too desperate.

The heavy, erratic shudder of his heartbeat told her it wasn't all right.

She jerked herself up, out of his arms, her gaze swinging wildly around the room. "Where am I? How did you get here?"

"You're in Mitso's house. I walked up this morning. There was a note on my door." He settled her back down on the pillow, pressing his fingers momentarily to the agitated pulse in her throat. "Rest, Alexa. I'll get a cloth to wipe your face."

From a chair across the room, Spiro watched them. "Just wait a minute," Damian said to him on the way to the bathroom. "Give her a chance to collect herself."

When he returned with a moistened towel, Alexa had managed to sit up, braced against the headboard. "What am I doing here?" She looked around, bewildered, fighting the fog that made her thoughts thick and sluggish.

"I hope you can tell us," Spiro said without coming closer.

Her gaze flew from Damian to Spiro and back again. Then she gave a little sigh of pleasure as Damian used the warm, wet towel to clean her face and hands. The black cat suddenly jumped up onto the bed, kneading the quilt a couple of times before he settled down.

"I was wondering where he'd gotten to," Damian muttered. "I was afraid he might attack the doctor."

"Doctor?" Alexa echoed. "Where is Mitso? And what am I doing in his bed?"

Damian hesitated, but he knew he couldn't put off telling her. Seeing Mitso's body would be more of a shock for her, and he suspected she'd had enough of those. "I'm sorry, Alexa. Mitso's dead."

"Dead?" Her fingers plucked frantically at the sheet. "How could he be? He was fine yesterday."

"It looks like a heart attack," Damian said gently. "Do you remember anything, like why you came up here? Did you want to talk to Mitso again?"

She wrinkled her brow. An eerie echo started far back in her head. *The sword of Dimitrios. Where is the sword of Dimitrios?* She closed her eyes, pain stabbing her temples. "I don't know. I don't know," she said, on the point of weeping. Why couldn't they understand?

"What don't you know, Alexa?" This time Spiro, who had come to stand next to the bed, asked the question.

"I don't know where the sword is."

Damian and Spiro looked at each other. "Is that what it's all about?" Damian asked. He turned back to Alexa. "Who asked you where the sword is?"

"Someone . . . a man, I think. But I'm not sure. All night long I kept hearing a voice, saying over and over, 'Where is the sword of Dimitrios?' I was so tired. I wanted to sleep but he kept waking me up. Someone else was there, shaking me and demanding that I tell him. But I don't know anything."

"Where was this?" Spiro asked.

"I don't know. It was dark, like the inside of a grave."

"The storage shed," Damian said.

She stared past him at the window, then at the yellow puddle of sunlight on the floor. The laugh she gave bordered on hysteria. "It's not dark anymore."

"No, it's morning now," Damian said soothingly. "Do you remember what happened yesterday, how you got here?"

"Yesterday?" Her fists knotted in the quilt. "I went for a walk. In the woods." Something else. Something she'd pushed behind a closed door in her mind. Her gaze lit on the dresser by the television, and her eyes widened. "What's that?" Her voice rose in panic and she pushed herself away from Damian, huddling into the corner of the bed. The black cat hit the floor with a thud and scooted under the bed, where he sat growling irritably. "Where did you find that?"

Spiro picked up the white garment. "How did this get here?" He held it out to Alexa. "Yours?"

A cold sweat broke out on Alexa's skin. "Yes, it's mine."

Spiro frowned. "You wouldn't happen to know how it got here, would you? I presume you didn't bring an overnight case."

"I brought the nightgown," Damian admitted. "I found it this morning on our front step along with the note from Mitso." He paused. "In view of what's happened, I don't think the note was from Mitso, or if it was, someone forced him to write it. Someone wanted me to come up here. I was worried about Alexa and came as fast as I could. I carried the nightgown along without even thinking."

"It was in my room, in the closet," Alexa whispered, the quilt drawn up to her neck. "That's why I ran from the hotel. I'd had a bad dream in the night. When I found that, I knew it was real, not a dream. Otherwise it wouldn't have been muddy. I must have been sleepwalking again."

"Well, you weren't sleepwalking yesterday afternoon. What happened?"

Damian's intense look burned her. She had to give him an answer. If only her brain didn't feel as dense as cotton wool. She loosened one hand from its grip on the quilt, bringing it up to touch the side of her face. The skin was rough and sore; she winced as she explored the tender spot.

"A sack," she recalled suddenly. "Someone jumped me in the woods and put a sack over my head. I felt a prick in my arm, and the next thing I knew, I was on a cot in a completely dark room."

"What else do you remember?" Damian asked.

She thought about it, frowning deeply. Then she shook her head. "Just what I told you. A voice asking about the sword of Dimitrios. And later, I was in a different place, I don't know where. It was so cold."

"I found you lying on the floor next to Mitso's leather chair," Damian said. "No sack, and you weren't tied up. But I found one of your hair clips in a storage shed out back."

"With a cot and a boarded-up window?" Alexa asked eagerly, sensing their skepticism of her story. In fact, her mind still felt so fuzzy she was inclined to wonder if she'd dreamed the entire episode.

"Yes," Spiro said. "Did the men say anything when they grabbed you?"

The images flooded back, bombarding her with sensations—the serenity of the woods changing to an ominous silence, hard hands, the sudden darkness, the dry, metallic taste of terror in her mouth. The pressure in her temples increased but she steeled herself against the pain. The more she remembered, the better the chances of catching her abductors. "I lost my watch. When they knocked me down. I felt the clasp break. The men sounded angry when I struggled. I couldn't understand them. But someone else came up and spoke to them in Greek."

"Did you recognize his voice?"

Alexa shook her head, although a sense that she was missing something important nagged her. "No. It was muffled."

"Mmm." Spiro grunted noncommittally. "You think they gave you an injection?"

"I felt a prick on my arm. Everything went black. I woke up in a dark place. A man came and brought me water and a sandwich, bread and cheese. The bread was dry." She coughed painfully, remembering how eagerly she'd eaten, how she'd blacked out afterward. "He must have drugged either the food or the water, because I passed out or fell asleep again."

She pressed her face against Damian's shirt, taking comfort from the rich, clean scent of him. She was truly safe; no one could touch her now. "Could I get up and go to the bathroom?"

Damian stiffened; she felt the tension that flowed into all of his muscles. She lifted her head, met his eyes. The grim set of his mouth told her everything. "That's where Mitso is, isn't it?" she said in a scared little whisper. "It's all right. I can wait."

A sound at the door brought her head around. The doctor—she recognized him from the morning at Angelo's house—came in, struggling with the unwieldy arrangement of poles and canvas that formed the old-fashioned stretcher.

Damian held her close while Spiro and the doctor went into the bathroom to see to Mitso. She couldn't stop herself from looking when they walked by. The old man was a pathetically narrow mound on the stretcher, covered with a gray wool blanket, just like the one that had covered Angelo.

She shivered violently, her eyes dry but her throat tight with unshed tears. Too many times she'd witnessed such a scene.

With a shock she realized that it hadn't been only in the past week. She'd seen this before, long ago, when she must have been only a child.

A man on the ground, then a group of men around him, arguing. She'd huddled out of sight. When they'd taken him away, she had crept out of her hiding place, stared for a long time at the blood on the flattened grass. She hugged her arms around her, unable to keep away the cold seeping into her soul.

The eagle wheeled across the sky, crying in the wind. She'd looked up, seen the blood-red sun on the horizon. Her mother would be looking for her. If she could only get home, she would be warm again.

Chapter Sixteen

Two hours later, Alexa lay between crisp white sheets in Damian's bed. Despite her protests that she felt well enough to get up, that she'd suffered no physical damage, the doctor had insisted on giving her a thorough examination and further directed that she spend the day in bed.

"Without a blood test, we can't be sure what drugs you were given," he had said, "but I'm certain you were given something, possibly even a hallucinogen. I don't want you having a relapse and hurting yourself."

And naturally Damian concurred.

He had waited with her until Spiro had brought the car back to the bottom of the hill. He had carried her down and driven at a snail's pace to Lisandro's house, where the doctor had met them.

Lisandro came into the room, leaning on a cane. Her heart ached at the sight of him, the painful, labored cadence of his steps. "Lisandro," she said.

"My dear Alexa," he said, sinking down on the chair next to the bed. He dropped the cane onto the floor with a grimace of distaste, and took both her hands in his. "Damian says you got lost in the woods and spent the night at Mitso's house. I'm happy to see you're all right, but you must be more careful."

"It won't happen again," Alexa said fervently, masking her relief that Lisandro accepted the story she and Damian had concocted in the car earlier.

He didn't appear well, she noted, pain squeezing her heart. He looked fragile, breakable, his skin pale and tightly drawn over the prominent bones of his face. The jagged scar on the side of his face stood out in ugly contrast, a bluish purple slash across the closely shaven skin.

She touched it gently. "It must have hurt."

He shrugged. "Compared to pains of the heart and soul, it was nothing. You grew up without a father. That must have been infinitely more painful."

"I had my mother," she said simply. "And the stories she told, how my father was a hero."

"If you don't find him, what will you do?"

She was silent for a long moment. "I'm not sure I expected to find him," she said at last. "I didn't really believe Kritikos's story. It was too vague, with nothing to substantiate it. It seems to fit the facts, but his informant could have been mistaken. It could be some other man, not my father at all. My father would be a very old man by now. It would be a miracle if he were alive."

"Will you look farther than Elatos?" Lisandro's voice was low, somehow filled with sorrow. His hands held hers as though he were afraid she would disappear if he let go.

Now where did that notion come from? Alexa almost laughed at her absurd fancies. "I've written an advertisement that I'll give to the car rental agent when he brings my tires. I'll ask him to drop the ad off at the Ioannina newspaper when he goes back. It may bring a result."

"So you'll be leaving soon." This time his voice was neutral, emptied of emotion. "We'll miss you, Alexa."

Tears stung her eyes, and she had to swallow hard before she could reply. Would Damian ask her to stay? Or would that damnable pride of his stand in the way? "I'll miss you, too," she managed to say.

ALEXA GOT UP FOR LUNCH, overriding Damian's protests. "I'm fine," she said. "I have to get up. I need my things from the hotel."

"I'll pick them up for you," Damian said, his jaw set stubbornly.

"Doesn't Spiro want you back at the police station to give a statement?"

Damian groaned. "Yes, and if he sees you out, he'll be grilling you again."

"No, he won't. You know he talked to me again after the doctor left. I've told him everything I know. By the way, is Kritikos still around?"

"I guess so, although I didn't see his car. But Poppy says he hasn't checked out. You're not thinking of talking to him again, are you?"

She lifted her chin and gave him a level look. "And if I am? Damian, he's my only lead."

"Then let Spiro talk to him. Kritikos knew Angelo. Spiro should be more aggressive in finding out if he knows anything about Angelo's murder, what enemies Angelo may have had."

"You'll be careful, won't you, Alexa?" Lisandro said with a worried frown. "Don't go off by yourself."

"I won't. You can count on it."

A MAN ALEXA HAD NEVER seen before waited on the hotel steps when they pulled up. For an instant she wondered if he were the rental company representative, but figured it was unlikely since she saw neither tires nor another car.

The man, probably in his sixties, greeted Damian with a broad smile and a firm handshake. Damian turned to Alexa. "This is George, the teacher I was telling you about."

Alexa shook his hand, her heart pounding with excitement. "You've finished translating the diary."

He nodded, picking up his briefcase from a nearby bench. Unzipping the case, he extracted the diary and a sheaf of typed papers. He smiled as he handed them to Alexa. "I translated it into modern Greek, then had my wife type it up in English, as well. She used to teach English in Ioannina before we retired. I thought that would be easier for you."

"Thank you. I'm sure it will." Alexa groped in her purse. "How much do I owe you?"

"Nothing at all," George said forcefully. "It was a pleasure to read an authentic document from one of the most interesting times in Greek history. You must be proud of your heritage, such a fascinating family."

"Did you know my father, George?" Alexa asked.

George shook his head. "I had a grandfather who came from Elatos, but he left when he was still a young man. I've only lived here during the summers of the last three years, since I retired." He shook her hand again and clapped Damian on the shoulder. "Thanks again for letting me read the diary."

Alexa let out her breath in a little puff, anticipation surging through her. "You're due to see Spiro, aren't you, Damian?"

He grinned. "Trying to get rid of me?"

She smiled back, giving him a little push. "Yes. But I'll let you know what it says as soon as you're back."

"I won't be long," he promised. "Spiro said he had only a couple of questions, and he wanted to see the note that was on my door this morning."

His expression grew serious as he laid his hands on Alexa's shoulders. "Lock your door, Alexa, while you're packing. Wait downstairs with Poppy when you're done. And stay away from Kritikos. I don't trust the man. So don't start playing amateur detective."

The intensity in his voice scraped at her nerves, dampening her excitement. "Do you really think he might have had something to do with what happened to me?"

Damian rubbed his hand over his face. "I don't know. But he's after something. It could be the sword. After all, it's no secret that there's supposed to be a fortune in diamonds hidden in the hilt." He bent his head and kissed her, an all too brief contact. "I'll be back. Be careful."

ALL THE WAY UPSTAIRS, Damian's words of caution echoed in her head. Poppy had greeted her in the lobby, but she'd been busy with a wine salesman, to judge by the samples laid out on the counter. The door to Kritikos's room was closed, the hall silent.

Her own room was locked. Poppy must have secured it. Alexa opened the door with the key she still had.

Everything was as she'd left it. Hard to believe it had been only twenty-four hours since she'd discovered the muddy nightgown, she realized with surprise.

Was Kritikos behind all the incidents that had happened to her, as Damian had implied? Well, he wouldn't be able to touch her at Lisandro's.

She sat down in the chair by the window and sifted through the papers she held. Rather than struggling with her imperfect knowledge of written Greek, she skipped straight to the English version, skimming until she found the references to the sword.

An hour later she sat back in the chair, closing her eyes. The sword, wherever it was, definitely belonged to the Doukas family, to her father. Or to Alexa, if he no longer lived.

But did she want it? The sword, a valuable artifact even in the early nineteenth century, had been given to the Doukas family as payment for a debt of honor.

Still, Angelo hadn't been far wrong when he'd told her the sword belonged to his family; it had, at one point. The Thetalous and the Doukases had descended from a common ancestor, a certain Dimitrios who had carried the sword to the Crusades. By the time of the Turkish occupation, the two families had been friends, blood brothers, and partners in business, for generations.

The alliance had ended when a young, headstrong Thetalou had betrayed an equally young Doukas to the Turks, over a woman, it seemed. The Doukas youth had been executed and the shamed Thetalou family had relinquished all rights to the sword, presenting it to the Doukas family. The Doukas family, in turn, finding the weapon a painful reminder of their dead son, had arranged for it to be kept in the village office ever after.

Oddly, there was no mention of the diamonds. Alexa gnawed thoughtfully on her lower lip, wondering if that story had started after the disappearance of the sword during her own childhood. It would add romance to the missing village relic.

Apparently, someone still believed the diamonds existed. Valuable as the antique weapon itself must be, diamonds were more readily disposable than the sword, with fewer questions asked.

A knock sounded on the door, followed by Damian's low voice. "Alexa, are you in there?"

She pulled open the door, closing it after him. Smiling sheepishly, she indicated the suitcase, lying on the bed. "I'm sorry. I haven't started."

Damian gestured at the papers in her hand. "What did you find out?"

"That the sword belongs to the Doukas family. In other words, even if my father took it, it was his to take." Briefly she gave him a rundown on the tragic story.

"So it's yours," Damian said when she finished.

"I guess," she said, her voice tinged with uncertainty. "But I think it belongs to Elatos. If it shows up, I want it to stay here." She held up the diary. "Would this legally establish ownership?"

"I would say so. I'm sure that the records department in Ioannina wouldn't have any trouble authenticating the existence of your ancestor." He picked up the suitcase, handing it to her. "Why don't you pack so we can go home?"

She looked at him quizzically, puzzled by his abrupt tone. Shrugging, she began to fold her clothes.

DAMIAN COULDN'T EXPLAIN the turmoil inside him. Walking over to the window, he stared out, his hands pushed into the back pockets of his jeans.

Home. Yes, he wanted her to think of his house—not really his, but close enough—as home. The thought of her leaving opened up a painful void inside him, one he knew he'd never fill.

As soon as he'd entered the room and seen the suitcase, he felt the hollow sinking in his stomach. He didn't want her to leave. In fact, for an instant, at the sight of the unmade bed, the bed she'd slept in, probably scented still with her elusive perfume, desire had slammed into him. He'd wanted nothing more than to tumble her on that bed and love her passionately. Until he imprinted himself upon her and drove every thought of leaving from her mind.

But he couldn't. He had no right. How could he expect her to give up her exciting life in Canada to live in a mundane Greek city with him?

He had nothing to offer Alexa, not even a name that was his own. Orfanos was not the name bestowed by his mother, but one he'd taken for himself when he'd first realized she didn't want him. Later he'd made it legal.

Meeting Lisandro, growing up and achieving success in his career had finally dulled the sense of isolation, the loneliness of feeling unattached to any other human on earth. Of course, there had been other women along the way, but meeting Alexa had given him hope; with her, for the first time in his life, he felt complete.

Nevertheless, she was leaving. She would take his heart when she left, and probably not even know it.

"I'm ready."

The low music of her voice washed over him, and he closed his eyes. Alexa. How can I bear it?

In virtual silence they drove back to the house. In Damian's room, Alexa unpacked only the items she would need for a day or two, assuring Damian that he needn't empty drawers or closet space for her.

She'd spent most of the day consciously blocking out the events of the night and early morning. And soon it would be night again, enveloping her in a darkness filled with terrors. Whenever she thought of the image of the narrow path over a bottomless void, she shivered.

Someone was after her. She frowned, her hands stilling as she folded a sweater and laid it on a chair. The marmalade cat came around the edge of the door, pushing it slightly ajar. He meowed plaintively and coiled sinuously around her ankles. She sank down on the bed, picking him up and hugging the warm, furry body to her chest.

Someone was stalking her. She should be afraid of this unknown person who tormented her. But the cold emptiness in her stomach grew more icy at the thought that maybe she was imagining the whole thing.

Abruptly she turned off the thought, went to the window and looked out over the woods and gray rooftops.

Damian was in a strange mood, she mused, stroking the cat. She'd expected him to be excited over the information in the diary, but instead he'd been quiet and moody. What was he thinking when he looked at her, his midnight blue eyes shadowed, his expression veiled?

Would he miss her when she was gone? She would miss him; even now she found herself looking for excuses to extend her stay. But she couldn't afford the time. She'd exhausted the resources in Elatos; it was time to look farther afield if she expected to find anything on her father's fate at all.

She had to go. Then why did she feel as if she were tearing out a vital part of herself at the thought that she would never see Damian again?

"Would you like to go for a walk before dinner?"

She spun around. She hadn't heard him open the door. Go out? Yes, the idea appealed to her. Fresh air would clear her mind, postpone facing her fear of the coming night.

"Yes, I'd like a walk," she told him quietly, avoiding his eyes lest he see the misery in hers.

DRY LEAVES CRUNCHED under their feet as they walked through the wooded paths. Alexa lifted her face to the westering sun, breathing in the scent of pine. Yesterday's wind hadn't returned, nor had the storms that warned of winter to come. Today the weather was almost as hot as summer.

Without realizing it, she directed her footsteps toward the birch grove. She still couldn't shake the feeling that it held a special significance to her. "I wonder if I came here as a child," she said aloud.

"You lived here less than a year," Damian reminded her. "And you were very young. Would you have gone this far from the village center?"

Alexa shrugged. "Perhaps my parents liked to go for walks. And you know how children are, always exploring. There must have been more children here at the time."

"You still don't remember, do you?" Damian's eyes searched hers as he clasped her hand to help her over a fallen log.

"No. If I did, maybe I would know what happened. Maybe I wouldn't have this feeling that there's something I'm missing, something that I should be seeing."

"Well, somebody thinks you know something," Damian said. "Whoever abducted you yesterday."

They entered the birch grove, a small circle of golden light, seemingly shut off from the rest of the world. "Unless I dreamed it all," Alexa said, her eyes troubled.

She dropped his hand and clambered over a pile of rocks. Intrigued, he followed. They found themselves in a sheltered little hollow, carpeted with brown, summer-dry grass and hemmed in on all sides by rocks and brambles. "How did you know this was here?" Damian asked.

She looked around, her face bewildered. "I—I didn't. No, that's not quite true. Somehow I did know."

"Maybe you remember more than you think, Alexa."

She made a small sound of distress. "Then why didn't I come to this spot the other times I visited the birch grove? I didn't remember before."

"Does it matter?" Damian asked gently.

She hesitated. He could feel the tremor that shuddered through her, as if she was poised on the edge of flight. Then the tension left her body. "No, I guess not."

He drew her down to sit on the soft grass, warm from the day's sunshine. Pulling her close to him, he held her, resting his face against the fragrant silk of her hair. Her scent filled him, and he wanted to freeze the moment in time. If they could stay here, like this, together, forever...

In that thought lay the roots of pain and disillusionment.

"Alexa, will you leave tomorrow?" he asked, brutally checking that part of him that dared to dream, that dared to keep hope alive.

"If the tires come in the morning."

Before reason prevailed, he knew he had to take the chance. He couldn't let her go without trying, without letting her know she hadn't just passed through his life without touching it.

"Alexa," he breathed.

She lifted her head, her wide brown eyes meeting his. "Damian?"

"I want to make love with you." There, he'd said it. Tensely he waited for her to jump up, to run.

She did neither. Her eyes held his, the tenderness in them making his own eyes burn. "I'd like that, Damian."

Her face blurred, and he had to blink away tears to bring her back into focus. He couldn't speak, his heart expanding until it lay like a great stone in his chest. He lowered her to the grass, stretching himself beside her. For long moments, they clung together, their bodies perfectly aligned, their breathing and heartbeats slowing and synchronizing, until they became one.

Damian kissed her, slowly, softly, moving his mouth over her face, wordlessly telling her how much she meant to him. She murmured her pleasure, and his pulse sped up, excitement surging through his body.

She responded, moving against him and pulling open the buttons on his shirt. She pushed it off his shoulders, then jerked her sweater over her head. Beneath it, she was naked.

Groaning, he lowered his head, kissing first one breast and then the other. She arched under his hands as though his touch had activated a live wire within her. "Please, Damian," she whispered urgently.

"Yes," he gasped with equal urgency.

He removed her jeans, then his own, pausing only long enough to grope in the pocket, tearing open the package with his teeth. Alexa sat up. When she touched him with gentle fingers, he closed his eyes, fighting for control. "Wait—"

"No waiting," she said, guiding him to her. "Now."

"Yes, now." Biting his bottom lip, teetering on the brink of exploding, he entered her slowly, gently, closing his eyes at the profound satisfaction of joining with her. He moved his mouth over her, kissing her eyelids, her cheeks, her lips, losing himself in the luscious taste and texture of her, pleasure echoing in every cell of his body, inexorably building.

He wanted it to last but Alexa surged upward, her legs clasping his hips. "Damian," she cried out, and she came apart in his arms, pulling him into the shock waves of her climax.

He let go, giving himself to her, hurtling toward an ecstasy he'd never experienced before.

That he'd never experience again.

THEY WALKED SLOWLY HOME in the gray dusk, aware only of each other and the sleepy twittering of roosting birds in the trees along the path. Somehow they got through dinner, Lisandro casting them odd looks when they didn't seem to be taking up his conversational leads.

Finally, dinner over, he gave up, standing up to go to his room. "When you're back in the real world, let me know," he told him, his faded eyes twinkling. "I guess you won't be needing blankets for the cot tonight, Damian," he added, laughing at the shocked look they gave him. "Don't worry. You're both adults, and I'm not too old to remember how it was. Good night." He winked at them and disappeared into his room, closing the door for the first time since he'd come to the little house.

NIGHT WRAPPED THE ROOM in deep shadows when Damian awoke. He reached for Alexa, sparing only a single instant of surprise that it seemed so right for her to be sleeping beside him.

She was gone. The realization slammed into him like a sledgehammer. He leapt off the bed, jerking his jeans up his legs. Zipping them with one hand, he used the other to feel her side of the bed. Not cold, but not warm, either.

He checked the bathroom. Empty. Lisandro's room? No, Lisandro lay in his bed, snoring faintly.

Back in the hall he saw that the front door stood ajar, swaying lightly in the draft. He shoved his feet into his shoes and ran out, nearly tripping over the cat who growled once and leapt down the path ahead of him.

Damian rounded the first bend. He saw her, a slender figure dressed in a long white nightgown. In the midst of his anxiety, he permitted himself a brief smile. She'd been naked in his arms an hour ago, but apparently even in sleep had enough propriety not to go outside without putting something on.

Catching up with her easily, he reached for her, thinking to get her turned around and back to the house. He remembered what she'd told him, that sleepwalkers are very suggestible. She would be back in bed in five minutes and not know she'd been out.

But he remembered something else, as well. She only sleepwalked when she was under some kind of mental strain. He would follow her, make sure nothing harmed her, but he would see where she went. If nothing else, he could reassure her in the morning.

Keeping pace, he watched her. She could have been awake. Her eyes were open although she blinked at about half her normal rate. She didn't seem to see him, but her footsteps—she'd remembered to put on slippers—were steady on the rocky ground, skirting rough places with uncanny accuracy.

They reached the place where the path forked; she turned right. They passed Vassiliki's house, dark and shuttered. A little farther on, she turned right again. She paused at a gate in a rusted chain-link fence, looking around as if she were puzzled.

Then she opened the gate, walked to the door of the house and pushed it open, as well. She went inside, walked to the fireplace and sat down on the floor. After a moment she began to sing, a soft lullaby that Greek mothers used to soothe their infants.

Damian stood in the doorway, a bewildered frown creasing his forehead.

Why had she come to Angelo's house?

Chapter Seventeen

Alexa found herself alone in the bed when she awakened the next morning. The spot where Damian had slept beside her was already cold. Only the indentation in the pillow told her last night had been real, that she hadn't dreamed he'd made love to her, once sweetly and tenderly, and a little later with fierce, almost desperate, abandon.

She got up, dressed and went into the kitchen, stopping only to wish Lisandro, still in bed, a good morning. And it was a good morning, sunlight streaming in through the window and pooling on the flagstone floor. She smiled to herself, a sense of well-being filling her.

Her euphoria lasted about a minute, dissipating like mist in the sun when Damian turned from the stove to greet her.

Without being able to explain it, she saw he had changed. The sensitive lover of last night was gone. In his place was a man whose shadowed eyes held speculation when they rested on her, a man who had drawn his emotions, so much on the surface last night, into a remote place in his mind.

Alexa felt a cold lump invade her chest where her heart had been. Was that all it was to him, a quick roll in the hay?

While she had given her heart and her soul, trusting that he would cherish them in tender hands.

He served her bacon and eggs and delicately browned toast, not saying much. She could hardly force any of the food down her throat, and kept her eyes downcast to hide the hurt in them.

When she took her plate to the sink, she saw that his food, too, was virtually untouched. She looked at him, noting the tension that etched hard lines in his face. "Damian—" she said tentatively.

But he lifted his hand. "Please, Alexa, not now."

He brought Lisandro his morning coffee. Alexa tidied the room where she and Damian had slept, feeling faintly left out as she listened to the sound of their voices.

What was wrong with Damian?

"Alexa, Vassiliki is here. We can go down to the square." His voice from the doorway startled her. She realized she'd been standing in the middle of the room, woolgathering, for who knew how long. Picking up a sweater, she left the room.

AN UNFAMILIAR CAR stood in front of the hotel. Next to her car, a young man in a crisp white shirt crouched on the ground, fitting a jack under it. Four tires mounted on rims were stacked beside him.

He jumped up when he saw her. "Mrs. Thetalou, my name is Paul. I'm so sorry this happened, and that we couldn't take care of it sooner."

She shook the hand he offered. "It's all right. How soon will the car be ready?"

Beside her, Damian muttered something.

Paul looked at his watch. "In an hour or so. I will have to get you to sign a report. And get a copy of the police report, as well."

"Spiro said he'd have it ready. Oh, here he comes now."

The policeman crossed the square with his slow, deliberate gait. "Good morning, Alexa, Damian. Could I speak with you for a moment?"

They sat down in the far corner of the empty dining room, ordering coffee. Poppy brought it promptly, smiling at them both. "That terrible man, Kritikos, is gone," she said. "He checked out early this morning."

Now that Alexa thought about it, she realized she hadn't seen his car. "But that leaves you with no guests, Poppy."

Poppy shrugged. "Better no guests than one like him, in and out at all hours."

Damian lifted his brow. "What do you mean, all hours?"

"Some nights he was in early, like a normal person, but he'd go out at two or three in the morning. Other times, he would be out all evening and half the night. I heard him sometimes when I worked late and even once or twice after I'd gone to bed. I'm a light sleeper and the stairs creak." She bit her lip, looking at Spiro. "I'm sorry. I shouldn't go on like that. I'll leave you to your business."

"Wait," Damian said. "Did you ever hear Alexa going out?"

Poppy colored in embarrassment. "Yes. The first night you were here, Alexa. You went out on the step in your nightgown. I spoke to you but you didn't answer. In fact, you looked right at me and didn't seem to see anything. It scared me."

Alexa patted her hand. "It's okay, Poppy. I was sleepwalking."

"That was before Kritikos came," Damian said, unable to hide his disappointment. "Poppy, did you hear Alexa go out any other time?"

She pursed her mouth, thinking. "I didn't hear her but she was out another night. The night it was raining."

"It's rained on several evenings lately."

"I know. This was the night before she got lost in the woods. It must have been nearly midnight. I thought I'd heard a noise about ten minutes before, but I'd just gotten out of the shower. When I came out of the bathroom, I looked around but I didn't see anybody. Then I went upstairs to get towels from the linen closet. Alexa's door was open."

Alexa stifled a gasp. That was the night that she'd awakened in her bed and seen the chair still jammed under the doorknob. So she must have relocked the door when she came back. Unless the intruder with the muddy shoes had done it. "Poppy, did you hear me come back that night?" she asked, urgency edging her voice.

Poppy nodded. "About an hour later."

"You didn't think to tell anyone, or to go look for her yourself when you saw she was gone?" Damian demanded.

An embarrassed flush crept up Poppy's cheeks. "I thought if she was out, it was to meet you, Damian. I didn't even think she might have been sleepwalking again. I'm sorry."

Damian gave her a quick smile. "It's all right, Poppy. You couldn't have known. Now, what about Kritikos? Did he come back in after Alexa that night?"

"I don't know. I only heard Alexa go up the stairs, and I heard her lock her door. I don't know if Kritikos was in or out. His door was closed. I didn't see him until breakfast in the morning."

Not too enlightening, Damian thought. Inconclusive, at best. "Thanks, Poppy."

Spiro had been following the conversation with interest. "Had this Kritikos been bothering you, Alexa?"

She shook her head. "Not really. Not in any way I could put my finger on, but he sometimes made me uncomfortable, the way he looked at me."

"Could he have been one of the men who abducted you?"

She'd thought about it before, coming up blank. "I don't know. I just don't know."

"Spiro, do you know something about Kritikos that might point to him, other than that he's a stranger in town?" Damian asked, recalling Lisandro's suspicions about the man.

"I ran a check on him," Spiro said, "Based on his license plate and the identification card he showed Poppy when he took the room. It checked out. I got a Volos address, but when I searched further back, I came up with nothing. Prior to five years ago, Kritikos doesn't seem to exist, at least under that name." He shrugged. "Of course, there are many reasons a man might change his name, such as his family disowning him. It doesn't make him a criminal. However, that's not what I wanted to talk to you about."

He made a little business of sipping his coffee and setting the cup precisely back on the table, apparently reluctant to get to the point. Dread walked icy fingers up Alexa's spine. Had he learned something new on Angelo's death?

"I'm afraid we may have another murder on our hands," Spiro finally said.

"Another murder?" Alexa said incredulously. "You can't mean Mitso."

Spiro nodded ponderously, as if the case weighed heavily on him. As it must, Alexa thought in dismay. Probably nothing had happened in this place in the past twenty years, and now they had two murders in a week. The very week she'd been there.

She glanced up, half expecting to see a little black cloud hovering over her head. A hysterical laugh threatened to erupt from her mouth and she pressed her knuckles against her teeth. No, it couldn't be because of her that two men had died. She would really go crazy if she let herself believe that. It was just a horrendous coincidence.

"I'm sorry," Spiro said. "At first it looked like a heart attack. After all, the man was nearly a hundred years old. But the autopsy showed bruises on the body. He'd been beaten before he died. Severely enough that it could have triggered a heart attack in such an old man."

He turned to Alexa, an intent look in his dark eyes. "You haven't remembered anything else about that night, have you, Alexa? Something that you might have missed before?"

Alexa hugged her arms around her waist. "No. I'm sorry. It's all mixed up, like a terrible nightmare." She grimaced. "And I know all about nightmares. I've had them all my life."

"The time you and your mother left Elatos was not a happy time," Spiro said. "You're probably reliving that fear."

"Did you know my father?" Alexa asked. "No, I suppose you couldn't have. Unless you're a lot older than you look."

"No, I didn't know your father, Alexa. I didn't live here then. In fact, almost no one who lives here now was in Elatos when your father disappeared. They either left after the trouble here, those who were still alive, or they've died since. Mitso was probably the last person who was a first-hand witness to all the upheavals Elatos has suffered."

Did that have significance? The question flitted through her mind, swallowed in the sudden realization that there might be no one left on earth who had known her father. At least no one she could trace. Except the mysterious Albanian Kritikos had told her about. And finding him was likely impossible. After all, Angelo and Kritikos hadn't even agreed on when the man had told the story, and she had no way of knowing if either or both of them had lied to her, simply to further their own ends.

The records in Ioannina might still have something, but she had little hope that searching them again would produce results. Just because he wasn't listed among the deaths in the past five years, in records that she'd thoroughly checked before coming to Elatos, didn't mean he was alive. He could have died anywhere, under any name.

Or be alive anywhere.

And she wouldn't know him if she fell over him. He would have changed so much over the years, and her memories were so vague, that he would be a complete stranger to her.

She closed her eyes in despair. It was hopeless. Unless the ad she was putting in the Ioannina paper paid off, she'd never find him, especially if he didn't want to be found.

Old political enemies might still be after him, or he might keep his identity secret from her out of shame for not contacting her and her mother. Perhaps if they had known he was alive, they might have felt differently, but they had dealt with their grief and made a life without him. Even now, with the faint hope that he might be alive, Alexa couldn't resent him for his past actions. He had provided a means of escape for them both, and they had never felt anything but gratitude for that. It had been a faint ray of comfort amid their sorrow on hearing of his death.

If Alexa saw him again, she would let the past lie, she decided, and not allow it to cloud their reunion. She would embrace and cherish the chance to see him again.

"I'm sorry, Alexa," Spiro said, jolting her back to harsh reality. "I wish I could help you. I know how much you wanted to find your father. But at least you had the chance to talk to Mitso."

Beside her, Damian stirred, touching her for the first time that morning. He took her hand, holding it firmly in his. His palm was warm and some of the chill in her body receded.

But when she looked at him, her perplexity at his behavior this morning returned. His eyes were remote, emotionless, as if he'd erected a barrier between them.

Spiro pushed back his chair, dropping a handful of coins onto the table. "Enjoy your coffee," he said, smiling faintly. "Even though I've spoiled your day. Alexa, if you're leaving, let me know."

"I will," she said. "And could you speak to the man outside? He needs the report on the slashed tires. For the insurance."

"Paperwork." Spiro's mouth twisted wryly. "I'll see that he gets it."

Alone with Damian, Alexa fidgeted in her chair. A thousand questions crowded her mind, but she couldn't corral them into any kind of order. Something was eating him, but what?

She sipped her coffee, making a face as she tasted the bitterness. It had gone cold.

"I'll get you some fresh," Damian said. He half rose from his chair, but she laid her hand on his thigh. The hard-muscled thigh she'd caressed less than twelve hours before. Heat flashed through her and she snatched her hand away.

"No," she said. "I don't want any. I want to know what's wrong."

He didn't meet her eyes. "You're leaving," he said at last.

Was that all? And would he admit it, this man who kept his emotions to himself except for those rare occasions when he'd let down his guard with her? The conviction hit her that he was throwing a red herring in her path. "Yes. I have to," she said. "Damian, you know that."

"I know." His voice was flat, and her spirits dropped further.

"But that's not all of it, is it?" she said impatiently, wanting to shake him. After last night, didn't he trust her? "Something's wrong."

He sighed heavily. "Yes. Alexa, do you remember all of last night?"

His sweetness, her response, the ardent movements of his hands and mouth over her as he made her feel as if she were the most beautiful, the most desired, woman in the world. Yes, she remembered all of that, but somehow she didn't think that was what he referred to. "I was sleepwalking again, wasn't I?" she said in a resigned tone.

Somberly, his eyes dark with pain, he nodded. "You went to Angelo's house. Why, Alexa? Why? Can't you forget him?"

"Angelo's house?" she said incredulously. "Why would I go to Angelo's house? And what do you mean, can't I forget him?" Her eyes widened. "You think—you actually think I'm still in love with Angelo or something? Damian, I told you—"

"You've been there a number of times. I don't know what to think."

"Damian," she said with exaggerated patience. "I'm sorry Angelo's dead, but that's all. I haven't loved Angelo in years and I'm not mourning him now. There has to be another reason why I went there. What did I do at the house?"

"You sat in front of the ruined fireplace. You sang this song I haven't heard in years, a children's song. And then you got up and walked home and went back to bed. You don't remember any of it, do you?"

She shook her head. "Nothing. Not a thing." She twisted her fingers together tensely. "Damian, maybe that's how I got to Mitso's house. Maybe I fell asleep in the woods or the birch grove and sleepwalked to his house. Maybe I dreamed the part about the men and the sack."

Damian covered her hands with one of his, stilling their nervous twitching. "Alexa—"

"Don't try to smooth it over, Damian," she cried. "What if it's true that I'm going crazy?"

"You're not going crazy, Alexa."

The words didn't comfort her. She just stared at him in numb misery, wondering if her world would ever be right again.

THEY DROVE HER CAR up to Lisandro's house, to save carrying her suitcase down the path again. The house was silent, the living room and kitchen deserted although a pot of bean soup simmered on the stove. "Vassiliki must have gone home," Damian said. He moved past Alexa, gazing down the hall. "Odd, Lisandro's door is closed."

Three long strides brought him there. He threw it open and had to hold on to the doorframe to keep from falling. Alexa's low cry ripped through him.

Kritikos stood behind Lisandro's chair, holding a knife at Lisandro's throat. The old man's face was white but his eyes blazed with defiance. "Get out of here. Bring Spiro." He gasped, the desperate words cut off as Kritikos tightened his grip on his shirt collar.

Damian reached back and gave Alexa a nudge. "Go," he said out of the corner of his mouth.

"And come back to find Lisandro dead?" she said flatly. "Like Angelo, like Mitso."

Damian clenched his teeth. "I won't let it happen."

"We won't," she said, and pushed him out of the way.

She stood in the middle of the room, her eyes on Kritikos's face. "What do you want with an old man, you coward? Do you think you can get to me through him?"

Damian stared at her. What was she up to? The uncertainty, the despair, he had seen in her at the restaurant was gone. She looked like Athena about to go into battle.

"It was you all the time, wasn't it?" she said. "You who came into my room, who followed me to Angelo's."

"Yes." Kritikos sneered, his crooked tooth looking like a fang. "That part was easy."

"And that night the lamp was off and it rained, did you relock the door and put the chair back, and then leave through the window?"

"Yes, and all for nothing. Missy, you didn't scare easily. I couldn't get anything useful out of you. It's time to try something else." He gave Lisandro a shake. "I think the old man knows more than he's letting on. Why would he suddenly, when he's dying, come to a benighted place like Elatos if he didn't have a connection with it?" His knuckles whitened on the knife, the point pricking Lisandro's skin. "Tell me, old man, who are you?"

"More to the point, Kritikos or whatever your name is," Damian said grimly, "who are you, and what are you after?"

"Why, the sword, of course. The diamonds. They're mine, by rights."

"The sword belongs to Alexa. The Thetalous gave it to the Doukases." Damian clenched his fists, calculating whether he could jump the man. "The diary confirms it."

"That's why Angelo wanted the diary," Kritikos said. "He was afraid of something like that, and he wanted to destroy it. But I don't need the diary. I only want the sword. And Dimitrios Doukas."

"What?" Alexa demanded. "If you wanted him, why didn't you follow up the story the Albanian told you, that he was alive?"

Kritikos's eyes narrowed craftily. "Because, my dear Alexa, your late, unlamented husband was the one who heard it from the Albanian. And it wasn't by chance. He had detectives working for him. He didn't see fit to tell me what he'd found out until a month ago. By that time, we knew you were coming and hoped you'd do the work for us."

"So you and Angelo were working together."

"You could say that, but Angelo didn't have the stomach for the job when it got serious. You might as well know, Alexa, the way he felt about you might have been a perverted obsession most of the time, but it wasn't all bad. In the end he didn't want you hurt. And he knew I might have to hurt you. We disagreed. He fell and hit his head."

"You killed him." A chill ran through her, making her knees tremble.

Kritikos inclined his head. "It was necessary. And I used the knife. I saw Lisandro coming toward the house. He was near Vassiliki's. I realized it was the perfect opportunity. Using a short cut, I ran to his house, climbed in the window, which I knew was always open, and took the knife. I doubled back to Angelo's and got there before the old man. It was easy since he walked so slowly."

"Why?" Damian cut in. "Were you planning to frame Lisandro for murder?"

"Not necessarily. I wanted to do something to shake his isolation from the village. Like the police coming to question him about the knife."

"It didn't work, did it?" Damian said. "Spiro didn't even know where the knife came from."

Kritikos shrugged. "Anyway, Angelo was dead before I stabbed him with Dimitrios Doukas's knife. The symbol of irony. Angelo stabbed by the knife of the man who killed his father."

"My father didn't kill Constantine Thetalou," Alexa said through gritted teeth.

"Mitso said he did."

He'd told them the same thing, but Alexa still didn't believe it. "He was confused. My father wasn't a murderer." She gasped in horror as his statement sank in. "Mitso told you this? When did you talk to Mitso?"

Kritikos shrugged. "The night he died. He talked plenty when I said I'd give you for a night's fun to the two men I hired to grab you." An evil smile crossed his broad face. "He was a tough old bird. I didn't expect him to drop dead. He fought to the end."

"You bastard." Infuriated, Damian lunged forward.

Kritikos let go of Lisandro and grabbed Alexa. Damian stopped dead in his tracks, glaring at Kritikos, who smiled triumphantly. "I figured she'd be a better pawn in this. Both of you care about her. Now prove it."

Alexa hardly dared to breathe as Kritikos pressed her to his body. His belly felt soft and flabby but his arm closed like a band of steel around her. Her stomach clenched in revulsion. The knife blade lay cold along her neck. His breath fanned her cheek, hot and repulsive. "Tell me everything, or I'll slit her throat like an Easter lamb's." One finger stretched out to touch her skin. "Such soft, pretty skin. Too bad it has to be like this, Alexa. But there's still time. I can save you for later."

Damian growled savagely, deep in his throat, his fists opening and closing helplessly. Without taking his eyes off Alexa's dead-white face, he moved to Lisandro's chair, crouching beside it.

Lisandro squeezed his hand. "I'm all right, Damian. He didn't hurt me. But you should have left when you saw what was happening. I'm old. It doesn't matter what happens to me. But you and Alexa have your whole lives ahead of you."

"Nobly said, old man." Kritikos sneered. "Now, what'll it be, the truth or dear Alexa's blood running on the floor? And you can bet I'll make it last a long time. I won't kill her easily."

Lisandro lurched forward in the chair, then fell back, his hand coming up to clutch his chest. "She's innocent," he cried, pain making his breath rasp in his throat. "She doesn't know anything. She doesn't know where the sword is."

"Mitso thought she did. He said the little girl saw everything."

Lisandro's face turned a ghastly shade of gray. For a moment, he stopped breathing and his eyes rolled in their sockets. Damian gasped in horror, sure he was losing him. He reached for his wrist, feeling the thready, uneven pulse.

Miraculously, Lisandro rallied. He made two attempts to speak before the words were audible, but then they came out, strong and ringing. "Mitso is mixing up his daughters' murders with the death of Constantine. He didn't know what he was saying."

"I think he did," Kritikos said, pulling Alexa's head back by clasping a handful of her hair. The knife caressed her exposed throat, and she tensed, bracing herself for the pain, her mind filled with incoherent prayers. *Even if I die, let Lisandro and Damian get away. Let them live.*

"Mitso said Constantine told him everything when he lay dying," Kritikos went on. "The little girl saw him hide the sword."

"Constantine took the sword?" Damian said.

Kritikos laughed. "Yes, he took it. And Angelo found out about it when he returned to Greece last year. Don't ask me how. From some old papers of his father's or something. He's been looking for it ever since. He finally contacted me, to ask my help."

"Why you? What are you to him?"

"Let's just say I had an interest in common with his father. When he was killed, our cause was inconvenienced greatly. I wanted to get that murdering Doukas who killed Constantine."

"You're a fine one to accuse a man of murder," Damian said scornfully. "You killed Angelo."

Alexa stifled a cry as Kritikos's fist jerked at her hair. "It was an accident," he said. "More like self-defense. He jumped at me when I suggested we use Alexa to find the sword. She was here as a child, and Mitso was always talking about the little girl with the sunshine hair. It had to be Alexa. Angelo told me about the sleepwalking, how easily suggestible she'd be. But he didn't like the methods I wanted to use."

"Hypnotic suggestion," Lisandro put in. "Brainwashing techniques taught by the secret police. You worked for them, didn't you?"

Kritikos smiled. "Good guess, old man. I learned my lessons well." The smile slid off his face, the knife pricking Alexa's skin, a faint sting overshadowed by the larger, spreading pain in her scalp. "But it didn't work." He yanked her head viciously back. "She kept going back to childhood, but she didn't tell me what I wanted to know."

"You drugged me," Alexa said in a strangled voice. It hurt to talk but she had to know. "How did you do it?"

"The jug of cold water you brought up to your room most evenings from the kitchen fridge. It wasn't a strong drug, only a mild hallucinogen. I figured if you thought you were back in the past, you would lead me to the sword."

In spite of her pain and terror, Alexa felt relief. She wasn't going crazy. The realization washed through her, momentarily clearing her mind. Kritikos still held her but the hand tangled in her hair loosened slightly. She fought to keep her fear at bay, fought the panic that made her want to struggle. If she could get him off guard for even a second, she had a chance.

She suddenly relaxed her muscles, allowing her body to fall limply forward, as if in a faint. "Oh, no, you don't, my pretty. You're not going to fool me like that."

He shifted his hold, grasping her around the waist once more, the knife lying coldly along her cheek. The sharp point pricked her skin, and she could feel warm blood trickling down her neck.

Her breath frozen in her throat, she focused on Damian's face. He was pale and his eyes glittered ferociously. His hands moved restlessly, fists clenching and unclenching, as if he wished they were around Kritikos's neck.

Beside him, Lisandro slumped in his chair, his head drooping. He looked so white; the only sign that he still lived was the rapid, uneven motion of his chest as he dragged in every agonizing breath.

Kritikos pushed her closer to the chair. "Old man, look up. Where is Dimitrios Doukas? I want him. Angelo always maintained you were hiding something, coming here and living like a recluse. We're finished with the games. Tell me now, or Alexa dies."

Lisandro opened his eyes, the light behind them gone. He raised his head, slowly and painfully, as if it were too heavy for his neck. "I'm the man you want." The words were slurred and desperate. "Dimitrios Doukas is dead. Lisandro Cosmos lives. Kill me, and take your revenge."

Chapter Eighteen

A burning pain flashed through Alexa's head, as if lightning had struck her. She knew. Suddenly she knew.

"Papa," she whispered, then louder, a mixture of joy and disbelief, "Papa."

In the same instant she became aware that Kritikos stood with his jaw slack, as astonished as she was. Twisting to the left, she slipped out of his grasp. He groped to regain his hold but only caught the end of her hair. She gasped in pain, but pulled free, leaving several strands hanging from his fingers.

Damian leapt forward and kicked the knife out of Kritikos's hand. Snarling like a wolf robbed of prey, the man lunged toward him. Damian got in the first blow, hitting Kritikos squarely on the jaw. The man only staggered, shaking his head. Raising his fists, he connected with Damian's nose. Blood spurted out, crimson drops spraying on his white T-shirt.

Damian dragged the back of his hand across his face and took another swing at Kritikos. Ready this time, Kritikos moved in, dodging the blow as his fist clipped Damian under the chin. Damian fell to the floor, reaching out at the last minute and dragging the man with him.

They rolled over and over, each trying to pin down the other. Horrified, Alexa stood next to Lisandro. Damian was fitter than Kritikos but the other man outweighed him by twenty kilos, which were working to his advantage.

It couldn't go on. Alexa cast her glance around, searching for a weapon.

The two men rolled again and this time Kritikos ended up on top. He wrapped his hands around Damian's throat, his face contorted in a triumphant snarl. Damian heaved his body upward but it was clear he was tiring and no match for the superior weight.

Alexa jumped to the hearth and snatched one of the swords that hung there. It was old and beginning to rust. She hefted it, noting that the balance was perfect. Gritting her teeth, she swung it, slamming the flat side of the blade down on Kritikos's head. The man collapsed like a punctured tire.

Gasping painfully for air, Damian shoved him to one side. He sat up, his chest heaving, fingerprints livid on his throat. "Thanks," he managed to say.

He stared at Alexa, eyes blazing, standing over Kritikos's prone body with a sword in her hand, a warrior who would always defend those she loved.

Was it light-headedness from lack of oxygen that made him see clearly all at once? *Alexa, I love you.* The words echoed within his soul, his doubts and fears vanishing like smoke on the wind. He did love her, with a fierce certainty that brought tears to his eyes. And he would ask her to stay with him. *I'll take the chance.*

"What is going on here?" a shocked voice cried from the doorway. "I go out for a moment and I come back to this. Damian, you're bleeding."

He touched his nose and stared at his hand, laughing shakily. "So I am. Vassiliki, go get Spiro, would you please? And leave me your apron."

Untying the immaculate white garment, she handed it to him, only flinching a little when he pressed it to his nose, staunching the dripping blood. With a dignified sniff, she turned and walked out the door.

Alexa knelt beside Lisandro's chair, her arms tight around his waist. His gnarled hand caressed her hair. "My dear girl, can you ever forgive me?"

She raised her eyes, her heart so full emotion choked her. "Papa, there's nothing to forgive."

"Damn you." Kritikos's vicious snarl cut across the room.

"Keep struggling and I'll tie you tighter," Damian said grimly, knotting the bloodied apron securely around the man's wrists. "I ought to tie this around your neck."

Lisandro straightened in his chair, leaning forward, his hand remaining on Alexa's head as if he couldn't bear to break the contact. He stared at the angry Kritikos as Damian hauled him to a sitting position on the floor. "Why? Why did you spend all these years chasing Dimitrios Doukas simply for revenge? Surely not for a political cause that died twenty years ago?"

"You killed my brother," Kritikos screamed, a blue vein throbbing in his temple. "Constantine Thetalou was my brother."

Comprehension lit in Lisandro's faded eyes. "So that's it. Pavlo. You're Pavlo."

"Why didn't Angelo ever mention you?" asked Alexa.

"Because Angelo didn't know me well," Kritikos said. "Our parents died when Constantine and I were children. Constantine grew up in Elatos, with relatives. I was sent to another branch of the family, in Crete."

"Hence, the name, Kritikos," Damian said.

Kritikos nodded. "We kept in touch and later we were in business together in Athens. In the early sixties, when politics became turbulent, Constantine moved back to Elatos. He got himself elected mayor here, didn't he?"

"And tried to win everyone over in support of the military government," Lisandro said. "Something few were inclined to do, voluntarily."

"And you killed him," Kritikos said, tendons standing out on his neck as he struggled against his bonds.

"I didn't," Lisandro said calmly. "You've been after the wrong man. Mitso was the one, so you accomplished your purpose, after all. He killed Constantine. Apparently Mitso had some misguided idea that Constantine had had something to do with the rape and murder of his wife and daughters. Which was, of course, impossible, since Constantine was hardly old enough to be involved in a war at that time. The day Constantine was killed, I was looking for Alexa, who had gone for one of her walks in the woods. I saw Mitso bending over Constantine's body. He must have heard me because he ran off. Constantine was dead. I couldn't help him. But the police grabbed me."

"You didn't find Alexa, then?" Damian asked.

"No," Lisandro said. "Her mother found her later, hiding in the woods. That's why I considered them to be in danger, all those years. Why I wanted Alexa protected now. I never got a chance to talk to Olympia, but I was sure that even if she hadn't seen what Alexa must have witnessed, plenty of people would think she did and kill her to keep her quiet. Once I was arrested, the real killer would be free, but he would always be in danger of discovery if Alexa or her mother talked. So I sent them away and didn't contact them, to keep them safe." He looked down at Alexa, his eyes tender. "What did you see, Alexa?"

At his words, the memory flooded back. Alexa cried out as images tumbled through her mind, a man shouting and a bloody knife plunging again and again into a man lying on the ground. Blood turning the grass scarlet, a dark blot in the mountain meadow. Overhead, an eagle screamed.

"I was there," she said, her lips so stiff she could barely force out the words. "I saw him."

Lisandro's hand stilled its motion of stroking her hair. "Saw who, Alexa?"

Was that fear she heard in his voice? For an instant, doubt swept over her. Had it been Lisandro she'd seen, and finding the shock too great, had she blocked it out of her mind? She closed her eyes, reliving the memory, snatching at fragments that drifted in and out of her mind with maddening elusiveness.

A face. Yes, through the screen of grass and wild flowers, she could see a face, contorted with rage as the knife rose and plunged. Rose and plunged. She didn't know the face, any more than she'd known the face of Lisandro was that of her father.

But one more nebulous memory floated to the surface. The killer didn't have a beard. She knew she'd rubbed her cheek over her father's soft beard a thousand times. The man was not her father.

"I didn't know the man. I'd never seen him before."

"How long were Alexa and her mother in Elatos before this happened?" Damian asked.

"Maybe five or six months," Lisandro said. "We came in the winter. I went back to Athens to work, and only visited several times. In April, after the coup, I made arrangements to get Alexa and Olympia out of Greece should that become necessary. After the killing of Constantine, I couldn't even talk to Olympia without a guard present, except to tell her to use the escape plan if more trouble came. I was only able to escape because I still had friends who risked their lives to help me."

He rubbed his hand over his face. "Most of them paid a high price for that," he said in a low, strained voice. "I had seen Mitso with the body but I couldn't implicate him, poor lost soul, half insane with grief all those years."

"Constantine was shot in the head, wasn't he?" Damian said.

"Mitso didn't shoot him." Alexa dragged in a long breath. "At least I don't think so. I heard a gunshot. Someone ran through the bushes. I waited and then crept closer. I saw a man lying on the ground. Then another man, pulling out a knife and stabbing him. That must have been Mitso."

Lisandro nodded. "So Constantine was dead before Mitso came. I always thought Mitso wouldn't have killed in cold blood. And I suppose we'll never know who shot Constantine."

On the floor, Kritikos ground his teeth. "The official version was that Dimitrios Doukas killed Constantine."

"The official version was wrong," Lisandro declared. "But it was a good excuse, since they wanted to get rid of me. Alexa, I beg your forgiveness for never getting in touch with you, and I wish I could ask your mother the same. But even after I came back, it was this *official version* that hounded me. And not knowing if Constantine's real killer was still around and would get rid of Alexa and Olympia to protect himself. I couldn't take any chances. It was safer for all of us if I took a new identity and cut all ties with the past."

Alexa wasn't sure she would ever understand. Growing up in Canada, she'd been protected from the Greek conviction of conspiracy in every event, the almost paranoid fear that even the simplest situations have hidden motives and dangerous repercussions. But she could not blame her father for his actions. He had handled it the best he knew how, with sincerity and integrity.

Damian walked over to the chimney and replaced the sword Alexa had used to end the fight with Kritikos. Thoughtfully, he touched the knife that hung below the swords. "It's almost identical, isn't it?"

Lisandro laughed a little sheepishly. "I was hoping you wouldn't notice, especially since you knew that I was out that night."

"Did you go to Angelo's house?"

Lisandro nodded. "I did. I thought it was time to confront him. I didn't like what I heard about his attitude toward Alexa. But the house was dark so I assumed he was sleeping and came home."

He shifted in the chair. "The missing knife was as much a surprise to me as it was to you. But I replaced it with a similar one I had, hoping you wouldn't notice and feel you were concealing evidence. Even though nobody in Elatos was likely to recognize me, I didn't want the police to come around, asking questions." He ran his fingertips over the scar on the side of his face. "With this and without the beard, not even my own daughter recognized me."

"I wonder if I would have if I hadn't lost my memory of that time," Alexa said softly.

"It doesn't matter." Lisandro took her hand in his. "God has been good to me. We'll have a little time together."

And Damian watched them, happiness mixed with an emotion he didn't want to admit might be jealousy. Not that he begrudged either of them their reunion. No, it was just the bittersweet realization that Alexa would stay a little longer, but for Lisandro, not for him.

Lisandro smiled at Damian over Alexa's head, and winked slyly. Damian grinned, his heart lightening. He lifted his thumb in understanding.

A brief knock on the door announced Spiro's arrival. "So he didn't leave, after all," he said, fixing his gaze on Kritikos who sat on the floor, still cursing. He turned to Damian. "Maybe you could give me a rundown on what's happened here."

Damian did so, identifying Kritikos as an old political enemy of Lisandro's, leaving out Lisandro's true name. If Spiro needed that information, he would have to ask for it.

"It was his knife in Angelo's chest." Kritikos twisted his head around to address Spiro. "And he's Dimitrios Doukas. He's wanted by the government."

Spiro looked at him with a faint smile. "That government no longer exists."

Spiro dragged Kritikos to his feet and sat him down on one of the chairs Vassiliki brought from the kitchen. "Let's hear your story," Spiro said. "And be careful what you say. I'm taking it all down. You might want to wait until you have a lawyer."

"Plenty of time to get a lawyer if you can make the charges stick," Kritikos snapped. "You've got no evidence at all, so it's my word against theirs. And I might as well warn you, I have important friends who could bust you to patrolling a beat in a town more benighted than this."

"I wouldn't count on it," Spiro said mildly, his pen busy in his notebook. "As for evidence, there was a fingerprint in the pool of blood under Angelo's head, a very good print which we haven't been able to match up. I've a suspicion that once we check your prints, we'll have our evidence."

He turned to Lisandro. "I've always thought there was more to you than meets the eye. But as far as I'm concerned, a man can use any name he wants as long as he's law-abiding in my jurisdiction. You don't have to tell me anything, even now. However, I would have appreciated it if you'd told me your knife was missing. We could have dusted your windowsill for fingerprints."

Lisandro faced him squarely. "I did what I thought best."

"And you, Damian," Spiro added. "Did you think the knife was Lisandro's and you said nothing?"

A faint smile curved Damian's lips. "I wasn't sure about the knife. After all, there are several like it in the village museum. And I'll venture that you would have done the same, in my position, if by keeping your mouth shut, you could save your dying father unnecessary anxiety."

Spiro's expression softened. "You're right, of course. Without hard evidence, any of us would have acted the same way. One more thing, Lisandro, why was Angelo asking questions about you and why did he want to see you alone?"

Damian looked surprised. "How did you know about that?"

"I have my sources," Spiro said complacently. "Well, Lisandro?"

"According to Kritikos here, he wanted the diaries, especially the old one." Lisandro frowned. "Everyone in the village knew about the diaries that were found in the rubble of the old house, but not about their contents. I kept them for Alexa. I was going to get Damian to mail them to you, after I die."

Spiro turned back to Kritikos. "How about you, Kritikos? Was that all Angelo was after?"

"He thought Lisandro might have known Dimitrios Doukas, or if not, at least his brother, Elias, since land records show Elias sold Lisandro the old house and the lot. He thought they might have known what happened to the sword. Angelo wanted the sword and the diamonds."

"So, none of you have any idea where the sword is," Spiro said, looking around at all of them, including Vassiliki standing quietly in the doorway.

They all shook their heads. Alexa's negative response appeared a bit uncertain as she gazed off into the distance. Damian looked at her speculatively. But he said nothing.

After several more questions to clear up minor points, Spiro left, herding Kritikos, securely handcuffed, ahead of him.

Lisandro had a thousand questions to ask Alexa, wanting to catch up on the last twenty-seven years. But Alexa, seeing the weariness in the lines of his face and the alarming pallor that turned his skin the color of clay, gently suggested that he rest first. She led him to the bed and helped him to lie down, removing his slippers and setting them on the floor. She kissed his forehead and tucked the blanket around him. "Sleep for a while, Papa. We'll have plenty of time to talk later. If you need anything, Vassiliki is here."

Eyelids drooping, he nodded, too tired to speak. He gripped her hand for a moment, then his fingers went lax. Alexa gave him another kiss and stepped back, tears blurring her eyes. So little time, but she would make the most of it. Both of them would.

In the meantime, there was Damian to deal with.

He stood beside the door, arms crossed over his chest, his expression inscrutable. Only his eyes gave him away, the deep blue filled with shadows and questions.

"Well, Alexa," he said, keeping pace with her as she headed for the kitchen, "what happens next?"

She spread her hands, palms up, then went over to the sink and drew a glass of water, drinking it thirstily. Vassiliki stirred a pot on the stove, muttering to herself. "I knew I shouldn't have left him alone this morning. But he said he felt well, told me to go." She shuddered. "When I think of what that horrible man could have done to him—"

Damian patted her shoulder. "Don't worry about it, Vassiliki. It's okay now. He's in jail and will stay there."

Alexa stood by the sink, staring into the distance. "What is it, Alexa?" Damian asked. "Do you remember something?"

She started, as if she'd been on another plane. Then she smiled faintly. "No, but maybe I know something I don't know I know."

"Makes sense," Damian said dryly.

"That fireplace in Angelo's house. There has to be a reason why I keep going there."

"Maybe you followed Constantine that day," Damian said thoughtfully. "Remember what Mitso said—the little girl saw him. Only the killing? Or something else? It has to have a significance."

Alexa wrinkled her brow. "Maybe if I go there when I'm awake, I'll remember something."

"It's worth a try," Damian said. "Vassiliki, could you please keep an eye on Lisandro, in case he worries when he realizes we're not here? We won't be gone long. He should sleep for a while."

"I will, Damian. And when you come back, will you please sit down and eat?"

Alexa laughed for the first time that day.

THE DOOR OF ANGELO'S house creaked as they pushed it open. Inside, it smelled musty and damp. A puddle of water from the leaky roof glistened on the living room floor despite two days without rain.

Alexa paused in the middle of the room. She cleared her mind and tried to focus her thoughts on the past. "Maybe I was never in this house when I was a child," she said in frustration. "My father and Angelo's were enemies, after all."

"By all accounts they weren't thrown together often. And your mother and Angelo's were friends," Damian reminded her.

"I suppose." She looked around uncertainly, seeing the moldy plastered walls, the heap of bricks in the fireplace. "Where did you say I sat last night?"

Damian walked over to the space in front of the hearth. "Right here."

Alexa shuddered. "Where Angelo died." She could only be grateful that someone, probably from the police, had mopped up the blood. "Maybe that's why I came here. Guilt."

"You've no reason to feel guilt," Damian said wearily, catching her around the shoulders. For a brief moment, he held her close. "Alexa, I think the best thing is to assume the fireplace has significance. Let's get to work."

He crouched down and together they began shifting the pile of bricks, tossing them into the middle of the room.

"That's odd," Damian muttered when they'd cleared away the rubble. "The fireplace cavity seems intact. The top half of the chimney outside collapsed, probably in an earthquake. I guess they filled the space with bricks to keep out the wind and rain."

"Unless they were covering something hidden here, like the sword." Alexa crawled into the soot-blackened opening, peering upward. Splinters of light came through the ruined chimney but she couldn't see the sky as she'd expected to. "Damian, did these fireplaces usually have a damper?"

"Only rarely."

"Well, this one has a damper." Alexa's voice rose with excitement, echoing in the confined space. She crawled out, soot decorating one cheek. "See for yourself."

Damian crouched down, squinting against the drifting ash. "You know, you're right. And it looks as if the handle's been broken off." He crawled farther in and grasped the jagged end that was left, grunting with exertion. A tortured creak told Alexa it was moving, then it opened with a thump, showering gritty soot on Damian's head.

He backed out, shaking his head. "What we need is a flashlight. Can you have a look in the kitchen?"

She found one in a drawer, although the feeble beam told her the batteries were dying. Damian directed the light up the chimney. "There's something up there."

Alexa's heartbeat sped up. "The sword?"

"Don't know yet." He reached up and tossed out a battered bird's nest, then groped farther. "Maybe if you held the flashlight?"

Alexa took it, wedging herself against his hard-muscled body. Using both hands, Damian pried the halves of the damper farther apart. More soot rained down, as well as another cluster of twigs and feathers.

The muscles of his back pulled taut as he strained to reach above the metal plates. "I've got it." His voice rang with triumph.

Another shriek of metal against metal assaulted Alexa's ears. She backed out of the fireplace to give Damian room. He stood up, his T-shirt as black as a chimney sweep's.

In his hand he held the sword. Slowly, he extended his arm, offering it to Alexa. "This is rightfully yours and Lisandro's."

She took it, unable to repress a shiver. She gazed at it, feeling no pleasure or satisfaction. The long blade showed orange patches of rust, and the carved, silver hilt was black with tarnish. It lay heavily in her hands, as though it carried the weight of the souls of those slain by its once-sharp edge.

"Ironic, isn't it?" Damian said softly. "Kritikos and Angelo were so close and they didn't know it."

Alexa swallowed, tamping down her uneasiness. "What will we do with it?"

"Let's ask Lisandro."

VASSILIKI GREETED THEM at the door. She eyed the sword curiously. "So that's what all the fuss was about."

"Why, hadn't you seen it before?" Alexa asked. "It was on display once in the village office."

"Me?" Vassiliki shrugged her substantial shoulders. "I've only lived here five years. Alexa, Lisandro is awake and he's asking for you."

"I'll be right there." Alexa looked at Damian. "Should we bring it in?"

"I don't see why not."

Lisandro sat up straighter in bed when they entered the room. "Alexa, you found it." He put out his hands to take the sword from her. She was startled to see tears flowing down his weathered cheeks. "Now it can go back to its rightful place."

"Are there really diamonds in the hilt?" Alexa asked.

"Let's see." Lisandro ran his fingertips over the silver hilt. Grasping it firmly with one hand, he twisted the knob on the end with the other. The two parts separated.

Alexa was surprised to note the lack of rust. "The thread was kept well oiled," Lisandro explained. He tilted the sword, blade up. "Hold out your hands."

Alexa did so, cupping her two palms together. A cascade of crystal poured out into her hands. Alexa's eyes widened. "Are they real?" They looked no more distinctive than shards of glass.

"They're real," Lisandro assured her. "Hold them up to the light. You can see the fire within them." He screwed the round knob back onto the hilt and laid the sword beside him. Leaning back against his pillow, he folded his hands. "So, children, what do we do with them?"

"You mean we don't have to give them to any government department or the police?" Alexa asked.

"They belong to our family," Lisandro stated. "No one is left of the Thetalous, unless you count Kritikos. In Ioannina I have documentation that goes beyond the diary you read, Alexa. When the partnership between the two families dissolved, most of the assets they held together were liquidated. The diamonds are the Doukas share. They and the sword belong to the Doukas family. That means it's yours."

Alexa backed away, a reflex she couldn't help. "By tradition, it belongs to the village of Elatos."

"The sword, not the diamonds." Damian spoke for the first time.

"The diamonds aren't going to do anyone any good in the village office," Lisandro said. "And they'll be a target for the next opportunist who comes along."

"Give them to a charity," Damian suggested. He'd seen Alexa's discomfort that bordered on antipathy when she'd touched the sword. "The money they bring can help somebody. And the sword can stay in the village museum, or you can give it to a museum in Ioannina, since I suppose it would be considered a national artifact."

"Good idea, Damian," Lisandro said approvingly. "Is that all right with you, Alexa?"

"Fine," she said, relieved that it was out of her hands. She'd never considered herself psychic, but the sword made her feel queasy.

Alexa spent the rest of the day quietly, talking with Lisandro, catching up on the details of their separate lives. During her fatherless childhood she'd often fantasized what it would be like if her father turned up again, imagined the closeness they would share.

The reality was nothing like her dreams, however. A bond between them existed, but she couldn't help feeling that it had been forged in the past week. In that short time, she had grown to love Lisandro. The revelation that he was her father only cemented the closeness between them, forming an immutable union breakable only by death.

Death. Alexa's heart clenched painfully in her chest. She had just lost her mother. Now she would lose her father, as well.

As if he sensed her thoughts, Lisandro got up from his chair and hugged her close. "You'll stay for a while, won't you, Alexa?" he asked, his voice shaking.

Tears clogged her throat. "Of course I'll stay. As long as you want me." *As long as you're alive.*

"And Damian?" Lisandro looked straight into her eyes, the deep brown eyes still as clear and honest as they'd been when she was a child.

Damian. Feeling a blush heat her cheeks, Alexa hid her face against Lisandro's chest. He chuckled. "I was young once, too, Alexa. I loved your mother. I see the same love in you for Damian. It's all I've ever prayed for, that you would be happy and that he would be happy. I never dreamed you'd find that happiness together."

"Even if I love him," Alexa said sadly, "I'm not at all sure Damian feels the same way toward me."

Again Lisandro chuckled. "Maybe he's afraid. Men often are, afraid to give their heart. It's up to you to show him."

DAMIAN AWOKE with a start, abruptly aware that Alexa no longer lay beside him. Sleepwalking again? His stomach tightened. If only she could put the past and its traumas behind her.

He sat up in bed. Out of the corner of his eye, he saw a movement by the window. Relief made him briefly dizzy as he realized it was Alexa, half hidden by the lace curtain.

He must have made a sound, for suddenly she spoke, still facing the window and the night outside. "If the business with Kritikos hadn't happened, would he have told me?"

Before he could frame an answer to the unanswerable, she turned. "I don't want to know," she said.

"No," Damian agreed. "It no longer matters."

He ran his tongue over dry lips. There was still something standing between them that had to be resolved, even though he was sorely tempted to take the coward's way out. If he didn't tell her, she would never know. Lisandro wouldn't ever mention it. Yet, with the insight he'd gained in the past week, knowing Alexa and her honesty, it seemed to him that secrets were time bombs waiting to explode. He had to tell her.

"Alexa, he told me."

Alexa turned and stared at him. "He told you?"

"Yes, a few days ago. Kritikos came to the house, said some things to Lisandro that were more than oblique threats, against Lisandro and against you. He didn't want to give Kritikos a weapon but at the same time, he felt he had to tell me so that I would be better able to protect you, if that became necessary." Damian raked his fingers through his hair, the hair that she had so recently tangled with loving hands. "I hope—" He broke off, wishing he could read what she was thinking.

"You knew." Her quiet tone was more frightening than a shout.

His heart sank. "Alexa," he pleaded desperately, extending his hands to her.

She didn't turn away. She ran to him, flinging herself into his arms. "How terrible it must have been for you when you knew Kritikos meant to harm Lisandro. Damian, of course you couldn't say anything."

"You're not angry?" His voice cracked.

She hugged him tighter. "How could I be? If it had been me, I would have felt torn in two, but— No matter. It's over. We'll go on from here."

His chest heaved with the force of his relief. "Alexa, what will you do?"

"You mean afterward?"

He nodded, his heart aching anew for Lisandro. No matter how much they tried to deny it, Lisandro would die. He might have days, or weeks, but he didn't have forever.

While they...

"Alexa, would you stay? Forever?" The words surprised him as they came out. Until today, he'd never thought in terms of forever, hadn't dared to. But today he'd understood the reason for the empty desolation that filled him every time he'd thought of her leaving.

He dragged in a deep breath. It was time. Time he told her he loved her.

"Forever, Damian?" she said quietly. "Do you believe in forever now?"

He smiled. "I think you can convince me."

"My job?"

He shrugged, hardly daring to hope, to believe. "Ioannina isn't a village, and it's prosperous. You can sell mutual funds to the Greeks. I think we're about ready for more complex investments."

He held out his arms, and she came willingly to lie beside him. Damian let out a sigh of pleasure at the feel of her, the scent of her, the reality of her. His. Forever.

"I love you, Alexa. I want you to be my lover and my wife and the mother of my children."

Even in the dimness of the room he could see the worried frown on her face change to joy. He'd gambled his soul and won. "Alexa, I love you. I love you." He laughed in sheer exuberance. "I never thought I'd say it. I never dared to dream I could ever feel this way."

"And I love you, Damian," Alexa said simply, deeply, her voice husky with emotion. "Forever."

INDULGE A LITTLE 6947 SWEEPSTAKES
NO PURCHASE NECESSARY

HERE'S HOW THE SWEEPSTAKES WORKS:
The Harlequin Reader Service shipments for January, February and March 1994 will contain, respectively, coupons for entry into three prize drawings: a trip for two to San Francisco, an Alaskan cruise for two and a trip for two to Hawaii. To be eligible for any drawing using an Entry Coupon, simply complete and mail according to directions.

There is no obligation to continue as a Reader Service subscriber to enter and be eligible for any prize drawing. You may also enter any drawing by hand printing your name and address on a 3" x 5" card and the destination of the prize you wish that entry to be considered for (i.e., San Francisco trip, Alaskan cruise or Hawaiian trip). Send your 3" x 5" entries to: Indulge a Little 6947 Sweepstakes, c/o Prize Destination you wish that entry to be considered for, P.O. Box 1315, Buffalo, NY 14269-1315, U.S.A. or Indulge a Little 6947 Sweepstakes, P.O. Box 610, Fort Erie, Ontario L2A 5X3, Canada.

To be eligible for the San Francisco trip, entries must be received by 4/30/94; for the Alaskan cruise, 5/31/94; and the Hawaiian trip, 6/30/94. No responsibility is assumed for lost, late or misdirected mail. Sweepstakes open to residents of the U.S. (except Puerto Rico) and Canada, 18 years of age or older. All applicable laws and regulations apply. Sweepstakes void wherever prohibited.

For a copy of the Official Rules, send a self-addressed, stamped envelope (WA residents need not affix return postage) to: Indulge a Little 6947 Rules, P.O. Box 4631, Blair, NE 68009, U.S.A.

INDR93

INDULGE A LITTLE 6947 SWEEPSTAKES
NO PURCHASE NECESSARY

HERE'S HOW THE SWEEPSTAKES WORKS:
The Harlequin Reader Service shipments for January, February and March 1994 will contain, respectively, coupons for entry into three prize drawings: a trip for two to San Francisco, an Alaskan cruise for two and a trip for two to Hawaii. To be eligible for any drawing using an Entry Coupon, simply complete and mail according to directions.

There is no obligation to continue as a Reader Service subscriber to enter and be eligible for any prize drawing. You may also enter any drawing by hand printing your name and address on a 3" x 5" card and the destination of the prize you wish that entry to be considered for (i.e., San Francisco trip, Alaskan cruise or Hawaiian trip). Send your 3" x 5" entries to: Indulge a Little 6947 Sweepstakes, c/o Prize Destination you wish that entry to be considered for, P.O. Box 1315, Buffalo, NY 14269-1315, U.S.A. or Indulge a Little 6947 Sweepstakes, P.O. Box 610, Fort Erie, Ontario L2A 5X3, Canada.

To be eligible for the San Francisco trip, entries must be received by 4/30/94; for the Alaskan cruise, 5/31/94; and the Hawaiian trip, 6/30/94. No responsibility is assumed for lost, late or misdirected mail. Sweepstakes open to residents of the U.S. (except Puerto Rico) and Canada, 18 years of age or older. All applicable laws and regulations apply. Sweepstakes void wherever prohibited.

For a copy of the Official Rules, send a self-addressed, stamped envelope (WA residents need not affix return postage) to: Indulge a Little 6947 Rules, P.O. Box 4631, Blair, NE 68009, U.S.A.

INDR93

INDULGE A LITTLE

SWEEPSTAKES

OFFICIAL ENTRY COUPON

This entry must be received by: JUNE 30, 1994
This month's winner will be notified by: JULY 15, 1994
Trip must be taken between: AUGUST 31, 1994-AUGUST 31, 1995

YES, I want to win the 3-Island Hawaiian vacation for two. I understand that the prize includes round-trip airfare, first-class hotels and pocket money as revealed on the "wallet" scratch-off card.

Name____

Address ________________________ Apt. ______________

City____

State/Prov.__________________ Zip/Postal Code____________

Daytime phone number__________________________________
(Area Code)

Account #____

Return entries with invoice in envelope provided. Each book in this shipment has two entry coupons—and the more coupons you enter, the better your chances of winning!

 MONTH3

INDULGE A LITTLE

SWEEPSTAKES

OFFICIAL ENTRY COUPON

This entry must be received by: JUNE 30, 1994
This month's winner will be notified by: JULY 15, 1994
Trip must be taken between: AUGUST 31, 1994-AUGUST 31, 1995

YES, I want to win the 3-Island Hawaiian vacation for two. I understand that the prize includes round-trip airfare, first-class hotels and pocket money as revealed on the "wallet" scratch-off card.

Name____

Address ________________________ Apt. ______________

City____

State/Prov.__________________ Zip/Postal Code____________

Daytime phone number__________________________________
(Area Code)

Account #____

Return entries with invoice in envelope provided. Each book in this shipment has two entry coupons—and the more coupons you enter, the better your chances of winning!

© 1993 HARLEQUIN ENTERPRISES LTD. MONTH3